Acknowledgements

My sincere thanks must go to my wife Jo, for all her patience and time. She has looked at every word of this manuscript and her suggestions have invariably been on the nail. Every chapter is more succinct and coherent thanks to her interventions. Thanks to my step-mother, Jean, for suggesting the first trip to Gemmano, and for accompanying me, and to my editor Seonaid Francis for all her work and support, and for pulling the manuscript down to earth when it threatened to get away from me. A big collective thanks is required to the town of Gemmano whose people have been unfailingly helpful and open, in discussions and interviews. And of course thank you to my father who, astonishingly, maintained a diary through these appalling days, from which I have drawn significantly.

Dedication

For my wife, Jo, with all my love and thanks.

For the people of Gemmano.

And, of course, for Dad.

Greetings to Jane &
Budleigh library
with all best wishes

Will

Chapter 1
August 31st 1944, morning
Toni

He pushes his nose through drifts of dried brown leaves lying over the forest floor. Shoving them aside like a pig hunting for truffles he uncovers soil beneath semi-decomposed vegetation, punctuated with pale, sun-starved shoots of grass. His eyes cross and he perceives blurs of mud on the end of his nose. He breathes slowly, enjoying the musty smell of the soil deep in his lungs. He feels that once upon a time he gestated in this earth, took his form from the minerals and the rocks, the roots and the worms, and then arose from them like a new day. He is of the hillside, like the creatures all around him.

There is a shift, the faintest brush against his shoulder, and he remembers what he's doing here. He opens his eyes and places one hand lightly on Remo's muzzle, so the dog knows to stay still. Stretching his neck he raises his nose out of the soil as slowly as grass growing. The dry wind whips away the scent of the soil and, dizzy, he places a hand flat on the ground to steady himself. He watches his body with care. He notes each sensation; a leaf has caught in his straw blonde hair and is rotating halfway within his vision. There is cramp in a toe, a frequent result of his having shot up in height over the past eighteen months. A broken branch pushes into his all-too-obvious ribs. He eases it away with fingers that have dirt jammed under the fingernails. He is aware of each movement, and observes one limb at a time in order to keep his focus pure. Now he raises his head, which allows him to see over the leaves he has piled up and hidden behind.

He observes the tops of the nets. His eyes follow his handiwork, tracing the supporting cord to each branch or trunk where he has tied it off. The nets hang to the ground and he has sewn up the moth holes as best he can with bits of string, hoping they will withstand the coming scramble. The old boards that form the back of the trap, and hold back the mess of brambles behind it, will prevent prisoners and net from getting irretrievably tangled.

Prisoners. The word is a trigger and from his core he feels the spasm coming. He almost groans, partly at the thought that he must imprison a living creature, and partly at the onrushing loss of physical control. Worse still, he fears the groan itself will reveal him, and catches the sound just before it bursts out of his mouth.

The spasm will be debilitating, and it will follow directly the sudden nausea in his gut. It may grip his head and shoulder, but a severe one can overtake his whole body, turning his legs to rubber. He will grope for support, collapsing on the ground and gasping for breath. Sometimes he will piss himself. Sometimes he will black out.

When younger he got the strangest looks from other villagers, particularly the parents of his friends. Emilio's mother wouldn't let him come and visit them again after one incident. Mama tried to talk about them once.

'Toni, you know when you have these little episodes. What is that? What happens?'

'I don't want to do it,' he said, carefully.

She laid down her demi-luna chopping knife and watched him closely. He shrugged, 'I dunno why. I dunno.'

She never raised it again, but the truth was that he did know. Blood. It was as simple as that. The idea of violence always threatened to cause him total physical incontinence.

But Papa said blood was like air. 'Everybody needs it, Toni, and we all need to eat to live. You must be able to kill.'

So he didn't tell anybody what the sight, the thought, the smell of blood could do to him. He learned to see the spasms coming, and to control them.

Now he senses this one like a lithe willow rod that has inserted itself into him from his throat to his belly; it's a rising sensation that will spurt to his muscles and burst out of his body as a powerful convulsion. Carefully he observes the stirring, watching it creeping into his skull. He knows that as long as he holds it in his eye, the potential spasm remains just that. Observed, it appears unable to make the jump to his muscle and sinew. He has learnt to neither suppress it nor expel it. He simply observes, never shifting his attention for a moment, for the briefest lapse in concentration will release it, to his extreme humiliation.

He mutters inwardly, 'You are eighteen years old. This is a child's affliction.'

After a time the feeling eases and shrinks beneath his gaze, retreating down his spine. Eventually it fades, and returns to its home in the depths of his bowels. As he gains control over it he is able to turn his attention elsewhere. For now the word *prisoners* loses its potency.

Again there is a shift and a brush against his shoulder and this time he issues a warning, a short, sharp exhalation of air hissed through his teeth that can be heard no more than feet away. Beside him Remo releases the faintest of sighs and rests his muzzle on the forest floor.

'You must be able to kill, Toni,' said his father. 'Now you are ten I'm going to show you how.'

He shuddered, 'I've seen you already. I've seen you with…with the chickens.'

'The chickens are the chickens. You're going to earn your living from the land, like all of us. You know the creatures we have to deal with here – pigs, sheep, goats. What do you think is in that spezzatino you like so much, hmm?'

Mama turned from her cooking pot to where they sat at the bare wooden table and laid her hand on Papa's shoulder. 'Guido, so soon?'

Papa was of medium build, his forearms and shoulders powerful from labour. He grasped a chunk of cold polenta on his plate, mopped some gravy and shoved it in his mouth. Then he stood up, wiped the gravy off his black moustache and looked Toni in the eye.

'*Amore*, I was trapping rabbits two years younger than him. He's never brought home even one rabbit.'

He walked out and Toni, head hung down, followed him without looking at Mama.

They collected their jackets from the anteroom to the kitchen, and Toni pulled his shoes out from under the rows of tomatoes, maturing on wire shelves. They went down the wooden steps into the stall where the animals slept and then, in the fading light, passed through the vegetable patch and the rickety gate.

Their house sat a little way outside the arched gate that gave access to the walled village of Gemmano. Perched on the eastern end of the ridge, the village confidently surveyed the surrounding

3

countryside as far as Rimini on the coast to the east, and the jagged cliffs of San Marino to the northwest. Toni's house huddled below the village on the saddle that ran west along the ridge towards the little peak of Monte Gardo.

From their back door they descended the first of Papa's two fields, lying on the north face of the ridge. In search of distraction Toni peered across the Conca valley to where, atop a lower ridge, the village of Croce surveyed the valley between them. It always seemed to Toni that red-roofed Croce glared up at her bigger sister, sticking out her tongue and warning her not to look down her nose at her sibling.

Papa put his arm around Toni's shoulders. 'Don't worry, Toni. Marta's old and tired. It's her time and we have many uses for her. Her coat, her bones for broth, her heart for the pig. This time I'll do it. I just want you to understand how.'

Papa didn't believe in naming the animals and usually pretended not to know that his wife and children had done so. Toni was grateful for this small concession and he prayed his Papa wouldn't feel his shaking shoulders. As they climbed the stile into the second field Papa said, 'I can't see properly, it's so nearly dark. You'll have to identify her. You know her? She'll be at the bottom of the field lying beneath the *castagna*.'

Toni lingered behind as they walked down, unable to ignore the nausea in his belly. The mighty chestnut threw a shadow over the bottom corner and it became hard to see little more than his father's solid, erect silhouette. Papa turned to him, 'Come on, Toni. Keep up. Which is she? I can see two.'

He couldn't even bear to look. Glancing sideways he pointed at the one that looked weathered and shrunken and, as if knowing what was coming, her companion suddenly rose and trotted away.

Papa came back to him. 'Okay, so you take the knife like this, and hold it like this, huh? Always take this knife. It's sharp and the handle gives a good grip.'

Toni had his hands behind his back but his father grasped one of them and pulled him forward until, five or six paces away, Toni's feet refused to take him any closer, and he could only look at the sheep from the corner of his eye. Papa glanced at him, uttered a brief exhalation of frustration and walked over to Marta who was sitting up and trying to follow the other sheep. Getting a leg over her back he reached under her head and grasped her jaw.

'Now pull her head up like this, so her throat is exposed. Put the blade here…not too low…or you can't do it with one cut. Up here, see? Now press hard and one long motion.'

Toni barely saw the blade move for his legs began to shake. He sat heavily on the ground and wrapped his arms around his body. His head twisted away with a snap. He felt acid vomit rise in his gorge, burning his throat as it spurted out. Darkness pulled a merciful blind over his senses and the next thing he knew he was lying on his back in the arms of Papa who was wiping his face with a handkerchief.

'Toni, Toni. Are you there? *Porca miseria!* Toni?'

He sighed by way of response and his father's eyes rolled heavenward. 'Thank God. What happened to you? No,' Papa sighed, 'don't say anything. I already know.'

A deep pain spilled upwards from his stomach like the vomit a moment earlier, filling his chest and making him groan. This was not shame that he had passed out. After all, it was not a deliberate act. Partly he was sorry Papa didn't understand, though how could he be expected to? He was almost resigned to this and to the fact that his passing out would reinforce Papa's opinion of him. Mostly the pain was sorrow for old Marta. Each day she had fed off their land, grazed their grass, and faithfully given milk. She had hurt nobody, asked for nothing, offering her wool each spring. Now in her old age they had spilled her blood all over this corner of the field. Papa would dismember her and feed her heart to the pig. He felt his eyes filling with tears and jerked himself from his father's arms, rubbing his face by way of clearing his head.

'I am all right. I am all right now.'

He stood apart composing himself as his father picked up the boning knife, and then turned away so as not to watch the dismemberment.

There was a rustle in the hedge beside him. It became a repeated scrabbling and after a moment a lamb emerged from the hedgerow and uttered a distracted bleat. It moved this way and that, unsure of where to go, and then took a few paces towards him. He bent and reached out his arms to it but at that moment it spotted the other sheep, standing a little away. It stumbled over to her, bleating as it did, and was about to duck under in search of the teat when the sheep rounded on it and butted it firmly away. The lamb tried again and was rejected still more vigorously. Toni and his father looked at each other at the same moment, and then his father raised the head of the corpse and peered through the gloom at it.

'Ah! This isn't Marta. It's the mother! You pointed at the wrong sheep! That's Marta over there.'

Remo nudges him, and he nudges back sharply. He wants no noise or movement from the dog now. Up in the trees he has spotted a blur, the beating vision of a bird on the wing. With a whirring sound it arrives on the ground before the trap and looks around itself. Almost immediately others join it, until half a dozen of them stand there like a collection of dignitaries outside a bar. They are pigeons, their plumage faded as if a little bit of life has drained out of them.

This is familiar ground for them, though they have been slow to become accustomed to the nets. They initially refused to land and, when they did, they would peck and forage without approaching the entrance. But today he has run a trail of stolen breadcrumbs out through the gap in the nets.

'Toni, you have not eaten all that bread!' cried Mama this morning. 'Now we have nothing for tonight.'

'I'm sorry, Mama, I didn't know. I was so hungry,' he said, carefully stashing the remaining bread under the rope that held up his trousers.

She brought her eyes close to his. 'You know the Germans have taken most of our food. So now you will forage for wheat for bread. Go to the mill and wait around the back, scrape what you can into this bowl. And think of your hungry sister!'

She knows he hates this nearly futile job but he nods without comment, eyes on the table. Knowing he will go nowhere near the mill, he salvages his conscience over Francesca with the thought of the proud moment when he produces pigeons for Mama to make into a pie. He is sure to garner an approving nod from Papa. Meat is scarce now, the war has seen to that, though they are more fortunate than most. Papa, being a smallholder, hides their few remaining animals down in the cave during the day, to be butchered in an emergency. They have a pig, two sheep, a mule and of course Coco the cow for milk.

The pigeons maintain a distance from the nets, shuffling around the carpet of leaves, and he fears they will not be tempted. An idea comes to him and he thinks that if he makes a dash at them perhaps one will fly in by accident. But he knows this is a plan born of desperation and that patience, and silence, must be his tools.

To his left there is a movement up near the top of the trees, which he catches out of the corner of his eye. He looks sharply at the spot, risking movement as he does, unable to prevent himself. He doesn't think it is a bird. Something in the quality of the movement disturbs him.

He searches the branches carefully. No, not a bird.

So, one of them?

He stares intently at a gap between the trees, which opens and closes as the branches wave in the breeze.

Was it? Well? Was it one of *them*?

A gap is where they'll appear, if they do. They seem drawn to space. Leaves dance across each other, stirring the light and making his vision uncertain. He feels a tug of fear in his stomach as he narrows his eyes. This uncertainty has been the hardest part of his whole life.

His gaze does not flinch from the spot. But he comforts himself that it's rare for them to come to him in the woods; they prefer buildings like the church, or the school, or occasionally an open space. Once he's satisfied that he's alone, he breathes more easily and turns back to the task at hand.

There is a tiny whimper to his left and he reaches out, as quickly as he dares, and lays a hand on the scruff of Remo's neck. He has no need to feel for Romolo who has not moved, perhaps has not even breathed, since they took up position.

The first pigeon has spotted the crumb trail. There is a larger piece that it struggles to swallow, and its efforts catch the attention of another who struts over and steals it away. Now there is competition between them and the two begin working their way up the trail towards the heap of crumbs sitting in the middle of the trap. Aware of the development the other four scurry up behind and in a group they cross the threshold and into the nets. Toni waits until they get to the pile and tuck in.

Now is the moment. Centimetre by centimetre he draws his legs under him, at the same time raising himself onto his elbows and then the palms of his hands. He takes hold of his cap, lying beside him. Still hidden behind the pile of leaves he is able to watch them eat. He hesitates. He knows he should move now but they are enjoying the feast so much. They are hungry too. Do they not deserve a final meal, some last moments of bliss before he strikes? They peck and coo contentedly and he can almost imagine them sitting back in a few moments, putting the tips of their wings over their stomachs and burping in contentment. This thought amuses him and he is forced to grit his teeth and stifle a snigger.

'You must go now!'

He leaps across the leaves scattering them everywhere and hurls himself at the entrance, yelling and waving his cap to drive his prey to the back of the trap. Romolo and Remo are a fraction of a second behind but they skid to a halt as Toni leaps inside the nets and pulls them together, tying the entrance closed with prepared scraps of string. He holds up a finger and the dogs sit and go quiet.

Behind him there is frantic scattering and fluttering, and he turns to face his prisoners. His prisoners. For a moment the blackness sweeps across his vision but he shakes his head and dismisses it. Miraculously not one pigeon has escaped. Two are on the ground, cowering in a corner, and one has got caught in the nets. Three are still trying to fly, blundering into each other, and then one crashes directly into him. He turns his attention to these three, beating at them with his cap, not to kill, but to confuse. They dance around the cap briefly but he strikes again and again, catching them with glancing blows, and with their equilibrium unsettled and their senses stunned they fall to the ground.

He grabs for one with its back to him, clasping around its wings so that they cannot flap and cause the bird further distress. He holds it firmly and raises it up until it is close to his face. This one is dark grey, with lighter flecks across its wing and back. Around its neck is a green patch, faded and barely visible, and its beak hangs slightly open. It shivers as he looks into one orange, staring eye.

'Do not fear. It is nearly over.'

He lowers his head until his nose is touching the feathers on its back. 'I thank you for your body. I thank you for the meat on the table. Father, may this soul fly to you. May it soar on high, up to you. May it be radiant, may it be free. May it suffer no pain.'

Without allowing himself to consider the violence he is about to perpetrate, he turns to a corner of the trap where he has already set a large stone. Getting down on one knee he grits his teeth, raises the pigeon a little and brings it down in an arc so that its head smashes against the stone. It goes limp but he hits it again to be sure it is dead. He pauses a moment and looks away, and then he lays it by the stone neatly, with its wings tucked in and its head under its wing.

As he stands he feels the spasm grow inside him and the darkness sweeps up to envelop him. He drops instantly to his hands and knees, closing his eyes, observing the feeling. He sees the panting of his breath, the rise and fall of his shoulders, the growing willow inside him. He cannot slow it so his attention rises to the top of it, near his throat, and he clears his head of anything else. Just he, and the tip of the rod are all that exist. It shrinks, then grows again, shrinks and grows in time with his breath. The darkness roars over him like a mighty wave on a beach, and it blots out all sound. He consciously relaxes his chest and shoulder muscles as he breathes out, then his stomach and then his limbs. Gradually, painfully slowly, the roaring dark diminishes and the rod begins to shrink.

From the corner of his eye he can see a pigeon scrabbling under the net. In a moment it will be gone. All he need do is reach out and grab it but he dare not. The rod must remain his focus until it returns to its place of origin. The darkness still swirls around at the bottom of his consciousness, like a mist around his feet. He can feel his attention being dragged away by the escaping bird and refuses to look at it. He closes his eyes and remains with the threat until it is gone.

When he looks once more the pigeon is almost out, but he is too scattered to make a dive at it. The bird hops forward and under the net and launches itself skyward.

Recovering his composure he re-applies himself to his task. He grabs the next bird, which does not resist. He says his prayer without rushing and then kills it, two blows to be sure. He places it gently at rest next to the first corpse, and then the one after that. As he stands and looks at the three bodies in a row the nausea rises once more. Fighting off the blackness he grabs for the fourth bird. Without a prayer, without even looking at it, he swings it against the rock and drops it, like a piece of hot magma. He turns away panting and then his attention is caught by the scrabbling and fluttering of the not-dead bird. He groans, picks it up, strikes it again and drops it on top of the others. He falls to his knees once more, his head spinning, and waits until his breathing slows.

There is one pigeon left. It has got tangled in the nets at waist height and has given up its struggle, its chest heaving as it looks over its shoulder at him. Suddenly he is very calm. Quietly he picks the net off the pigeon, easing strands from around its neck and ankle. He checks to see if the wings are intact, and indeed the bird appears unhurt. He lifts it out of the net, and raising it to his face he looks into its orange eye.

He whispers, 'You are like a cat. You have more than one life. You can fly now. Live for your friends who are dead.'

He unties the entrance and steps out. Romolo and Remo look up expectantly at lunch, the reward for their patience. To their disgust he raises the bird above his head and releases it with a shove. 'Fly.'

The pigeon soars up through the trees and is gone.

Chapter 2
August 31st 1944, lunchtime

He has invaded land he has no right to be near. By setting his nets in this copse atop the small hillock that is Monte Cerpello, he has strayed into Zollara territory and his presence, if detected, will not be welcome. Indeed he is surprised that the nets have gone unnoticed by locals, though he plunged as deeply into the copse as he could. He knows this absence of vigilance is only because the land is owned by the dead. War weariness has sent so many of the elderly to their graves over the last eighteen months. The inheritors are in other parts of the country, perhaps fighting as partisans, perhaps in the King's remaining army advancing northwards with the Americans and the British. Perhaps dead or fleeing. No bureaucrat has the time or the inclination to follow up on death notifications now Mussolini has fallen, and dances like a puppet for Hitler in Gargnano.

Poised out of sight, several steps back from the edge of the field, Toni examines it for activity. It falls away to his right, a hump running across its centre, and the grass has been harvested for hay. It is stacked in golden piles at intervals throughout the field. He peers across to other copses on the far side but can detect no evidence of locals at work. He cranes his neck around trees that block his view, determined to be thorough.

His stomach rumbles and he remembers how hungry he is. He has forgone any lunch, lying in wait, so his entire consumption for the day consists of a piece of bread, a little goat's cheese and a square of yesterday's focaccia. His hand moves to his belt, and he touches and counts four soft, bloodied heads. The family can look forward to a good dinner tonight, and there will be more vegetables for him.

But he knows he will never come to these nets again. It costs him too much.

He catches something out of the corner of his eye. It is not so much a movement as a modification in the quality of…the light? …the air?…his perception? In a piece of music it would be the background tone of an organ clearly but subtly changing chord just once, underneath the harmony of string and wind sections that are the trees and the breeze. The symphony plays on, yet there is an undeniable shift in the atmosphere.

Reluctantly he raises his head until he is looking above the treeline. His instincts have not deceived him and he flinches. One of *them* is rising above a large oak. It needs the space above the vegetation and he steps well back from the edge of the field, letting the forest surround and cloak him. It will not find it easy to approach him down here. He stills his trembling, and narrowing his eyes he glares at it. This rarely makes any difference, but here, today, it shows no sign of coming down. After a time it drifts behind the tree and he senses, rather than sees, that it has gone.

He half turns and without taking his eyes off the treeline he calls out, 'Romulus, Remus.'

Remo rushes over and bumps into his legs, rubbing his flank along him and grinning up. He is taller than Toni's knees, his short, wiry coat a deep rusty colour that tapers to the tip of his almost black tail. Toni rubs Remo's head. He knows they are wary of the dogs, and unlikely to approach.

Romolo also trots up, and sits a yard away looking at him, ears cocked as if to say, 'Why do you name us in English like that?'

Reassured by his presence Toni grins and continues in English, 'I like the show off, you know, my English. I like the practice.'

Romolo is black, of lighter build, his hair longer and shinier. Toni is regularly to be found untangling objects from his coat.

'Sie mag meine Sprachen?'

Romolo lies down, his paws facing straight forward. 'Yes, we know you speak German too, though aren't you being a little formal with me?'

Toni switches back to English, 'Is because I speak English better. German – mm, German I understand but to speak is hard.'

Romolo looks into the distance as if bored by the discussion on linguistics. Toni says, 'What about you? You speak two languages too. The professor taught you when he was teaching me, remember?'

Professor Carter taught him his first words in English by working with the dogs. 'Sit', 'lie down', 'come', and other commands were amongst his earliest encounters with another language, and Toni delighted in using them to bend the dogs to his will. He did not even know where the professor had come from, only that the year before the war he'd arrived in the vicinity with his two young dogs. Out collecting wild asparagus one morning Toni had come across him perched on a fallen tree making notes in a leather diary, peering over his glasses at the hillside and then at his notes again. Toni was so surprised that he stopped dead and simply gaped. The professor left off writing and looked at him, addressing him in faultless Italian.

'Don't be afraid of the dogs. They're very friendly.'

'I'm not afraid of dogs. I had a beautiful dog with thick, long, black and white hair, but she died last year.'

'And what was her name?'

'Aurora, but I called her Aura, 'cos I couldn't say her name properly when I was a little boy. We went everywhere together.'

The professor raised an eyebrow. 'You know the area?'

Toni flicked his wrist at the surrounding countryside, 'Aura and me went everywhere. Villa. Farneto. We even stayed out all night once when we went over to Croce.'

'And what were you doing way over there?'

'We were following an injured pheasant, to help it, and it ran all the way down into the valley, over the Conca river, and up the other side. Can you believe it?'

'Indeed I can't. That must be over two kilometres!' said the professor in admiration.

'But it got dark and when we got back down to the Conca we couldn't find the crossing, so we slept there and Papa found me in the morning.'

'Wasn't he cross with you?'

Toni considered for a moment, 'No, he was happy. Well, relieved anyway.'

'You wouldn't happen to know a place called Casa Menghino over there, would you? I have to meet some people there.'

'Of course. But today I have to find asparagus. I can show you tomorrow.'

Toni attached himself to the professor without any conscious decision. He'd watch the same spot each day until the professor showed up, and then he marched with him over the ridges of

Croce, Zollara, Villa and Farneto, the professor scribbling notes, the dogs at his heel. When the professor sat to survey the view Toni would practice instructions with the dogs.

'Romolo, play dead!'

The dogs did as they were told, partly because they liked him, and partly because the professor's authority lurked in the background. Besides, when they obeyed him they got their tummies rubbed. Romolo would get bored first, wandering off and sniffing in ditches and rabbit holes. Remo would grin at him, and push him with his nose for more tickling. Eventually when Toni had had enough he would edge close to the professor.

'How do you say that, in English?'

'This? This is my notebook. Notebook. And this is my pen.'

'What are you writing?'

'Well, I'm…'

'No, tell me in English so I can see if I understand anything.'

Slowly the professor told him that he was in the region studying the state of Italian agriculture for his university in London. He was observing methods and degrees of mechanization.

Toni laughed. 'Okay, now tell me again in Italian.'

Afterwards he had run home as fast as he could. Arriving at the stall he slipped past the pig and up the steps to the kitchen door, announcing to his startled family, *My name is Toni.*

Mama turned from the fire to her husband, eyebrows raised. Francesca said, 'I think he is telling us his name is Toni.'

Mama looked astonished. 'I know his name is Toni. I brought him into this world.'

I am twelve year old.' He held up ten fingers and then two more to emphasize the point.

'Why are you speaking like that? I can't understand you,' grumbled Mama.

Toni danced before the kitchen table, slapping his head, accidentally kicking a pot into the broad fireplace. 'I am speaking English. I learnt it today from an English professor. *I am twelve year old!*'

He laughed out loud and Francesca laughed with him. Mama retrieved the pot with an oven cloth and told him to be more careful. Then she, and everybody else in the room, turned to look at Papa. He was seated, as always, at the head of the table, pipe in hand. The gloom of the kitchen somehow emphasized the bushiness of his moustache and at the same time hid his ears, which stuck out a little. He put the pipe on the table.

'Who is this...professor? Is he a real professor?'

Toni knew he must be quiet now and give Papa his full attention. 'I think he is real. He can write – pages and pages. He wears a tie and good boots and a jacket that looks new. He has two dogs.'

Papa's face softened in understanding. 'Ah, dogs. So, if he's English how can you speak to him?'

'He speaks Italian like you and me.'

'Maybe we should meet him. Invite him to dinner.'

Mama flapped her apron, 'Here, to this...?' she gestured about the main room of the house, 'You cannot bring a distinguished foreign professor to this house. It's too poor. Look at the state of the sideboard. And you need to paint the walls again. They are becoming black from the fireplace.'

Papa glanced around himself. 'My house is good enough for anybody. We can invite Father Morelli too, if you like. Anyway, I want to know who Toni is spending time with.'

'But what will we say to him? How will we speak to him?'

'You heard Toni. He speaks Italian. I want to ask him about England. I want to know if they will stop Hitler.'

Toni's eyes glistened, 'And he knows lots about farming.'

'Why do you love speaking English so much?' Mama demanded. 'They're all just foreigners.'

Papa held up a finger. 'In the White War there were often communication problems. They could cause great confusion and many deaths, and there were times when we needed to speak English. It's good to speak another language.'

'So I'll ask him then,' Toni interjected quickly.

The professor charmed everybody. He talked to Papa about new ways to feed livestock and fertilize fruit trees, and he made a show of taking notes while Papa explained the best way to keep olives. He thrilled Mama when he said dinner was better than the food in the finest restaurants in Bologna. Francesca giggled shyly while he pulled out a map of Britain and showed her where he lived and worked, and all the while Toni played with the dogs who were not allowed over the threshold. When the food arrived

Professor Carter watched without comment when Toni was served a 'minestre' while the rest of them ate a boar casserole on polenta. Toni explained, without embarrassment, 'I don't eat meat any more.'

The professor nodded politely, 'And why is that?'

Toni said, 'I don't want to kill animals so it seems hypocritical if I should eat them.'

Toni saw the professor glance across at Father Morelli, also invited by Papa for the security of having a familiar, authoritative figure around.

'Vegetarianism is not so strange. There are eastern religions, such as Buddhism, where none of them eat meat.'

'What is Buddhism?' Toni asked.

The professor and the priest took turns to explain the concepts of reincarnation and meditation as best they could, answering a variety of questions from Toni, until Papa grew bored and drew the professor back into agricultural conversation. Father Morelli smiled at Toni and ruffled his hair.

As the professor left, Mama slipped him a slice of vegetable pie wrapped in a napkin and Papa handed him a bottle of his own wine. 'You must come again. Send word with Toni and stop by any time for a glass.'

After he was gone Toni said, 'Papa. Now Aura is gone we should be thinking of getting another dog.'

Now Toni creeps towards the edge of the copse. The August sun beats down on the field, harvested and peppered with haystacks. He watched the women from his hiding place some days ago, forking the hay up against a triangle of timber, so that the stacks stood straight and strong with walls and a roof like a circular hut. On other days he might track along the edge of the field before emerging at its narrower end, leaving himself less exposed to the locals. But today he is hungry, and the birds hanging from his belt strengthen his resolve. He feels lighter, more confident. He peers again to left and right, and over at the copses on the other side of the field, but sees nothing to alarm him. He will take the quicker route.

He steps onto the field, and into the feeling that he is standing stark naked in the school playground. His skin crawls. It crawls in a way that's out of proportion with simple apprehension of locals. But the dogs, taking his lead, bounce into the open. They bang shoulders as they playfully snap at each other's faces, breaking off to sniff around the base of the nearest haystack. Toni stops and turns a full circle, watching the edges of the field and the top of the treeline, all the way around. It couldn't be quieter. The dogs continue to trot about, sanguine, and this reassures him. Touching the heads of the pigeons he sets off, maintaining a steady, careful gait, glancing to either side. The tufts of cut grain crunch and bend beneath his feet, and although the surface is uneven he is sure-footed, even in his worn-out, string-repaired shoes. He gives a brief whistle, for Romolo is ranging further afield than he would like.

As he approaches a dip in the field he halts. There is a haystack ahead and to his right, perhaps thirty metres away, and he cannot see the base of it for the dip. The breeze flows over him and whisks away the noise he thought he heard. He cannot say what kind of noise, only that he wouldn't expect to hear it. He closes his eyes and listens, but there are only the trees swaying in the copse behind him. He is poised for flight, from what he has no clue, and then Remo disappears around the haystack. He hurries after the dog.

There is an exclamation from behind the haystack and then a roar, and Remo leaps into view heading across the hump. He runs with his hind legs tucked up, and as he glances over his ears are laid back. Toni is about to whistle when a figure stumbles into view. He is in German uniform, though his jacket is open and his shirt undone. He wears no helmet and his short, fair hair is dishevelled. He bends over, spits some liquid from his mouth and grabs a stone. He launches a poorly aimed throw at Remo who has turned to survey the effect of his incursion, and is not even aware a missile has been hurled at him. The German bends, seeking another stone, and then he spots Toni. He lurches upright and stops, one hand on his hip.

'What have we here?' he says in German, then raises a warning finger as Toni glances around for an escape route. 'No, no, no, my handsome young fellow. Don't move. Please, don't move.'

His face is slim with soft lines around his jaw, a small mouth and prominent lips. He is slight of build. He glances back at the haystack, 'How long have you been standing there?'

Toni plays dumb. The German wipes his mouth with his hand, glances at it and then cleans it on his trousers. He approaches Toni and then looks across at Romolo who is close by and beginning to growl. 'Is that dog dangerous?'

Toni shrugs and begin to walks towards Remo who has started circling them nervously. Toni knows he won't respond to the whistle unless he can calm the dog first.

'*Ferma*,' cries the German, in Italian, and Toni does.

Before anything else can be said another German emerges from behind the haystack. This one is large, heavy, with a square haircut. Toni has heard German soldiers referred to as 'squareheads' and supposes this is why. He has no jacket or shirt on and is buttoning up the flies on his trousers. He pulls his pistol from its holster.

'Stefan, where is that dumb animal?' he demands, though Remo is directly in front of him. He raises the pistol, takes brief aim, and fires. Remo catapults into the air. To Toni it seems like his body is suspended in time and space, hung six feet above the ground, half upside down and twisted, his tongue hanging sideways and his rear legs splayed. He can see the grey hairs around his eyes and muzzle, and the fine white stripe down the centre of his forehead. Then the dog collapses on the ground motionless.

It feels as if a shock wave from a nearby bomb has hit. His senses are knocked out of him and all he can hear is a buzzing noise that fills his head and forces him to his knees, clutching his head. The field spins and he doesn't know which way is up. Bile rises up into his throat and a black wave assaults him. Through the dizziness he can see the German aiming again at the prone body of Remo.

With a cry he hauls himself to his feet and staggers over to the dog, brushing off a restraining hand from the blonde German, Stefan, who tries to hold him back. He hurls himself over Remo spreading his arms and legs as wide as he can, trying to cover every inch. Looking back at the German he can see the gun is pointed at him and the German is shouting, 'Get off, or I will kill you too!'

'Don't shoot, don't shoot,' he cries in Italian, still trying to

18

maintain the illusion of incomprehension. The German steps threateningly towards him and brings the pistol up to his eye, pointing it straight at Toni's face.

'Get off the dog, or I will kill you. You understand me. Oh yes, you understand me.'

'I cannot,' he cries, 'I cannot.'

There is a roar of pain nearby and they both look over at Stefan who is leaping about and clutching his arse. Romolo has observed him trying to restrain his master and has raced over and bitten him hard.

'It bit my bum, it bit my bloody bum,' yells Stefan.

To Toni's surprise the heavy German bursts out laughing. In other circumstances Toni might have been amused himself at the little fellow hopping about the field, and now the other is doubled up with laughter, almost dropping his pistol.

Stefan shouts at him, 'Yes laugh, Wolfgang, laugh. That's all you can do, you brute. Why don't you shoot the damn thing? It probably has rabies in any case. Do something useful. Shoot it.'

His comrade is staggering around clutching his stomach, but he still has his pistol and now he starts firing off shots in Romolo's direction. But the dog is too quick, nipping behind a haystack, and Wolfgang is laughing so much that there is more danger he will kill Stefan. After a minute he gives up and sits, wiping his brow with his hand, occasionally glancing at Stefan and bursting into renewed gurgles of mirth.

In Toni's arms Remo twitches. He looks down where he is cradling the dog's head on his lap and examines the wound. It is easy to find, running blood as it is, but when he wipes it away with the cuff of his shirt he finds it isn't deep. It appears to be a glancing blow. Lowering his head he listens carefully. Remo is still breathing.

The two Germans are shouting at each other and as quietly as possible he begins to drag Remo up the slope towards another haystack some twenty metres away. He doesn't want to stand and carry him for fear of attracting their attention so he crawls, pulling Remo with him, still cradling his head as he does. From time to time he listens again, just to reassure himself that he hasn't imagined it, but yes, Remo is breathing. He is about five metres short of his ground when there is a shout. He freezes.

The heavy one, still grinning, has risen and is now strolling over towards him. The gun is back in its holster. He looks at the prone body of Remo in Toni's arms and asks in German, 'Your dog?'

Even if this were not a breathtakingly stupid question Toni has the presence of mind to look blank. He lowers his head and buries it in Remo's neck, but the German kicks him and makes him look up.

'What are you doing here? Are you spying on us?'

Stefan comes over rubbing his bottom. 'I don't believe he understands us, Wolfgang. Look at him, he's just a peasant.'

'We will see.' Wolfgang reaches for his pistol again but his comrade rests a hand, lightly, upon his arm. 'Leave this to me.'

Wolfgang shrugs as if the matter is of no interest to him and goes away to take a pee.

'Now, get up,' the other signals, and then says in Italian *'Si alzi!'*

Toni obeys, gently resting Remo's still-supine head upon the ground as he does. The soldier walks back and forth without speaking, looking him up and down, and Toni shivers.

'Dove vai?' he says suddenly, again in Italian.

'A casa.' Home.

'What were you doing here?' He asks this in German, as if it is too hard to formulate in Italian.

Again Toni looks dumb but the soldier, with a mixture of hand signals and finally a frustrated clip around Toni's ear, makes himself understood. Toni turns slightly to the left so that the pigeons may not be so obviously in view. 'Looking for mushrooms,' he says, hoping this is a city dweller unfamiliar with the seasons.

'Show…er…show them to me!'

Toni points at his mouth, and rubs his hungry belly.

The soldier appears satisfied, making a brief gesture with his head as if dismissing him. But as Toni turns Wolfgang calls over, 'Stefan, what has he there, in his belt?'

The soldier makes Toni turn. 'They're pigeons!'

'Take them from him. They'll make a good supper.'

Stefan reaches out and prevents Toni from leaving, and from a nearby haystack there is a deep growl. Stefan glances anxiously over and then snaps his fingers indicating that Toni should hand them over.

'Si prega di lasciarmeli. Please, please don't steal them. It is all I

have to feed our family. I have four young sisters and my mother has no food in the kitchen to feed them. We have hardly eaten since – well there is no food around in recent days. We are really desper…'

The soldier cuts him off with a sharp gesture, and Wolfgang asks, 'What did he say?'

Stefan looks exasperated. 'How should I know? I was taught the same phrases you were. I can tell him to put his hands up, or clean out the latrine, or write down his rank and regiment. Negotiating for dead fowl was not part of the orientation course!'

He puts his hand firmly on Toni's shoulder to silence him and then reaching down he removes three of the pigeons. The fourth he pushes surreptitiously around Toni's back and flicks his shirt half over it. He backs off looking Toni in the eye, and then with a slight wink he turns away.

The other German has watched all this closely. Not convinced and losing patience he pulls out his pistol again and marches over to where Toni is bending towards Remo. He puts the gun to Toni's head and grabbing his arm he spins him around. The nearby growling intensifies causing him to loose off a shot in that general direction, and the sound reverberates in Toni's head, like a ball bouncing back and forth between the walls of his skull. He holds his hands together in the sign of prayer but Wolfgang has a hard, dead look in his eyes and Toni is sure he is about to die. The soldier reaches down, grabs the remaining pigeon and rips it off him, snapping Toni's rope belt and causing his trousers to fall down to his ankles.

This triggers another outburst of mirth. Wolfgang turns to his comrade and points at what has happened, slaps his thigh and roars some more. Toni stands there, too afraid to be embarrassed until Wolfgang realizes he still has his gun in his hand. Chortling he slips it into the holster and waves Toni away.

The two soldiers gather the rest of their clothing from behind the haystack, dress quickly and then walk up the hill towards the Zollara road at the top of the field. Stefan glances across at him as they depart. Toni watches them go and then takes Remo in his arms without even bothering to pull up his trousers. The dog's eyes are now open, though a little glazed, and he flicks a grateful tongue at Toni's face in acknowledgement. But he is shaking too in a way that tells Toni he is in great pain. Romolo comes over and sniffs at Remo, licks the wound for a while and then lies down nearby.

Toni caresses Remo and talks soothingly to him. Then he lays the dog's head upon the ground and kneels beside him to make himself comfortable. He puts his hands upon Remo's head and neck and allows the heat to arise in him. He feels it come from his chest and his shoulders and he allows it to gather in his arms and flow into his hands. As smoothly as butter pouring from a saucer on a hot day the energy flows, his hands begin to warm and he rests them a little more firmly into Remo's fur. The dog relaxes. From a distance, were Stefan to glance back down the field, he would see the young man bowing over the dog, his head touching its coat, as if in prayer. After a while he would have seen the dog get to his feet and lick Toni's face.

Toni falls to the ground, instantly asleep. Remo and Romolo lie on either side of him in the middle of the field, keeping him between them. Romolo's eyes are never closed, though at times they appear so. He never ceases to glance around and over the bodies of his exhausted companions.

Chapter 3
August 31st 1944, afternoon

When Toni awakes the quality of the light has changed. The heat blazes upon the side of his face, which throbs in time with his pounding head, and he longs for a breath of cool breeze. The shadows are longer and sharper, and he pulls himself into the shade of the nearby haystack. It is as if a great hand has redirected the heat of the sun and he breathes more easily. His mouth feels dry. He leans against the haystack and takes Remo's head in his hands.

'How do you feel?'

Remo grins at him, his tongue lolling from the side of his mouth. His eyes are no longer glazed but there is a noticeable lack of energy about the dog. He buries his nose under Toni's arm and sits quietly. Romolo shifts and Toni sees that he too is thirsty. He looks over at the far side of the field. After the dry summer there is only one nearby stream that still has a trickle of water in it.

It is only as he stands, and his trousers fall to the ground, that he recalls the fate of his pigeons. As he makes repairs to his belt he sighs, knowing he will be in trouble for not having gone to find wheat for bread, and he will have no excuse. If he tells Mama about the pigeons she will only think he is lying.

Glancing up where the Germans left the field he can make out a motorcycle and sidecar parked under the plane trees lining the road, but there is no evidence of the pair themselves.

'You're a brave boy,' he says to Romolo, patting his head.

He does what he can with his trousers and heads across the field, watching his feet as he plods. He need not keep an eye out for the dogs; Remo is walking right in at heel and Romolo – well, Romolo does as he pleases unless he is told otherwise, and Toni trusts him to take care of himself. As he walks the throbbing fades and he finds himself feeling rested after his sleep. But he is a little fuzzy too, as if he has taken a second glass of Papa's wine.

There is no need to climb the fence at the edge of the field. It is so broken down as to be scarcely visible amongst the high grass and stray poppies. He steps over it and into the copse, knowing there is a nearby stream to his left with water in it. He turns to make sure Romolo is following.

'Sssssss.'

He freezes at the sound. The breeze brushes his ear with a hanging twig and he glances sharply to his right. He reaches up to the twig and strokes the leaves, and then looks reluctantly about him. A bee stumbles across the air, seeming to leave a space in its wake, a space into which he looks almost expectantly. It's been such a violent day that his thinking is panicked. Could one of *them* have followed him? Space is something they gravitate towards, and they like it when he is fuzzy too. He feels his chest constrict and his pulse quicken. But there is only the field, and now Romolo who pushes down the high grass with his chest.

In any case they do not speak, if indeed they have mouths. Had it followed him he'd have been aware of its presence before now. He knows he's being foolish and releases a long, slow breath.

'Ssssssss.' It is a human voice without a doubt. 'Here, over here.'

There is a rustle in the undergrowth behind him and he bends and peers. There is a face, almost at ground level, and a hand holding back some branches while the other beckons him. Beside him Romolo growls, and Remo looks on passively.

Resting a hand on Romolo's head, he steps cautiously towards the man. The stranger is hard to see with the mottled light of the undergrowth upon him, but Toni can make out a large moustache, dark hair and an unshaven, yet pleasant face. The hand that beckons him is so dirty he cannot make out the fingernails. Toni steps closer until he is almost within touching distance, when another growl from Romolo makes him hesitate.

'Who are you?'

'Come in and I will tell you.' The voice is educated, low and urgent.

'Tell me first.'

'Listen, I'm very sorry to do this but…'

The hand has disappeared and now re-emerges with a gun, which is pointed at Toni. It occurs to him that he has never had a gun pointed at him in his life, and now two within the afternoon. The second time is less startling and he crouches down, looking the man in the face. He is still semi-hidden but Toni can see the dark hair is curly and matted, with twigs and leaves snagged in it.

'What do you want? Why will I come in there if you don't tell me what you want?'

'I want to tell you. I *will* tell you, when we are safe under these bushes. At present you may still be seen by those Germans if they go past.'

This makes sense and their shared language, and apprehension of Germans, convinces him. Carefully he slips under the branches and into a dim, twig-strewn space that is surrounded by bushes and covered by a tree, which hangs over them like a giant umbrella. He holds onto Romolo, not trusting him to behave, and settles a little way from the man, an arm around each dog for reassurance. He finds his voice is trembling as he says, 'Now, put the gun away.'

The man puts the gun on the ground beside him. He is of medium build and wears the remains of a uniform that looks Italian, but it is badly ripped down one leg, with dark stains all over it.

'Why? Why do you have to point a gun at me?'

The man holds out a hand. 'Calm yourself. I'm sorry, but I don't know who to trust any more. I've met many people on my journey and some were cowards who turned me away, and on one occasion betrayed me. I have to be very careful.'

'What cowards? Germans?'

'Italians.' The man's eyes flash for a moment. Then his shoulders slump a little. 'But perhaps I shouldn't blame them so much. They had suffered terribly, and they were very afraid.'

'Where have you been?'

The man glances away for a moment, and his voice grows a little fainter. 'I've been a long way. A long, long way. And I have further to go.' He glances back at Toni. 'I will tell you, but first...'

He reaches into the breast pocket of his uniform and pulls out a rather crushed packet of cigarettes. He carefully extracts one slightly less bent, and leaning over he offers it to Toni, who shakes his head.

'No? Now I've seen everything.'

He pulls a packet of matches from the same pocket and lights the cigarette himself.

'My name is Lorenzo Bergamas. It's not my own name, but that's a story for later. I was with the king's army in Russia, fighting the Communists alongside the Germans,' he glances up sharply, 'but I am no fascist, hm?'

Toni persuades Romolo to lie down with Remo and the dog obeys reluctantly. Lorenzo shifts his leg as the dog lies close, and then groans and winces as he does. He lowers his head almost to the ground and Toni can see him clenching his fist and biting it. He looks again at the dark stains on the torn leg of the uniform. It is blood.

'Your leg. How bad?'

Lorenzo turns to him again, sweat mingling with the dirt on his forehead. 'Later. First I will tell you. I want you to trust me.'

Toni cannot help but be moved. 'No, first I will help you.'

He crawls over beside Lorenzo and begins to pick away the torn strips of the trouser leg. In places they are stuck to the leg by semi-congealed blood, and he peels them slowly. The fact that the blood has no effect upon him at all escapes his notice completely.

'Sssss. Careful. Careful!'

He works as gently as he can until the wound is exposed, though he can see little for the dirt, blood and leaves. In order to distract Lorenzo he asks, 'What happened?'

Lorenzo groans, 'It was this morning. I was trying to get through the Zollara hamlet when I passed by a garden. I wouldn't have gone in but I could see some tomato vines. I hadn't eaten for twenty-four hours and the tomatoes were big and ripe and red. I just wanted to take two, to feed my belly. There was a rusty iron fence around the garden with spikes on the top, so I had to be careful as I climbed over. But I think those tomatoes must be famous around here for he has a dog to protect them too! I didn't see it until I was all the way over the fence – as a matter of fact I believe it waited for me. It was a big, black brute with tawny streaks around the face and it came straight for me. It was snarling and all I could see was this big set of teeth.'

Toni knows the dog and is always careful to keep Romolo away from it. Romolo would not step back from a fight, but the other dog is very big and Toni is afraid for him.

'So what did you do?'

'I turned and leapt the fence, but I did it so quickly that I missed my jump and landed on one of the spikes, which went deep into my calf as you can see. I was so afraid of the dog I ripped my leg up and off the fence and fell over onto the other side. Anyway, at least the dog didn't get me.'

'There isn't too much blood, but this needs to be cleaned, or it will go bad and you may lose the leg. Wait here. Don't move.'

Instructing the dogs to stay, he pushes aside the branches of their hidden bothy, and makes his way down to the stream. He slips his cap under a tiny waterfall that gradually fills it, though he cannot resist cupping his hands and drinking the sweet water first. Then he goes searching in the undergrowth. He carefully selects a fistful of leaves and herbs, and then collects a couple of good sized, flat stones from the bed of the stream. When the cap is full he hurries back.

Lorenzo has his head bowed and his hands clasped together, as if he is praying. Remo is lying beside him. He looks up and asks, 'What have you there?'

'I'm going to make you a poultice. This herb is the most important one. Around here it's called *'Lingua Cane'* – the tongue of the dog. It's good for dressing wounds.'

'Will it work?'

'Don't worry, it has helped many a person. Now, tell me.'

He puts the larger, flatter stone on the ground and starts to grind his herbs; Lorenzo begins.

'I came back to Italy this year, after nine months in Russia. They were the worst nine months of my life, and the cold is something I will never forget, all my life. Even now I can't get warm at night. That peacock Mussolini sent us – he told Hitler he was going to help him, but really he just wanted to get his hands on the oil further east. Then we got caught by the Russkis on the River Don. They surrounded us and we couldn't escape. Our officers had no idea what to do, but we'd heard the Russkis were taking no prisoners so we said to them, 'Come on, at least let us die fighting to get out of here. We've got to break out.'

'There was one officer who listened to us. He got us together and we fought our way out, but I'll tell you something; there were less than nine thousand of us by the time we got repatriated back to Italy. You know how many were on the Don? Over thirty thousand!'

'Stay still,' says Toni, holding him down, 'I'm trying to clean your wound out.'

'Thirty thousand,' says Lorenzo subsiding against the trunk of the tree again. 'When we returned to Italy it was just in time for the surrender. They called it an armistice but we knew what it was. Badoglio was telling Hitler one thing, and negotiating a surrender with the allies behind his back. It was humiliating to be a part of it. None of our officers stayed around when the army was stood down; they all just buggered off home. Left us standing there! So we talked it over and decided we'd do the same. Some wanted to fight with the Nazis but not me. I'd seen enough of what they did in Russia to prisoners. No wonder the Russkis weren't taking any prisoners either. We used to hear the screams of the captured. We were told the Teds hung them up and then hammered used cartridge shells into their knees. Can you imagine it? And then they started behaving like that in Italy. You know, any Italian soldier who fights with the allies is being treated like a traitor and shot without trial!'

Toni doesn't speak, he is so overawed by this man's experiences. Lorenzo clearly needs to talk, so Toni concentrates on his work, grinding up the herbs and sprinkling water on the little pile. Now he wraps it in dock leaves and looks around for something to apply it. Reluctantly he takes off his trousers and rips a leg off.

'What are you doing?' says Lorenzo.

'They are old,' Toni shrugs. 'Mama hates them.'

He wraps the poultice more tightly into a kind of flat wad, soaking it all in his cap. 'Lie back while I apply this to your leg. Tell me how you got here.'

Lorenzo sucks air sharply between his teeth as Toni applies the poultice. 'Well, all I wanted to do was to come home. I had no news of my family, and they none of me. We were stationed near Florence so I headed south to try and attach myself to the allies as an interpreter – I speak English you see. I figured going north would be easier with them, rather than trying to make it on my own. Then later I got myself attached to the Canadians when they began their push towards the Gothic Line. I wanted the Canadians 'cos they were going up the east coast – ouch, go easy!'

Apart from an apology Toni remains silent. He can't imagine

the suffering of being separated from his family for that long. He finishes binding the poultice onto Lorenzo's leg.

'How did you learn to do something like that?' asks Lorenzo.

'My Grandpa taught me before he died. He used to take me into the woods a lot. There are all kinds of things in here for healing. It's better than the village store.'

'Will it ease the pain?'

'I don't think so – but it will stop the bleeding, and the wound will heal more quickly.'

With a sigh Lorenzo leans his head against the trunk and caresses Remo's head, lying on his lap. Then he squints down at Toni.

'You're a smart kid, aren't you? And brave. I saw you with those Tedeschi.'

'You were watching?'

'Yes, but,' he indicates his leg, 'I couldn't do anything to help. Good thing you don't speak German.'

'In fact I do understand it, a bit.'

'What, in this hilltop village?'

'When Italy declared war the government said we must have German speakers – that we must be able to communicate with our fascist brothers in arms. The Mayor organized a German teacher to come for a while. They thought, because I speak some English, that I have an aptitude for languages so they made me learn. Papa didn't like it much but he didn't say anything.'

Lorenzo nods. 'I thought that big brute was going to kill you for sure. That's when I knew I could risk contact with you.'

'It's the first time I've spoken to any of them really. They're normally down in the valley, passing through. It's only in the past few days that they've been into the village much, usually to talk to the priest.'

'Then you should know it's very dangerous for you to be helping me. If they find us like this, now, they will kill you as well as me. To them I'm a traitor and you are assisting me.'

Toni shrugs again. 'I can't just leave you here.'

There is a silence while Lorenzo caresses Remo's broad head and Toni pulls on his one-legged trousers. He sits besides Romolo and says, 'What are you doing here if you wanted to go up the coast? This isn't the way.'

Lorenzo glances at him. 'The Allies are very close now. Up the coast is the way home for me, but I heard the coastal route is well defended. I think that I have some relatives...er...near here, so I thought if I got to them maybe I could rest a while. So two days ago I slipped away from the Canadians.'

Toni is distracted as Lorenzo tries to ease his leg into a more comfortable position. The sweat is pouring from the man's forehead and he is barely able to suppress his groans.

Toni has never tried it on a human before. It has worked for the dogs, and he has helped injured animals but nothing more. Furthermore, he has never done it twice in a day, for it leaves him drained, and even though he rested in the field he doesn't know how much he has in him. He gets up.

'Lie down flat on the ground.

Toni props Lorenzo's head up with a pile of leaves, and then kneeling beside him he closes his eyes. Making himself comfortable he rests his hands on the injured leg, one above and one below the wound, and then he waits. For a moment nothing happens, to the point where he starts to feel foolish. Then deep in his chest he feels the heat rising into his shoulders and neck. He breathes deeply and allows it to gather in his arms and flow down through his hands into Lorenzo's leg. He feels him flinch and tightens his grip to prevent movement.

'I don't know what you can feel. You must tell me.'

Lorenzo says, 'It feels warm. Your hands feel warm! Hot even.'

'Okay, lie still.'

Remo and Romolo are the largest creatures he has ever laid his hands on, and this man must be over twice their weight. Not only that, the wound is deeper than anything he has encountered. Somewhere in his chest he is usually able to control the generation and the flow of energy, knowing each passing second drains more from him, using it as sparingly as he can. He knows this will not suffice here and focusing on his chest he watches the energy carefully and then, with an exhalation of breath he opens the flow completely. The heat surges into his arms and he hears Lorenzo give a gasp. It flows more powerfully than he ever imagined possible, and it seems to him that his hands must be glowing. Though not consumed by it, for after all it is he who generates it, there is nothing in his consciousness except for his hands and Lorenzo's leg. The outside world ceases to intrude upon him. He is able to hold himself in position for barely a minute before he can feel the energy subsiding, and an overwhelming tiredness assaults him from the edges of his senses. He removes his hands, and his head hangs down to his knees.

'The pain. The pain is almost gone.' Toni doesn't respond. 'That's unbelievable. Have you cured me?'

Toni shakes his head and whispers, 'It's only for the pain. Now I must rest.'

He falls beside Lorenzo, and just as sleep overwhelms him he says, 'The Allies are right behind you. We must see my father. We must warn the village.'

Toni is awoken by Lorenzo's hand shaking and shaking his shoulder. But it feels a long way back for Toni, from the depths of an exhausted sleep.

'I'm not ready,' he complains. 'I'm not ready to wake up.'

'You must. You must wake up. There are too many Germans around here. Look, there goes a truck along the track above.'

The light beneath the tree is dimmer though Toni can still see patches of sunlight outside. Everything is blurry to him, and his head is sore. It is hard to formulate words. He sits up and rubs his eyes and his face. Without looking at Lorenzo he says, 'You cannot walk.'

'Look at me!'

Toni glances up and there is Lorenzo standing with his hands wide apart and a smile on his face. 'You've cured me.'

Toni shakes his head. 'I told you, I have only eased the pain for a while. It'll come back and when it does it will be like before. That's a deep wound.'

'But I cannot stay here.'

'Didn't you tell me your relatives are close by? What village?'

Lorenzo says, 'Gemmano. That's the name I was told.'

'But I am from Gemmano! You can come with me. I will bring you to Papa and later we can find your family. We'll keep you safe until your leg is better.'

'Listen, before I hooked up with the allies I was making my way through German-occupied Italy alone. In one village I nearly got caught when they betrayed me because they were paid. I would not impose that choice upon your family.'

31

Toni is impressed by the honourable words. 'I will not bring you into our village. But you don't know my father. You can trust him. He's not afraid of the Germans. He fought them during the White War. Sometimes we help to hide partisans. We can do the same thing for you. Don't be afraid.'

'It's different now. This is almost the front line. Anyway, I don't want to meet partisans.'

'We have a good place to hide you. We just have to contour round Monte Gardo where the cross is. Close to Gemmano there is another copse like this one. Come, I'll take you now, and then I'll get Papa to come and meet you.'

Lorenzo has sat down again, and Toni can see the sweat on his brow once more. It won't take long for the pain to come back and there is absolutely nothing more he can do today, so drained is he. Instead he tells Lorenzo they should wait until twilight, and in the meantime he checks and rearranges the poultice. Then he searches until he finds a fallen tree from which he manages to break off a strong branch, still semi-green, that will bear Lorenzo's weight. He says, 'Have you anything in your pack we can wrap around the top in order to make it soft? It must fit under your arm.'

Lorenzo produces an old shirt that serves well enough, and he practices a little with the crutch, up and down, inside the bothy. When they judge it time, and can hear no evidence of moving vehicles, they slip out of the bothy and make their way up through the copse until they get to the track. Toni creeps out of the undergrowth first, pausing and listening as he does. Then he whistles the dogs out and Lorenzo follows, leaning heavily on his crutch.

As they make their way along the track away from Zollara, in the direction of Gemmano, Lorenzo looks behind them and tuts.

'Toni, walk on the side of the road. On the grass, not the dirt.'

Toni frowns and Lorenzo jerks his head backwards. 'Look at the dust we are kicking up in the road. If a German comes he will stop to investigate that straightaway. Believe me, I've seen it.'

Toni calls the dogs close and they continue on the edge of the road, stopping occasionally to listen. But it is quite late and they can hear only the evening birdsong and a goat bleating distantly. A gust of wind blows up a little tornado of dust off the road but this dissipates quickly enough. Lorenzo relaxes a little and says, 'Toni, that thing with your hands. How do you do that?'

The mere thought of what he has done causes a heavy veil to descend over his eyes and it feels like a huge weight pushing down on his forehead.

He says, 'I dunno. I always could. The first time I remember was lying at home in front of the fire with a cat who was hurt. I think I was about six. I did it with her and somehow I knew it helped her. Then I started to do it with dogs and other animals. But I never did it for a person before.'

They are coming to a bend where the road goes right, contouring around the hill. Toni knows it is very exposed until it turns left and into the trees once more. Better for them to come off it, climb over the rise through the trees, and join it on the other side.

Before he can explain his plan there is the sound of a heavy vehicle starting up. Toni can tell it is heading towards them so with a whistle to the dogs he gets an arm around Lorenzo and helps him down into a large ditch that is covered with broad bracken leaves. The roar of the engine is getting louder, so making sure Lorenzo can't be seen he instructs Romolo to lie down beside him. Where is Remo?

Remo is standing in the middle of the road gazing vacantly down the hill.

'Remo,' he cries, but the dog doesn't appear to hear him. He leaps out from the ditch and Remo jumps away in fright as if seeing him for the first time. He tries to grab the dog's collar but Remo remains just out of reach, confused and afraid. The roar of the engine thunders in Toni's head.

Taking a deep breath he crouches down to Remo's height, and speaks as kindly as he can. 'Look Remo, it's me. It's me. It's okay. Come now.'

This sparks recognition and with a broad grin Remo trots up to him. Grabbing the dog he hurls them both back into the ditch, unable to do anything about the swirl of dust they have kicked up. He lies on top of Remo until he stops wriggling, perhaps understanding from the tension in Toni's body the urgency of the situation.

A half-track thunders into view. He can only see it through the fronds that are hanging over them and he is grateful for these. It is painted grey with the German cross on its side, and it is full of troops. It roars by in a cloud of dust, swamping the little that he and Remo kicked up. They lie flat and still as they listen to it blast up the road, and he gets a snapshot of a face beneath a helmet peering over the edge of the door down into the ditch. The face seems to look right into him. But there is no evidence that the vehicle is preparing to stop and after a time the roar fades.

The rest of the journey is uneventful. If Lorenzo is dismayed at the prospect of leaving the track and climbing through the wood he does not show it, though Toni knows it must add to his discomfort. They take it slowly and emerge on the road again with the red roofs of Gemmano showing through the tops of trees. They walk another fifty yards or so and then Toni glances off the road and says, 'In here.'

He follows a path that twists and turns through lichen-covered boulders, crossing a dried stream bed twice as it descends. There is a large oak tree to his left that has been cleft by lightning. It is not dead but split, and grows almost as two separate trees. Glancing behind he waits for the lagging Lorenzo. Then he steps off the path just beyond the oak and works through the trees until he comes to the ruin of a cottage. There is no roof left and only two walls, and he picks his way across what must have been the kitchen. There is a pile of large stones and rocks that were once a wall, arranged in such a way to look like the wall has collapsed. He sets to work clearing these to one side and by the time he has done so he has shifted upwards of a hundredweight of rocks. Scraping aside a smattering of sticks and dirt he reveals several flat planks, with others nailed across them to hold them together. Slipping his fingers underneath he lifts and pushes them aside, and beneath there is a hole the size and shape of a coffin.

'You will be completely safe here. Nobody will find you.'

Lorenzo looks startled. 'You want me to wait in here?'

'It is where we put partisans too, if the Germans are looking for them.'

'I'm not getting in there!'

'Look,' Toni points, 'There is a little shelf in there with a pan, which has water in it. And you can fit your pack there so you have it with you.'

Lorenzo pulls the crutch out from under his arm and sits on a crumbling wall. 'I will not get inside there. I will wait here and you can bring your father to me.'

Toni can't understand why he won't get in. Can it be that he doesn't like the place? To Toni, this seems unlikely. It is a place he chooses to come when it is not in use, so that he can lie in peace. But neither can he see a flaw in Lorenzo's plan so he says weakly, 'I think Papa would want you inside.'

Lorenzo speaks with authority. 'I'm perfectly safe here. The Germans are not combing the forest. We would know. If your Papa wants he can tell me himself when he comes.' Lorenzo groans and feels his leg, which has suffered from the journey. 'Please go and find him now, and if possible bring some food. I'm very hungry.'

Toni sighs. He can see Lorenzo will not be moved, so pointing out the water in the pan he whistles to the dogs and takes his leave.

Chapter 4
August 31st 1944, early evening
Lorenzo

Lorenzo eases the weight off his bad leg as he watches the boy turn away. Toni is unusual around here for his hair is hay-blonde and he has freckles around his nose. He is tall and thin, as if he has shot up in height in recent months but has yet to fill out. He walks slightly stooped as though surprised at finding himself so tall, and his clear blue eyes flit in and out of focus. Now he and the dogs merge back into the trees like ghosts.

The ache in Lorenzo's leg is returning in full force. Blowing out his cheeks he sinks to the ground, unable to take another step. He has no choice but to wait for Toni's return, so he stretches himself out on the grass, not too close to Toni's grave. He is tired beyond belief.

It feels as if he has been travelling for a million years, over a million miles. His entire life has been occupied by this journey, starting in Russian snow and ice, then stumbling about his own country, a country he no longer knows, and culminating in the long climb onto this ridge. From the bottom the slope had looked relatively benign. He'd slipped around to the north face, forced to detour around lagging German troops, and surveyed the ridge's silhouette in the early morning light. It was perhaps three hundred meters above him, higher in the west, to his right. It descended gently to a saddle, and then rose to where Gemmano sat on the eastern end looking out over the distant sea. Believing he'd seen troops in the village he climbed all the way around the western edge to where he'd encountered that cursed dog.

This life, fighting and travelling, seems like the only one he has ever known. Undeniably he can recall, in distant memory, a growing up, a maturing to adulthood with people who loved him, and with others who didn't. But these memories feel unreliable as if they are not his. It's like they have been told to him by somebody else.

He stares at the hole exposed by the boy and shivers, for here the past demands his attention. Large in his mind sits this stark memory of the hiding place that kept him alive, an aeon ago, in the outskirts of a distant Russian town, the name of which he can no longer remember.

As a platoon they were a ragged bunch. Looking for food, their clothes creaking in the cold, they had pushed too far into the centre of the town. He recalls looking at everything through a cloud of his condensed breath. The Russians had pretended to retreat and they, hungry fools, forged forward regardless. The Russians circled around in a pincer movement, doubtless guided by locals, and succeeded in cutting them off. They'd only realized this when gunfire to the rear made them turn, and they watched horrified as 'C' platoon was caught in a crossfire and cut down.

His lieutenant snapped an order and their platoon dispersed. Ducking down behind a ruined truck with Vito he watched as the Russians shot down those of C platoon who raised their arms in surrender. The soldiers, dressed in greatcoats, began to work their way up the street towards them. They were firing flamethrowers and tossing grenades into open doorways and upturned vehicles – anywhere they feared might conceal the enemy.

Spinning round at the sound of explosions behind them, Lorenzo saw other troops advancing and realised they were trapped. He and Vito gripped each other, the fear in his friend's eyes reflecting that in his own. Glancing to one side he saw a piece of waste ground that had once been allotments where the townspeople grew vegetables. At any rate there were familiar looking sheds and stray canes lying against them, long-deserted. Just maybe they could hide somewhere in the longer grass. He'd reached for Vito's shoulder when there was a crack of a rifle and a tomato exploded at the side of Vito's head. Like a coat that slides off its hanger, he sank shapelessly to the ground.

Lorenzo could not leave before making the sign of the cross and uttering a brief prayer over the lifeless huddle of his friend. Then he turned and hurled himself over a half-demolished wall. The sheds before him sparkled, the long grass brittle with frost. Crouching as low as he could, he sprinted to the first shed and ducked behind it. The moment he examined it he knew they would smoke it with their weapons for sure. He raced over the ground, but the far end backed onto houses that lined the patch from end to end, and offered no way out.

Frantic, he slipped behind the last shed and sank down against the door. To his surprise it fell in from his weight and he tumbled on top of it into the shed. The hinges must have rotted completely. Reason banished by panic, the only thing he could think of was to push the door back into place and hide in the shed. But as he lifted it he realized the shed had no floor at all. It had been torn up and a hole dug, and inside this was a frozen corpse. The man was wearing a suit and a tie, and he was clasping to his chest a small bunch of withered stems that had once been flowers. His hair was neatly combed and beneath the sheen of ice Lorenzo could make out a thin moustache. The ice gave the cadaver an unreal look, as if it had been produced in a waxworks museum, and then placed here and iced over.

The ground was so hard that the hole could never have been dug out in these winter months, so the work must have been done in the summer and the corpse laid in it later – perhaps recently. He couldn't imagine why anybody would bury a loved one in a garden shed, or not cover him over, but this was no time for speculation. Thrusting aside the thought of what his priest would say at the disturbance of a child of God, he gripped its shoulders and pulled. The body was frozen to the ground, but grabbing his bayonet he levered up the rigid corpse until the clothes tore and it came free. He climbed in the hole underneath it, using one hand to pull the door on top of them both.

The hair on the back of the cadaver's head was pushing against his face, and the rock-solid, angular bones were jutting into his body. Some of the frozen hair inserted itself into his nostrils and he snapped his head to one side in disgust. The cold from the ground seeped up through his uniform and into his own bones, as though death had caught him in its arms and was infusing itself into him. The cadaver began to make noises. It gave off a creak, then another, and then Lorenzo was sure he heard an expulsion of air from somewhere. One of the arms dropped slightly, resting on Lorenzo's own as if touching him reassuringly.

Now he could hear the blasts of flamethrowers and shouts in Russian as the comrades closed in, and before long there was a crash as the first shed collapsed and burned. Shed after shed crashed. He was shaking, though with fear or with cold he couldn't say. He had lost a glove and his hand was so painful from the cold that he felt its bite in the tips of his fingers. His hand was closing into a claw and he whined in torment. He couldn't help seeing the hand pinched and dry, clutching a bunch of flowers to his chest. He almost wished the flamethrowers would get to him, just to thaw out his hand.

As if in answer to his prayer there was a rush of heat above him, the crackling and spitting of fire, and the smell of burning kerosene. Then loud bangs as heavy boots kicked in the flaming walls so as to crush anybody inside. He felt three of the walls crash atop the door, upon the cadaver, upon him, and he closed his eyes and prayed to God, waiting for death.

After what seemed an age he found his senses again. He couldn't tell if he had passed out, and there was only silence around him. It was dark and the dominant smell in his nostrils was of burnt wood mingling with burnt flesh. His right, gloveless hand was numb and the rest of him ached with stiffness. He remembered the cadaver and began to push, but the body flopped recalcitrantly, half melted by flames, seemingly trying to fall back on him. Drops of fluid dripped from it onto his face and a wave of disgust and panic seized him. Surging up into a sitting position he thrust it aside and grabbed at the door, but he gripped a still smouldering edge. The heat seared through his glove and his skin before he could snatch his hand away.

It took him half an hour to crawl out from under the collapsed shed with its walls and door burnt on the outside, and round the edges, but miraculously almost unharmed on the underside. At one point the arms and hands of the corpse got tangled up in his legs, seeming to cling to him, imploring him not to go, and he kicked and kicked until he emerged into the night air. There was nobody around, and he collapsed in a state of physical and mental exhaustion.

Now he prods lightly the dressing on his leg and looks down at his hands. The seared, scarred flesh in the palm of his left hand is less debilitating than the two stunted middle fingers with missing tips on the other, where the surgeon cut them off to prevent the frostbite spreading. Lucky he was left handed, or perhaps unlucky. When he got back to Italy a captain came to see him in hospital and declared he could still fire a rifle. No way was he getting invalided home.

That was before the armistice. When he returned to the remains of his unit he found them camped in an olive grove. Sitting at night, listening to the crickets' chorus, smelling the wood, feeling the dry dirt beneath him, he felt he had returned to his country, but that this was not the same as coming home. As he laughed with his comrades each talked about his family and offered up snapshots of where he was from, what his father did (though Lorenzo didn't talk about his), what they cooked locally, and who was waiting for them. It was as if they were reassuring each other that the Italy they had grown up in was still there, waiting upon them – they who had fought for her honour and prosperity. They slapped each other on the back and passed the grappa round, speculating about their next posting or, hopefully, that they had done their bit and would be sent home.

They considered the political situation too, and that with Mussolini no longer in charge, perhaps the war would end. Perhaps the Tedeschi would get out of Italy and they would make peace with the allies. Then they'd be able to go home for sure. But during these discussions differing political camps emerged. Yes, they were brothers in arms, first and foremost. They had stood by each other under fire. They had supported the injured and the maimed, and they accepted that help when it was their turn to be shot or shelled. They all wanted to go home. But what happened after that was anybody's guess, and Lorenzo detected deep and diverse undercurrents of feeling amongst them that had, in their evolution, the potential for collision.

He didn't have time to muse on this for long, for shortly thereafter the armistice was signed and Hitler, hopping with rage at the Italian betrayal, instructed his troops to arrest the rapidly dissipating Italian army and ship it off to labour camps where it might be of some earthly use. The senior officers deserted and, emasculated by the vacuum of authority and years of discouraged initiative, the men and junior officers stood around looking at each other until the Germans arrived. Waiting to be herded into cattle trucks at a station near Siena the rumour spread through their ranks that they were being taken away from Italy again. It was more than he could bear. Once the head count had been completed and double checked by the German guards, he crouched to the ground and slipped to the back of the ranks.

There was a fence just behind them and not ten meters beyond that was some undergrowth offering effective cover. But he dare not break out of line for fear of being seen so he crouched at the feet of his comrades, still standing to attention along the platform.

It was evening and Lorenzo prayed the Germans might wait until nightfall before boarding. But twilight clung on while the order was shouted and his comrades shuffled forward to the trucks. He braced himself. Two of his friends, aware of his plan, started a noisy quarrel over a pack of provisions and for a moment the closest guards were distracted. Paying no attention to the guards down the platform he leapt the fence cleanly and plunged into the undergrowth. He might not have made it, but somebody who had the same idea further along was spotted as he jumped. The man was gunned down before he even hit the ground on the other side of the fence. Lorenzo lay amongst the plants, his heart pounding, dreading that the incident would precipitate a search, but the Germans seemed satisfied that they'd taken care of the escape and were more concerned about controlling their suddenly restless and angry prisoners.

After the train departed he worked his way south towards the advancing front, and as he did the old Italy embraced him. He found shelter in a tiny house in the country where two women, dressed in black, welcomed him in.

'My husband is also away fighting, may God bring him back safely,' said the younger of the two. 'Now I will prepare somewhere for you to sleep.'

The older woman gave him some warm food and later, as he ate, he heard them whispering in the next room, 'There is some milk we can drink.'

Realising they had given him their food for the night strengthened his resolve to continue south, join the allies, and help to push the Tedeschi out. People such as these were worth fighting for, and he fixed up their tattered chicken run just as he would at home, before he left them.

As he approached the front he was forced to hide more and travel less, laying low as the Teds marched north in good order. He skulked in wheat fields or olive groves and noted the landmines they laid in the roads, in ploughed fields, and even grenades hung in cherry trees attached to the branches. It was all useful information for when he must prove his sincerity to the allies. He slept rough at night, of course, begging from locals to keep himself alive. Eventually he hid in a cellar until the front passed over him and he was able to present himself to the British. He told them how his unit had been arrested.

'There is the *Corpo Italiano di Liberazione*, somewhat to the west,' said the courteous British commander in good French. 'Perhaps you ought to go there.'

Lorenzo had heard that the allies had better food and equipment, and though he would have liked to rejoin his Italian comrades he remembered the inefficiency of their officers, and how they had run out on the rank and file when the armistice came.

'Perhaps you can use me here, for translation and so on,' he said in halting English.

The commander's eyes lit up. 'I say, the very thing. Our translator was killed last week. We can't communicate with the locals at all. Lucky you managed to hole up in that cellar until the Teds were gone. Now, show me again, on this map, where these bally mines are.'

There is no sign of Toni. As he nurses his injured leg Lorenzo feels his stomach rumbling, and by way of distraction pulls his bayonet out of his boot. He cleans and then sharpens it on an old stone, which he carries with him, and reflects that this assignment was what led to his first encounter with the new Italy.

One day the British commander asked him to communicate with local partisans, for two senior officers had come into the British camp.

'We are here at extreme danger to ourselves,' said one, a heavyset peasant with snot in view inside his nose.

'We are all here at danger to ourselves,' commented the British commander to Lorenzo with raised eyebrow, 'Don't translate that! Ask them what they need.'

The peasant, whose name was Zuntini, sniffed and ran off a list of ammunition, equipment, clothing and food that would have satisfied a battalion for a month.

'What campaign is it you intend to mount with all that?' asked the commander, the sarcasm not lost in translation.

Zuntini pulled himself up. 'Last week we blew up a truckload of retreating Teds. The week before that we raided a Nazi-held village, occupied it, and then eliminated seven fascists.'

'You mean Germans?' Lorenzo asked, seeking clarification.

'Nah, the Germans we let go. It was the fascists we wanted.'

'Italian fascists?'

'Of course.'

Lorenzo asked, 'How did you know they were fascists?'

Zuntini laughed, 'We made the Germans point out those that had aided them.'

Lorenzo sighed, 'And were the fascists all young, strong men?'

Zuntini looked slightly disconcerted, 'There was one woman amongst them.'

The other, older partisan stepped forward and looked intently at Zuntini. 'You let the Germans go?'

Zuntini looked even more uncomfortable. 'We only captured two. They traded their lives and gave up the collaborators.'

The older partisan spat on the ground. 'Italians! They were Italians!'

The British commander shifted impatiently and the partisan turned to him. 'We are not looking to kill Italians. We don't need so much. Can you give us a few grenades? And of course if you have any food you can spare…'

Lorenzo said to the commander, 'I am not sure about these two. They are telling me different things. The big one – he has a vendetta going on with Italians sympathetic to Mussolini. Maybe a local thing, with some history.'

The commander looked bored. 'I'm not concerned with their petty squabbles. What can they tell us about German troop movements?'

Zuntini raised his chin. 'Give us the supplies and we will tell you all about the troop movements.'

The older partisan, who never gave his name during the interview, leaned forward. 'Show me your map and I will tell you what I can. But we are very local, and we have to live high up in the mountains, so we only see two or three main roads, and then infrequently.'

Afterwards the British commander ordered up some token

supplies and Lorenzo, not wishing to bother him further, took his compatriots for something to eat. As they sat outside, perched on boulders in the shade of a ruined house, Zuntini sniffed at the British food suspiciously. The older partisan nodded his thanks and began to eat.

Zuntini looked at Lorenzo, 'And you, what are you doing here? How come you are not with your unit?'

When Lorenzo explained about his unit in Russia, and later about their arrest here, and his escape, Zuntini shrugged and said carelessly, 'I too escaped.'

The older partisan, his mouth full, made a sound that might or might not have been a contemptuous laugh.

Zuntini narrowed his eyes. 'So then, you fought for Mussolini. You went to Russia with his army.'

Lorenzo put down his plate of food and stood. 'When you are in the army you go where you are sent. I'm a patriot. Don't you dare say I am a fascist.'

Zuntini backed down a little. 'It's a good thing you are with this British outfit. That way I can believe you. But fascists – all I am here to do is eliminate them.'

Lorenzo said, 'We all want the Germans out of our country.'

'That,' replied Zuntini, 'is not what I said.'

There was an implacable flatness to the statement that took the strength from Lorenzo's legs. The man's eyes burned with a hatred that he did not like to see in anything, far less when directed against his own countrymen. This Zuntini would not be the only one. The partisans were all over northern Italy. They had suffered at the hands of Mussolini's Salò Republic and they wanted a fresh start.

Later, as Zuntini loaded the 'meagre supplies' onto the cart and hitched it to the mule, the older partisan took Lorenzo aside, and put his hand on one shoulder.

'Listen, you seem like a decent fellow. You are doing what you can, fighting with the allies. But don't tell people about what you have done in the war. Understand?'

'Why not?' Lorenzo frowned. 'I have done nothing wrong. I have fought for my country. I am fighting for my country now.'

'Things are changing. People want to attach labels to you. Better to keep silent when you can.'

'I am neither communist, nor fascist. I just want to go home.'

The partisan looked at him urgently. 'Listen, that village Zuntini told you about, when they shot those poor bastards? I wasn't there or I would never have allowed it, but they told me about it afterwards. One of the people they dragged out for punishment was the schoolteacher. Yes, the teacher at the local school. You know why? Zuntini said he was subverting the youth of the country by what he was teaching them. And what did they find in his school room? The books identified by our government – Mussolini's government – as the core of the curriculum for our children's learning. This man was just doing his job, teaching what he was told to teach by his government, and for this he was dragged outside.

'But did they shoot him? Oh no. Zuntini made the others kneel down in a row outside the town hall and executed them publicly for collaborating with the Germans.' The partisan snorted, 'Collaborators! And who had identified them? The Germans! You have to understand, if you're dealing with somebody like Zuntini you are not dealing with an intelligent, or a reasonable man, hm?'

'And the schoolteacher?'

'Ah, the schoolteacher. Zuntini didn't like something about him, though I don't know what it was. He let him watch as he shot the others and then he dragged him to the middle of the piazza in the centre of the village. Then Zuntini grabbed a shovel and drew an outline in the dirt, the shape of a coffin. 'Now, dig a hole,' he told the schoolteacher.

'They give him a pick and made him get to work. The schoolteacher was a small man, not used to physical labour, and he often had to stop and catch his breath. Every time he did Zuntini would kick him and drive him on, cursing him and telling him he didn't have all day to bury him.'

'It took him an hour to dig the hole and at the end Zuntini made him kneel beside it. He was weeping, his hands were clasped together and he begged for his life. He said he'd only done what he was told and he would teach the children whatever they wanted. None of the villagers dared to raise a voice in protest – the bodies of the others were still lying in front of the town hall. Finally, two of our group protested.

Then Zuntini laughed and said, 'I never intended to kill you. Just make you think,' and he threw him in the back of a truck. They drove him up the hill for over three miles and Zuntini dumped him by the road, telling him to think about his life as he found his way back to the village.'

The partisan looked at Lorenzo, 'You see? You see how they will shape your history any way they want?'

Lorenzo watched him. 'And you?'

'I just want Italy free of foreigners, to let us get on with our own affairs. If that means fighting to drive the Germans out, then I will do it. So for now the allies are friends, though afterwards we must ensure they too leave. Even Zuntini I must tolerate.'

Lorenzo nodded and they walked back to the cart where Lorenzo waved them on their way.

Now he looks more closely at his hands. The seared flesh means it will always feel tight and uncomfortable when he makes a fist. The missing tips on the other hand make it hard to eat, especially using a knife, and these days he tends towards a fork, one-handed. He glances up. Now this boy wants him to get into this hole, this hole they use to hide partisans.

Chapter 5
August 31st 1944, early evening

Toni is slow going back to the path, glancing round frequently to where Remo is picking his way over fallen branches and pine cones. The dog pauses from time to time to look around as if unsure of his bearings. Toni gives a low whistle, and Remo pricks up his ears and comes forward again.

He is troubled that Lorenzo knows what he can do with his hands. Why did he reveal himself like that? Nobody knows about it. Nobody! The villagers would laugh, or worse might think it some form of demonic possession. Their priest seems like a nice man but you can never know, and Toni's trust for him certainly doesn't extend that far. He has never told his parents for it would give them the dilemma of helping with his cover up or else revealing him. Furthermore his other little foibles, like his unwillingness to butcher animals, means that his father already sees him as slightly odd and perhaps weak. He has no doubt of his father's love for him, regardless of this, but he is reluctant to give him anything that might reinforce this opinion.

Francesca suspects something. She once saw him crouched over an injured squirrel that then hopped away towards the trees. Later she said, 'Do you think that squirrel will be all right?'

'Yes.'

She looked at him, 'I believe you. You know these things. How is it you know?'

'I just know.'

'I think that squirrel knew you were being kind,' and she leant her head, her dark curls, against his arm. 'You are such a kind brother.'

'I love you too, Francesca.'

Perhaps it was because Lorenzo was a stranger; in truth he cannot say why he revealed himself. It was the thing to do at that moment, and he knew he could do it. There was nothing more to it than that.

Making his way back up to the track, he becomes aware of how exhausted he is. It is a deep weariness that blankets the depths of his soul, and his feet drag as if he is walking through ankle-deep mud. As he arrives at the track he stops to wait for Remo. He holds the dog's head in his hands and looks at his eyes. Remo smiles and grunts, enjoying the attention. He can see nothing unusual in the dog, but once again Remo walks close to heel as they trudge along the road, seeming to find in him a point of reference.

He will tell Papa about Lorenzo. He will know what to do. Imagining what Papa will say causes a disturbance to ripple across his innocent intention. In Toni's world the situation is simple. A man is injured and in need of help. He, Toni, is able to provide that help, and of course the place he will go for it is his house. For him the war has been a distant event, something that affected other people but which, except in indirect ways such as rationing, had little to do with their life in Gemmano. Indeed, there are times when he has felt almost benign towards the war, its outbreak being the catalyst for Professor Carter's sudden departure.

'I must take the train from Rimini tonight,' the professor had said, sitting in their kitchen. He held up a hand and smiled at Toni. 'I can see your question coming and I need to ask a favour. Will you take care of the dogs while I'm away?'

Toni's mouth had dropped open and excitement clutched at his breast. He put a hand to his mouth. 'Oh, Papa?'

Papa turned to Professor Carter. 'How long will you be gone?'

The Professor returned his look. 'It's very hard to tell. It may be months. Perhaps more. Who can tell when there's a war on?'

Papa nodded. 'Toni, you will have to take care of them. I don't have the time. Your responsibility, understand?'

'Yes, oh yes!' and Toni was out of the door and hugging the dogs as both men chuckled.

The war has had no greater effect upon Toni than this. But after today in the field things don't feel the same, and the injured Remo, trotting alongside, reminds him that a darkness looms over them. He thinks he recalls Lorenzo telling him of the danger in helping him, but Toni doesn't really believe this. Nobody is going to get angry with him just for bandaging up a man's leg. Yet he remains disturbed, his eagerness to get help for the soldier undermined. He halts with Gemmano in view. Suppose Papa helps this stranger – and how can he not? – then are the family also at risk?

He was so determined, mere moments ago that he can't believe he is now hesitating, especially when it is such a severe wound. Anyway, it is difficult to say what actually troubles him. He turns away from Gemmano, closes his eyes and lowers his head. Lorenzo is back in the wood. The family is up ahead. He stands here between them, the link, the point of communication. Why does he feel that to establish such a link would be dangerous? A moment ago the plan had seemed so right, so indisputable, that he hadn't even questioned it. Now he is contaminated by indecision.

Gemmano looms impassive before him in the pale light, and its edges seem hard and unnatural to him. It is alien to this landscape. He can smell the pine scent of the trees that waft in the breeze. When he kneels on the moss in the forest he can feel a connection with the ground beneath him, almost as if he has gestated within it and then sprung forth from the earthy womb. Each time he touches a tree, or holds an animal, he connects to the womb and he knows he will return there one day, and he does not fear that. Resting inside it cools his mind when indecision brings him turmoil. Now he kneels and lowers his forehead until it rests on the soft moss.

So, what now? He can only make his mind work through the process of eliminating possibilities. He cannot stay here. He cannot go back to Lorenzo and tell him to go away. The man cannot move, and in any case there is something innately decent about him that makes Toni feel he deserves all the help he can get. So he knows he must go on. Equally he cannot arrive home and say nothing, for Lorenzo will undoubtedly starve. He is quite unable to hunt or forage. So then, he must speak. Surely – surely that won't put anybody in danger. Not just speaking. Anyway, Papa will know.

He glances up sharply and puts out a hand to Remo. A shudder runs through him. One of *them* is hovering above the track, perhaps the same one he saw earlier in the day. He pants and feels faint. This is too much to cope with now. He hasn't possibly got the strength or the focus, both spent on the exertions of the day. If he is to meet it he must be fresh, his mind cleared and without encumbrance. He calls Romolo over, crouches between the dogs, and pulls them close. Their hackles rise and they peer outward. Their warmth gives him succour and holding himself very still he glares up at it. Long moments pass, and then to his inestimable relief it removes itself from his presence. He thinks of Papa. This is something that cannot ever be discussed. Not with Papa. Not with Mama. Not with Father Morelli. Not even with Francesca.

He follows the road towards Gemmano until he is in the Borgo Mazzini quarter, sat upon the saddle just below the village. As he approaches their house a neighbour, Paisani, sticks his head out of a ground floor window. 'What are you doing out, boy? Don't you know there's a curfew? Germans imposed it today. If they see you out they will shoot you and not even ask who you are!'

He nods silently and moves quickly between the houses, which are built by the road at the top of the ridge. These have the appearance of being lopsided, although they are not, their backs being lower than the front doors, which open onto the road. He goes down to their chicken run at the back of the house. He lets himself into the vegetable garden through the rickety head-high gate, stops at the outside toilet for a moment and then slips in through the stall. There is something wrong. He runs his hand along the back of the mule as he goes through, and he can hear the pig shuffling and quietly grunting to herself. But there is a gap on the other side of the mule where the cow should be.

He climbs a few steps, for the kitchen is a half level above the animals. There is a semi-enclosed area of glass before he enters the kitchen proper, where they all take off their boots and hang their jackets. Kicking off his shoes he is reminded of his one legged trousers. His late arrival is unlikely to excite much comment; Mama has long since given up nagging him to be home for dinner on time, knowing he prefers to prowl his fields and woods at twilight. His appearance may be a different matter.

As he opens the door he is surprised to hear raised voices. It is Mama who is speaking, and with a more urgent tone than usual.

'But where would we go? We have no relatives where we can hide.'

Papa says, 'Turrini is leaving. He said he is taking his family north in the morning. You know, we could take the mule and the cart with essentials. We could find help somewhere.'

Mama gestures impatiently, 'And where would that be? Turrini has family in Cesena. In any case I don't believe it. Why would the war come here? They have been telling us for months that this is a safe place. People are coming up *here* to hide. They arrive every day. Why would they do that if we are about to be attacked?'

Papa says, 'This time it's not the Italian authorities who are telling us. It's the Germans. They visited Father Morelli this afternoon and told him to get us all out. *All* of us!'

Toni steps into the kitchen. Papa is sitting at the wooden table sharpening a kitchen knife on a stone by the light of the paraffin lamp. Mama turns from her cooking pot over the fire.

'But what happened to your trousers?' She doesn't sound particularly upset.

'Where is Coco?' asks Toni.

Mama is short, dressed in black with a dark blue apron tied around her waist. Her face is square, solid, and she has the traces of a moustache. Her hair is tied neatly in a bun but she wears nothing on her head, at this time of night. She makes a face. 'Those cursed Germans took her. Just walked in and took her! So now we have no milk.'

She comes over and peers up at him, 'You look very tired. Take off these trousers. At least now I can throw them out! Why do you insist on going around looking like a tramp in the fields?'

'I have told you many times, Mama, if I wear decent clothes they will get damaged out there. Is there something I can feed the dogs?'

'Huh, *I Fratelli Collisioni*! The Germans have taken all our food and now you want me to feed them?'

Mama always refers to the dogs as the Collision Brothers and refuses them entry to the house on the basis that they crash into everything, and each other, and then knock things off the table. Toni protested the first time but his complaint was undermined by the knowledge that she was right.

'I can send Romolo out to hunt but Remo is hurt. Is there a bone?'

Papa looks up from his work. He's wearing a faded striped shirt and his braces are an equally faded plum colour. By the end of the day the growth around his firm chin is beginning to show, and his short, dark, curly hair is thinning on top of his now hatless head.

'You have a mark on the side of your face.'

He reaches up, realizing he has quite forgotten where the German cuffed him. 'I met a German soldier.'

By revealing this information he is forced to explain the incident in the field, which he does as succinctly as possible. As he speaks Francesca, who has heard him arrive from upstairs, enters the kitchen and stands beside him, kissing him lightly on the head. She is wearing a plain blue-grey dress which neither accentuates nor diminishes her slim figure, and which matches her eyes perfectly. Her hair brushes her shoulders as she turns and it makes Toni think of the schoolyard when his peers would look at her. He felt proud that she was his little sister and he watched his friends, if friends they were, warily.

'Are you hurt, Toni?' she says, putting a hand on his face.

Papa says to Mama, 'Now do you see what can happen? Toni's lucky he wasn't taken off to work for them. That's what I hear they are doing with the local boys now.'

Mama hands Toni another pair of trousers. 'Sit at the table, there are some ravioli left.'

'In a moment.' Going to the back door he opens it and lets Romolo out. He closes the door knowing the dog will return in the middle of the night, slipping through the dog flap in the fence, and sleeping in the stall with the pig. Remo stands looking at him vacantly, so he puts a bone in front of him, which Remo sniffs and then settles down to scrunch.

'Papa, I met another soldier today. An Italian soldier.'

As Toni explains, Francesca holds his hand and Papa keeps silent, watching him carefully without interrupting. Toni has long since learned to measure his words with his father, avoiding repeating himself, finishing his sentences and making sure he is saying something of substance. When he has finished Papa says, 'Good.'

Toni feels a little as if he has completed an exam and is pleased by the response. But he also feels irritated, almost petulant, as if he's being treated like a child, when what Papa should be focused on is the issue at hand.

As Toni starts to eat Papa looks at Mama. 'So you see? This man says the allies have crossed the Foglia. They are coming much faster than we thought.'

Mama continues to wash the dishes and says nothing.

'We need to tell the *Comitato*…and we need to decide what to do with this soldier.'

Mama doesn't turn round. 'This soldier? What do we know about this soldier? He could be anybody. He could be a spy. He could be a fascist. What if Ugalotti has sent him?'

'Mama, he is badly injured. We cannot leave him.'

Mama turns and looks at him. 'You are a kind boy, Toni. But you do not understand all the risks. Anyway,' she turns to Papa, 'how can the allies be close? They won't come this way. They will go up the coast. It's obvious. And didn't the *Comitato* get some intelligence or something? What was that General planning?'

'Ugalotti wouldn't send a soldier to walk around the countryside with a hole in his leg. And that so-called intelligence was very second hand.'

Mama turns back to the stone sink she is washing in. 'It makes no sense to me. They can't come this way. It is flat on the coast. Of course they will go up the coast, and through the valleys.'

Papa glances at Toni. 'Here is what I will do. I will go and see this Lorenzo. If I am convinced by him then I will take the information to the Priest, and he can pass it on to the *Comitato*.'

'But what about this soldier. You can't bring him here. It is too dangerous for all of us,' she gestures. 'What about Francesca?'

'*Amore*, he is injured.'

Mama's eyes blaze. 'No, I will not have him here. Not even in one of the caves. What if other Germans find him? What if they see you bringing him inside. What if Ugalotti sees you? I will not have it!'

Papa sighs. 'Very well, for now we will put him in the hole.'

Mollified, Mama says, 'I will give you some bread and cheese for him, and figs from the tree.'

Toni says, 'And something for a clean bandage.'

Papa collects a light, sleeveless jacket from its peg at the door, and a paraffin lantern unlit, and leads Toni out into the golden evening light.

'I'll close the door,' says Toni. 'I don't want Remo to follow. He should rest.'

The thought of rest is a wonderful one but he pushes it to one side as they make their way back down the road. Toni falls in step beside the slightly lopsided gait of his father, a limp in his left leg.

It is a little gift, as he puts it, from the old war.

'Papa, what is the *Comitato*?'

'It's the *Comitato di Liberazione Nazionale*. The CLN. They are the antifascists. Now the British are arriving the fascists will have to get out with the Germans, and so communists and others are getting ready to take over when they go. Father Morelli is our contact with them.'

'Is it dangerous to be an antifascist, Papa?'

'It's dangerous to be anything now, son. Just keep your head down and do what seems right. That's all anybody can do.'

When they get to the ruin there is nobody to be seen. Toni glances around and calls out, 'Lorenzo, it's me, Toni. I'm here with Papa.'

From behind the standing wall Lorenzo emerges and hobbles into view using the wall for support. He sits down heavily. 'I heard you before I saw you, and I couldn't be sure.'

Toni hands him the food, which Lorenzo grabs with both hands and begins to eat. Though obviously hungry he breaks small chunks off with his hands and chews thoroughly before taking another piece. Toni kneels, unwraps the makeshift bandage from Lorenzo's leg and begins to work. Although it is getting dim in the forest Papa doesn't light the lamp, saying he doesn't want to run the risk of being seen unless it is necessary.

Lorenzo says, 'You are partisans?'

Papa shakes his head abruptly. 'Who are you? What are you doing here?'

'I am a soldier. I have fought for our government, for our king. Now I don't know what that means. I am trying to get home.'

Papa observes him. 'You came up with the British?'

'The Canadians. I was translating for them.'

'So why would you leave them? It would have been safer to stay in their ranks, I think.'

'It was always my plan to leave them and get home when I could. It was just that travelling north through Italy it was best to be on their side until I could find my own way.'

'Until now?'

'Yesterday morning I saw my chance. I was with the 5th Canadian armoured and we attacked across the Foglia river, making for Morciola. We hit early morning, and hard, and I think the Teds are tired from all the defending. Anyway we gave them a very hard time and they retreated fast. They were all over the place. I can tell you it wasn't very typical. Usually you have to fight for every single metre against these bastards. Say what you want, they are good soldiers.'

Papa nods. 'They are good soldiers.'

'By the time we occupied Morciola we had moved so fast we had to wait for reinforcements and supply lines to be sorted. So the commander says to me, 'Go up to these villages and talk to the people. I don't think there are many Germans hanging around in the hills. They've headed up the coast. Tell the people we are coming, and that they will be liberated. Find out how many can put up troops for the night, and ask about mattresses or food.' So off I went up the hill.'

Lorenzo shifts uncomfortably on his leg. 'Lucky for me that the Commander trusted me. So then I was between the lines, with the German line in disarray and retreating fast, and the advancing allies pausing at the Foglia. I realized this might be the only opportunity I would get. Even better, the villages were inland, in the direction I wanted to go.'

Papa's eyes narrow. 'But you told Toni your home is up the coast. What are you doing here?'

Lorenzo holds up a hand, 'I'm coming to that. I walked up to the first village, around the wall and then straight on. I just kept walking when I could, stopping and waiting when I saw Germans retreating. I stayed off the roads unless it was really clear. An uncut field or a copse is a good place to duck down and hide in a hurry. Last night I slept in the country under a tree. I found a few figs to eat but apart from that, nothing. Then this morning I tried to get past Zollara,' he gestured at his leg, 'Christ, I can survive the entire Russian army but I can't escape one bloody dog!'

'Yes, but why? What is here for you? You must understand it is strange to find a soldier still trying to get home. Most passed by last year. The fascists have sent spies into the countryside to see who is abetting the partisans.'

'Believe me, I am no fascist. I despise them.'

Papa contemplates the man in front of him. 'Yes, you are a soldier. I believe that. But where are you from?'

'I live near Mestre. My village is Spinea.'

'I fought in the White War. I know the accent of a person from there.' Lorenzo shrugs and chews some more cheese. Papa continues, 'I fought in the White War when I was sixteen. I was at Caporetto in the rain and the sleet when the gas came down on our friends and comrades in arms. I got shot in the leg so then I came down from the mountains and stayed in a village outside Mestre. That village was called Spinea.'

Lorenzo looks up, 'My Mama is called Stephania, from the family Bergamas.'

Papa stares at him, 'And your father?'

'I never met my father. They say he died in that war. I was raised by my Mama and my grandparents, on their farm.'

'So what family could you have in Gemmano?'

'It is where my father was from. Mama told me. And I don't know for sure he is dead.'

Papa says nothing for a moment, but instead bends and fiddles with the lantern as if about to light it. Changing his mind he looks up again.

'So tell me the latest from the front.'

This takes Lorenzo no little effort and by the time he is finished Toni has his leg carefully cleaned and re-bandaged.

Lorenzo says, 'Thank you. But it still hurts. Your hands. Can you...?' Toni's eyes open wide and he frowns and gives a tiny shake of his head. '...can you see to tie it off all right?'

Toni nods, a wave of relief washing over him. 'There, that will last until morning.'

Papa says, 'We will try to help you. First I must take this information to the *Comitato*. Toni will take care of your leg. He is the best in the village for that. You will sleep here tonight and we will bring you more food in the morning.'

'But where must I sleep?'

Papa indicates, 'Toni showed you the hiding place, no? It's where we hide *partigiani* sometimes.'

'I cannot sleep there. I will not.'

'You must. There is no other safe place.'

'I prefer to go on to Gemmano then. Tell me how and I will set off now, under cover of darkness.'

Toni says, 'You are crazy. You will be exhausted after five minutes on that leg.'

'I will rest. I'll take my chances.'

Papa says, 'But I will not. Gemmano is still governed by fascists. What will they do to a soldier of the king, travelling with the allies? If they catch you they will give you to the Germans as a traitor. It is obvious you have been helped, and they will make you tell them. I guarantee that. I cannot have you travelling now.'

'Then I can sleep on the forest floor.'

'But now I must know where you are. I don't know you. I must know you are in that hiding place with boulders on top of you so you can't get out. We will come with food soon enough and let you out.'

Toni can see the sweat on Lorenzo's brow. His hand has crept towards the gun in his belt. Papa says, 'What are you going to do? Kill us both? Come on. I don't think it's so hard to stay there for some hours while you sleep. Toni comes here because he likes it!'

And so they bury Lorenzo. As they push the planks over him Toni's eyes meet his. 'For God's sake, come back for me soon. I beg you, don't leave me here too long.'

They pile up enough rocks to hold him down, and then calling that they'll be back in the morning they make their way out of the forest. As they emerge onto the road in the dim light Toni sees a dark shadow detach itself from the undergrowth and trot at his heel. Romolo has eaten. Toni says, 'How do you know you can trust him? Why do you believe him?'

Papa is silent for a moment before answering, 'Because I was billeted with a farmer called Bergamas when I was recuperating in Spinea, and he had a daughter by the name of Stephania.'

As they approach Borgo Mazzini they can see a figure standing silhouetted against the skyline a little above them. It is a man, short and with a paunch. The figure disappears against the hillside as he descends to the road to meet them.

Papa mutters, 'Ugalotti.'

Toni knows who he is talking about. This is a man who marches about the village in a uniform as if he owns the place. He is balding and wears rimless spectacles. Toni has noticed that people are always polite to him, though they never really talk to him.

Ugalotti says, 'You are out late, Mazzanti. And with your son.'

Papa says, 'As you say, with my son.'

'Where is it you have been?'

'You want to know where we have been?'

'That is correct.'

'Since when has it been necessary to explain – even to fascists – where I go in my evenings?'

Ugalotti sounds confident. 'There is a curfew. It is the law. I, as Segretario di Commune, have a right to ask this.'

Papa gives a short laugh, 'Not for much longer I don't think.'

Ugalotti sneers, 'You are thinking the English are coming. Don't be so confident. The Germans are digging a line in here. It won't be so easy to pass. They are going to protect the whole of northern Italy from the invaders. Mussolini's regime will remain intact.'

'You know, even you don't sound as if you believe that.'

Ugalotti snaps, 'Tell me where you have been. I demand it.'

'And if I don't?'

'I will take you into the commune jail.'

Papa pretends to peer around in the gloom, 'And who do you have here to help you do that? Your German friends are already billeted in quarters for the evening, I think.'

Toni sees Papa taking a firmer grip of his walking stick, and Ugalotti lays a hand on the holster of his pistol. Romolo begins to vibrate and growl beside him. Toni steps forward, 'We were looking for my dog. He ran off. Papa came to help me because I was afraid for him.'

Ugalotti looks at him. 'Your dog?'

'Yes, look. Here he is. We found him.'

Ugalotti is silent for a moment. He glances at Papa again and then he says, 'Very well. If that is the case.'

Toni takes his father's hand, 'Come Papa, we still have to feed the mule and the pig.'

As he is dragged away Papa spits on the ground, dangerously near to Ugalotti's feet, something the fascist chooses to ignore. When they get back inside Papa goes to the sideboard and takes out a bottle of grappa. He pours himself a glass and sits at the table glowering. 'Scum.'

Mama raises a finger, 'Watch that temper of yours.'

'Tomorrow morning I am going to see the priest. He needs to know about the allies advance.'

Chapter 6
September 1st 1944

Toni rises early, as usual. He emerges from sleep as from a deep and comfortable hole in the ground. An earthy smell fills his nostrils and his lungs, leaving him feeling nurtured and calm, and he is dragged reluctantly into the morning light. He takes a moment and steadies himself, then dresses quickly, for he must be ready to return to the woods and let Lorenzo out. He saw the fear in the man's eyes as they pushed the planks over his head. Mama is not yet around, and Francesca says she wants to come with him so they make coffee, dunk some of Mama's biscuits in it, and then slip out of the back.

They climb up the side of the house to the road. There are houses on both sides here with the biggest and most elegant, Casa Paisani, on the other side some thirty paces further along the road to Zollara. In the other direction there is a man leaning against a wall not far from the gate into Gemmano. He is chewing a straw and when he sees them he looks idly away. Toni sets off down the road but Francesca grabs his arm. She whispers in his ear,

'That man, he is a friend of Ugalotti. His name is Di Stefano. He's a fascist too.'

'What man?'

She points him out.

'So what?'

'Don't you see? He's watching our house. Ugalotti wants to see where you go this morning.'

'But I told Ugalotti we were looking for Romolo.'

She kisses his cheek, 'Toni, you are so sweet. Don't you know he didn't believe you? Why would he? He suspects something else.'

'But I have to let Lorenzo out. He really hates that hole.'

'You can't go just now. *And* we need to show this man a reason for us being out here. Come with me and we'll get some figs off the tree past Ca' Paisani.'

It takes them ten minutes to accomplish this and when they

return Papa is feeding the pig.

'We have to let him out, Papa. He'll be afraid.'

Papa shrugs, 'He'll live. For now you cannot go. You will lead them to him. Come to the church with me to see Father Morelli.'

Toni groans, 'Must I?'

'I know you don't like the church, but if we both go then Di Stefano will follow us, and maybe Francesca will have a chance to get down to the hole later.'

Toni struggles to think of a reason to avoid going but there is no time, and he cannot tell Papa it is because he is bound to encounter one of *them*. Papa is aware that something about the church troubles Toni, but no more than that. He was present when, aged eight, Toni got to his feet in church, stood apart from everybody else and stared at a spot above the pulpit while the rest of them queued to take the sacrament. Instead of moving forward with the family it was as if he was somewhere else, his lips moving silently, his eyes moist and fixed. He was frozen and when Papa whispered in his ear he did not respond. He simply shivered and muttered, the tips of his fingers twitching, a trail of drool emerging from his mouth. Then he gave a cry and ran outside in terror. Papa had followed him and found him vomiting in the gutter outside. Later, and ever since, Toni has refused to talk about it.

After that, each Sunday morning, Toni was up before daybreak and out of the house. While the villagers were at church he was in the fields, hidden away in a copse chatting to Aura, or investigating an interesting nest. As he grew older he began to understand that this caused his parents much embarrassment and from time to time he would attend a service to see if things had changed. The first few occasions differed little and he would bolt. As the years passed he sometimes forced himself to stick it out. Gripping Papa's hand, he'd allow one of *them* to manifest and after a time, even to approach. By the time he was sixteen he'd learned how to behave with them, so that it didn't overwhelm him for the rest of the day. Even so he could stand such an encounter no more than once a season.

Now Papa and Toni walk up to the arched gate, which opens onto the Gemmano piazza. It is still early but one or two German soldiers are washing their faces in the village fountain, or tying up their packs and making sure they are tight. As they cross the cobbled paving stones Toni glances around and sure enough Di Stefano has followed them into the village.

They walk across the little piazza with its regular, rectangular windows, faded green shutters, and walls that have long lost their original colours, and now shed patches of plaster after the winter. The archway surrounding the door to the commune has been painted more recently but is the only sign of upkeep. Ahead, at the end of the lane, they can see the front of the church, and Papa makes for it. Toni drags behind him. They can feel him entering the village; he knows it. He has a sense of them stirring inside buildings as they become conscious of his presence. They rise up chimneys and curl around the stacks.

As Papa pushes the heavy door of the church it groans back on its hinges and strikes the entrance wall with a thud that echoes into the church. The air is cool and they start up the aisle between the pews looking for Don Morelli, the priest. Toni finds himself treading as lightly as he can, as if this will save him from being observed.

Don Morelli shows himself near the nave, stepping out from behind a pillar, his hands clasped together in front of him. He is a handsome young man of about thirty with black hair neatly combed back off his forehead. He has broad dark eyebrows that give emphasis to his expressive brown eyes, and a firm jaw.

'Ah, Don Morelli, I must speak with you.'

The Priest frowns, gives a small shake of his head and glances back to where he was standing.

Papa says, 'There's a lot to tell you.'

The Priest rolls his eyes and frowns again, 'Mazzanti, I'm very busy at present. Now is not a good time.'

From the shadows another figure emerges. Tony starts, for it is Ugalotti.

'Come, Don Morelli. You must always have time for your parishioners, don't you agree? Let us hear what Mazzanti has to say.'

Papa stops dead, nonplussed. 'What are you doing here, Ugalotti?'

'Never mind that. It's Commune business, which is no concern of yours. Now, what is so urgent that you must tell Don Morelli?'

'It's not for your ears.'

'How suspicious that sounds!'

Papa looks around desperately and Toni steps forward. 'He means that he has to confess to Don Morelli, don't you Papa?'

'That is precisely what I mean,' Papa turns towards Toni and observes him with soft eyes. 'Thank you...for waiting, Toni.'

Morelli says quickly, 'Come then, over to the confessional box. As you say Ugalotti, my first priority is to my flock, so you will excuse me.' As they cross to the other side of the church the priest gives a knowing smile and adds, 'I fear we may be some time before Mazzanti is finished. He can be very comprehensive, you know. Perhaps you should come back later when I'm free.'

Ugalotti says he has no intention of going anywhere, and sits himself on one of the steps leading up to the altar. He watches Toni who turns uncomfortably away.

'You're a smart boy, are you not?' Toni chooses not to answer.

'Perhaps not as strange as they say you are, hm? You remember what you told me last night? I don't think it was true. If I think you're lying I can put you in the jail. Did you know that?'

Toni glances over to the confessional box into which Papa and Morelli have disappeared, and from which emerges only their faint mumblings.

'I wonder if you have just lied to me again.' Ugalotti shrugs, 'Very well. Remain silent. But you may regret it.'

Toni moves to the opposite side of the church from the confessional. He'd feel more comfortable nearer Papa but doesn't want to give Ugalotti an excuse to follow him and get closer to the box. In the event there is no need to worry. Ugalotti remains where he is by the altar, tapping his fingers on the step in frustration.

Toni's attention is caught by a window above his head, on the other side of the aisle. Light streams in as the sun begins to enter directly. He can see particles of dust drifting on the air and there is a small, downy feather that wafts into the dimmer interior of the church. In front of it Toni senses streams of space crossing each other, arriving from different directions that he cannot see, and as they meet the space becomes concentrated and grows. To Toni there is another invisible dimension between him and the window, and he feels that in this space parallel events are happening and other entities exist. He knows he cannot avoid this.

He holds himself very still and brings all his attention to the space before him. He hardly has to think any more in order to do that. It is just instinctive. Becoming aware of his breathing he puts his hands together and to his chest. He can feel a tension arise within his breast, but he also knows that he can hold this tension, and calm it, so he will be able to see clearly. This is important. If this entity is to leave him in peace he must stay with it until it is finished, and ready to leave.

Imperceptibly the presence becomes visible. It appears to do this in time to his breathing. As he draws in a breath it's like he draws upon it too, pulling it from its own dimension of existence into this one. Then, as he releases his breath it pauses, like a snail that halts and looks around before continuing its journey. The breath becomes a connection between them, the observer and the observed, and each time he breathes in he rocks back on his heels, while with the out breath he eases forward again. The connection becomes stronger until it seems he is physically pulling the entity into his presence, though he does not desire this. He knows better now than to fight it, or to run away from it. He tried both so often when younger, and he knows he is left deeply agitated. He feels he has failed something – somebody – in a profound and hurtful way. The feeling fills him with horror and can stay with him for many hours.

Somewhere in the background there are footsteps and urgent whisperings, but he cannot relinquish his attention now. He has no choice but to engage with the arrival.

The entity takes the form of a rolling, shifting cloud, made up of bubbles. These are almost transparent, and reflect the light around them. They are so small they are like the froth on top of Papa's beer, and yet not like it for they are clean and pure. The light immediately surrounding the entity dims as though being absorbed by it. Initially Toni can see only the edges of the manifestation, and then with every breath it grows firmer, and he sees that each bubble has its own individual movements. They are all connected to each other and yet each has an independent path within the overall entity, through which it rolls in perfect harmony to the others. The reflections of light shift and flicker, and sometimes Toni thinks they form the shape of a face. But the formation is gone too quickly for him to be sure.

Finally the entity develops no more, as fully manifested as he has ever seen one, and he finds himself ceasing to rock, his feet together, his hands across his chest. *Breathe. Breathe. Breathe.*

A bump appears in the entity, pulsing and growing. As it elongates it becomes more like a protrusion, and this stretches towards him, swaying and reaching. From within the entity comes a wail, but too distant for him to know what it expresses. It shifts and writhes, apparently in pain and another protrusion extends itself. The entity hangs above the pews, about head height, and appears unable to move away from its central point, though it continues to twist, and turn, and wail. Toni feels an anguish rising in his own breast to match the pain he is observing, and it is this he so dreads. *Breathe. Breathe.*

Turning his attention upon himself he watches the emotions arising, without judgement or any attempt at control. They become the core of his focus and he permits nothing to interrupt him. Though he still feels the entity's cries he doesn't allow them to penetrate his concentration, which grows in strength as he focuses. By observing his emotions he stills them to the point where they weaken and begin to sink once more into his bowels. Correspondingly he senses that the entity is weakening and the protrusions are retreating, the wails diminishing. In another moment or two it will be gone, and he will be calm.

A hand grabs him by the shoulder and spins him around. His focus is shattered, his thoughts flung about the church. He has a sense of the entity being sucked out of his view and he gasps for breath. He closes his eyes, doubles over and tries to find his equilibrium. He can hear a voice.

'Take your hands off him,' snarls Papa, from outside the confessional.

He looks up, his head spinning. It is Ugalotti, who now releases him and stands back, grinning. He says, 'What's the matter with him? What's he staring at?'

Papa sounds weary. 'You know. Everybody knows. He was like this at school too. It doesn't make him an idiot.'

'Indeed? Then let us see what he knows.'

'Leave him alone. He knows nothing.'

'In that case you must tell us.' Ugalotti turns and points directly at Papa who is standing with Don Morelli. They remain stubbornly mute, but then another figure emerges from the gloom around the back of the confessional. Di Stefano says, 'Don't worry, Ugalotti. I slipped into the church. I overheard everything.'

Papa puts a hand to his brow in despair, and Toni feels his bowels turn to water. Don Morelli spins round, 'You listened in on a confession?'

'It didn't sound like a confession to me. More like information passing.'

'That is not the point. The confessional is sacred. You should be ashamed.'

Ugalotti says, 'Come Don Morelli, this bluster will not keep us from the truth. What did Mazzanti tell you?'

Di Stefano says, 'He has met an Italian soldier and he has a lot of information about the front.'

Papa slumps in a pew, his face turned away. Di Stefano talks on for some minutes, occasionally pausing to answer a question from Ugalotti, but Toni cannot bear to listen. There can be no disguising what they have been up to now, and he fears terribly for Papa.

Eventually Ugalotti says, 'This information about the front cannot be correct. I have heard nothing from the Germans.'

Don Morelli steps forward.

'Well, they told me. They came here yesterday and said exactly the same thing. They said we should evacuate the village. Why don't you ask them yourself?'

Ugalotti says, 'Why would the Germans tell you and not me? This is nonsense.'

'That I cannot help you with.' Don Morelli knows better than anybody that the Germans generally communicate first with the priest of a community and only later with the civil authorities. He also knows how much this grates with the Segretaria di Commune.

Dismissing the priest, Ugalotti turns to Papa and says, 'So this Italian has deserted the front. He was fighting with the Germans and has run off.'

'He was fighting with the British.'

'Absurd! How could he have got through the front? And for what purpose? No, he has deserted, and he should be shot. You will take me to him.'

'I cannot do that.'

'Are you telling me you are aiding the enemy?'

'I am telling you that he has gone. After I talked to him he set off again, heading west. He said his family is in Parma.'

'Then you have helped him to escape. Less good for you.'

Di Stefano clears his throat and holds up a hand. He slips through the pews and comes over to Ugalotti in order to whisper in his ear. But Toni still overhears, even through his retching.

'Mazzanti said that the allies are coming very fast. Very fast. If the Germans are confirming this then they could be here in twenty-four hours. We have seen many German troops retreating, heading north. Perhaps we should consider how much longer we will hold power here.'

Ugalotti looks at him. 'We need to inform ourselves. We need to contact General Levelson.'

He turns on his heel without another word and, with Di Stefano at his heels, he strides up the aisle. At the door of the church he turns and points at Papa, 'I will be back for you, and then either you, or this soldier you are protecting, will be in my custody.'

They slam the door of the church on the way out.

Chapter 7
August 31st – September 1st 1944

The last thing Lorenzo sees as the planks are dragged over the hole is Toni's anxious face as he hands him his pack. He cannot say whether Toni is feeling compassion, which would be consistent, or whether he doubts from previous experience that he will find Lorenzo alive upon his return. He has no specific reason for fearing the latter, apart from a deep sense of despondency and hopelessness cultivated in years of war. If in doubt, things will probably turn out for the worse.

He can hear Toni and his father pack the stones back onto the planks. There are cracks of light, but as the stones are piled up these cracks become broken and smaller, until there is only one tiny sliver to let him know that an outside world still exists. He has hidden in so many places in these past months. He has cowered in an attic as Germans talked to the house owner below, and then searched the barn. He has holed out in the mountains with shepherds, eating bread boiled in a pot and then oil poured on it, and occasionally a mouthful of cheese. It is neither fear nor hunger that assails him now. It is a sense of being alone, abandoned, and no longer of this earth. The world he knew before the war is gone. The Italy he has travelled through evinces such contradictions, such cruelties, such confusing paradoxes that he does not know who to trust anymore.

They finish shifting stones and, after a brief exchange, the father and son depart. He listens to their footsteps as long as he can, but once they leave the ruin their steps are muffled on the soft forest floor. He goes on listening for anything that might give him a connection to the outside, and there is a breeze making the trees rustle, their collective sound forming a distant roar that could be a river. This in some way is comforting. His leg aches less following Toni's ministrations, and lying down does it no harm either.

Exhaustion overtakes him and he sleeps.

Of course he dreams he is in a hole with a corpse and the corpse is melting over him. Its arms drop slowly so that they come down on either side of him, and then he realizes that the corpse is face down and has him in a ham-fisted, passive embrace. After a while it begins to drip goo, which slips from its brain and out through the nostrils and teeth. At the beginning it is just drops of thin, clear liquid running off his cheek or his neck, but this turns to a kind of festering gunk which drips into his eyes and mouth. Its stench starts to choke him and he tries to turn away from it, but the embrace has grown firmer and he struggles against those arms. The gunk in his mouth is preventing him from breathing and his body convulses as it gasps for air. He twists and thrashes, and then he wakes and panic seizes his whole body and he surges upwards trying to force the planks off the hole. He suddenly has incredible focus and ceases to bang or kick. Instead he pulls his knees up as close to his chest as the hole will allow. He puts his hands at his sides to brace himself, and uses his huge back, stomach and thigh muscles to bring every ounce of strength to his task. Letting the adrenalin kick in he pushes up with his knees and feels the planks flexing under the strain. He even hears the shift of a rock as he strives and he sucks in another breath, knowing he has only one good push in him. But it is no use. Nothing else will move and his strength ebbs. He accidentally kicks his wound and this makes him wince and give up the effort. The adrenalin drains out of him and he subsides, sucking deep breaths as he does. Energy wasted is a serious loss; it is not something to be lightly spent. But he is calmer.

He doesn't know how long he has slept, and his efforts have extinguished the final sliver of light. Dark thoughts assail him. He is unwanted. The Germans, of course, intend to execute him. The British would like him back, but probably to shoot him for desertion. Mazzanti is afraid to have him in the village, for the fascists might see and betray him to the Germans. The Partisans don't approve of his war effort. Once again a sense of worthlessness begins to insert itself, insidiously, into his brain. If he dies here who is to care, who is to know?

He remembers there are some figs left in his pack. He gropes around for the pack, which has been pushed down to the end of the hole by his scrabbling. He hooks it with a foot and pulls it within reach. Carefully he slips his hand into the pack until he finds the figs. Some have been crushed or squeezed by his thrashing, and the jelly is oozing out, gunk-like. He forces that image out of his head and sticks a finger into his mouth, sucking on the sweet juice. It is like a ray of sunshine pouring into his prison. He pulls out one less smashed and turns it inside out, sucking out the pulp and leaving only the barest of skins. The grainy jelly washes around his mouth, the grains crunch between his teeth, the freshness of the juice slips to the back of his throat, and it makes him think of sun, blue skies, and walks in an olive grove with a girl he had known briefly called Antonia.

He had fallen sick after joining the British. It was a fever and the British were unable to care for him, on the move as they were. He was left at the door of a country farmhouse, and the family took him in and put him to bed. As he grew better and more aware of his surroundings he saw that the war had passed them by here, at any rate to the extent that the buildings were intact. Much livestock had been taken, aside from a few chickens they'd secreted away, yet the farmer and his family ate well enough on pasta and bread cooked in the outside oven. There were tomatoes and other rich produce from the vegetable garden. Antonia reminded him that there was something other than war. He would wake slowly and walk behind the house after breakfast. He could hear her singing at her laundry, her voice slipping over the stone windowsills and dissipating amongst the irises beneath. Sometimes he persuaded her to walk with him and he loved to hear her talking about the day-to-day minutiae of her life. She told him how one of the donkeys had hurt its hoof because it believed it was a goat, and insisted on springing down the terraces from great heights. She would explain to him the difficulties of cooking with rationing in effect, though she was more bothered by the lack of clothes.

One day she lamented, 'I need a new skirt. Look at this one. The patches have patches on them!'

'I could buy you one.'

'It's not the money. You just can't get them now. There's nothing in the markets. Everybody is selling their stuff to the Americans.'

'What, skirts?'

She pushes him. 'Of course not skirts! The material you buffoon.'

The ordinary nature of her conversation was like balm poured over his fevered brow. It felt like home and reminded him that there were still ordinary people who did ordinary things and wrestled with ordinary worries. Perhaps his Mama and his grandparents, his sisters and brothers, still had similar conversations. The commanders who ordered you into battle, the soldiers who stole gold fillings from the teeth of the dead, the people who hated you without knowing you, were not the only people in this world. The unforgiving nature of war, of military life, had made him forget that there was time for kindness, and gentleness. The prospect of future tragedies and pain lost some of their sting here.

Lorenzo remembers Antonia's soft brown hair and eyes, and the sight of the nape of her neck as he helped her down a steep path. That he was attracted to her there was no doubt, but his attraction was for her companionship and her nature. There was nothing carnal in his thoughts, and now he feels that he may remember her at any time and, so long as his thoughts are chaste, he can be sure the memories of their time together will give him succour, and peace, and ease his loneliness. Nobody can take that away from him and now he rests his head on the earth once more.

He thinks again about his family, and these thoughts mingle with those of Antonia. Might they not all meet one happy day after the war? Hope stirs deep down inside him, and a voice warns him that he is straying into dangerous territory. He ignores it, persisting in his daydream. Perhaps he will travel south and find her. He will ask to work on the farm and he will stay there and court her. If Antonia is willing he will marry her and bring her home to meet the family. Their reservations about his marrying somebody from another province will be overwhelmed by her good nature and character.

He has walked into the trap set by his agitated mind, for where there is hope and desire, fear must follow. To marry he must survive, and the threats array themselves before him. Daybreak, Toni had said, as Lorenzo lowered himself into the hole. He would be there with food at daybreak. Yet now Lorenzo can hear birdsong announcing the dawn. It must be soon. He waits and he waits. He knows the vagaries of country life mean he cannot expect Toni at a specific hour, and about this he is sanguine. It is the uncertainties of war, the interventions it imposes upon local communities that cause the fear to arise in his breast once more.

The waiting is interminable. The mustiness of the earth in his nostrils seems tinged with something gunk-like and he wants to gag. He tries listening to the birds as a distraction but grows still more aware of the passing of time. Last night Mazzanti was careful not to light his lantern, for fear of being seen. That means there are fascist spies or Germans around. Were Toni and his father spotted on the way home? Has Toni been arrested and forced to tell about this hiding place? Toni is a sweet, quiet boy and Lorenzo doubts his ability to stand up to any severe questioning. Indeed they may have caught him this morning, just as the birdsong arose, and then dragged him off to an interrogation room. He is in that room now, cut off from his family, alone and afraid, and it is surely only a matter of time before he tells them about the hiding place. Perhaps they will even make him bring them here.

Lorenzo knows he cannot lift the planks. But might he burrow out? He feels to right and left but after some brief scrabbling it is clear the hole has been dug between two foundation walls and these stones are not to be shifted. He cannot reach above his head to burrow in that direction and downwards – well, downwards he'd be dead of old age before he got out.

He feels around his belt for his pistol and to his horror he cannot lay his hands upon it. Panicked, he pats his hands up and down the hole as best he can, shifting his body from side to side for the feel of the pistol's unyielding form beneath him. There is no sign of it and he groans, banging his forehead on the wood above him and collecting a splinter above the eye for his trouble. Then he recalls removing it from his belt as he climbed into the hole, for fear it might go off. He put it in his pack! He feels around and there it is, cool and reassuring, sticky with fig juice. He has disassembled it a hundred times, blindfolded, so it is a simple matter for him to clean it and check that it is functioning. He lays back flat on the earth with his arms across his chest, holding the firearm.

There is the sound of footsteps coming across the ruin towards him and a muffled voice talking to somebody nearby. Lorenzo's finger slips over the trigger. There is scraping above him as the stones are shifted and the cracks of light again begin to appear through the planks.

Chapter 8
September 1st 1944

There are German soldiers all over the village now, and the queue at the fountain is longer. They are hurling equipment into waiting vehicles and then leaping in as the trucks roar off. The inhabitants of the village are keeping themselves to themselves, for the Germans do not look to be in the mood for interruptions. Certainly they are far too preoccupied to notice the two peasants slipping past the houses outside the church.

Toni is barely able to see where he is going, stumbling along the cobbled street, his mind scattered. Papa guides him, holding his head as he throws up outside the church, then walking with an arm around him, wiping his forehead with an old handkerchief. The noise in his head is all pervading and crushing, planted inside him when he was snatched away from the entity. The wailing screeches across his soul like fingernails down the black board at school. It isn't always this bad. Indeed, often the entity doesn't evince more than discomfort, or confusion, and these emotions leave less residue. Today's encounter is one of the worst ever.

He slumps at the kitchen table. Mama catches Papa's glance and she puts some milk she got from a neighbour over the fire to warm.

'I didn't let Francesca go to that soldier, Guido. I couldn't. Look at the village. It's too dangerous.'

Papa grimaces, but he sits and recounts the happenings in the church.

'That Ugalotti,' says Mama, 'his mother was such a fine woman. Died in childbirth to his stillborn brother.'

'That's as may be. But now I don't think we can stay in this house. Don Morelli says even the Germans admit the front is advancing quickly.'

Francesca says, 'But where can we go?'

Papa shakes his head. 'We cannot go south into the war zone of course, and we cannot go to the coast. The Canadians have already moved up towards Rimini. Look at all the refugees coming up here. If we go to San Marino the allies will follow us there and we will be travelling alongside the retreating German armies. We cannot expect any favours from them.'

'But *you* cannot stay here,' says Mama.

'Why not?'

'Are you not just finished telling me that Ugalotti is coming back for you and that…troublesome soldier? What will you do? Sit and wait here for him?'

'I cannot simply walk out and leave you all here.'

Mama places a bowl of warm milk in front of Toni who is staring at the table in front of him. 'But you must! We'll be all right. You'll see. The war will pass us by. It is Ugalotti you have to worry about.'

'You're wrong about the war, Donatella, but I do not know where else we can go.'

Francesca says, 'Papa, maybe you can stay in the cave today, at least until it's dark.'

'There's work to do, *amore*. We should be preparing now. We need to fill the water tank, make bread, collect our vegetables and hide them. Also Gerta. I don't want her to go the way of Coco.'

Mama snorts, 'How are you going to hide the pig?'

'I'll take her to the cave with me. And then hope they won't steal the mule. Meanwhile you must start making bread. Lots of it.'

'But Guido…'

Papa thumps the table, 'I insist! If we're not going to leave then at least we must prepare. Are we fools?'

Mama looks at him and nods briefly. 'So bread, and should we not butcher Gerta? But I have no salt. Nobody does.'

'In this heat she'll go bad very quickly. Keep her alive until we need her. Francesca, make sure we have plenty of firewood for the ovens. And bring the sheep in from the field. Tether them both outside so they can reach grass, but not escape. I'll bring them down to the cave later too.'

Toni puts his bowl of milk down on the table. 'I must go to Lorenzo. Now! I must go now.'

Mama rests her hand on his shoulder, 'You aren't well, *amore*. I've seen you like this. You need to rest a day or two.'

He looks up at her, 'I can do it. I can go. Who else if not me? If Papa goes he'll be seen.'

'And so will you.'

Toni stands and steadies himself against the back of the chair. 'He hasn't eaten. I am going now.'

He cannot easily express the deep sense of responsibility he feels for Lorenzo. The man's face, as they pushed the planks over, haunts him. The soldier doubted them – Toni saw it in his eyes. He feared they would never return, and suspected he had, of his own free will, just climbed into his grave. Nobody but the family knows where he is.

Moving slowly like an old man, he goes to the door and laces on his shoes. Papa stands too and says to Mama, 'He means it.' He speaks from the knowledge that once Toni has a cause to pursue he will not stray from it.

He turns to his son, 'Listen, I'll go first. Then, if Di Stefano is waiting I'll go off in a different direction and he'll follow me. Then you can get away. Which way are you going?'

'I'll go round to Villa. Then I'll cut off and go down to the Ventena river. I can follow it under Montefiore and round towards Farneto. If I hide behind the Farneto ridge I'll be invisible from the village.'

Francesca says, 'That's such a big circuit, and so much climbing up the ridge. I'm coming with you, Toni. You're tired. I can carry the food.'

Mama's eyes widen but Francesca tosses her head and pulls on her shoes.

Papa sets off in the direction of the three charcoal burners, for as he says, the Zollara road will be too close to Lorenzo for comfort. They give him five minutes during which Mama prepares the food and Toni fills a water flask. Emerging cautiously through the stall they walk down off the top of the ridge, crossing the field and descending towards the big chestnut tree. If stopped they will use the excuse of looking for the sheep, and the food will be easy enough to explain. 'It's breakfast,' says Francesca. Toni keeps the Collision Brothers to heel. Remo seems all right this morning though he is happy to stay close.

At the chestnut tree the entire vista north is spread before them. To his left Toni can see the ragged outcrop of San Marino dominating the province. There are purple ridges layered one on the other, all the way from there to here, and the Croce ridge lies directly before them, across the Conca valley. Behind Croce more ridges run all the way down to the distant sliver of sparkling sea, and Rimini crouching to the northeast. To his right he follows the Conca to where, just beyond the reach of his haze-limited gaze, the river flows through Morciano.

They are out of sight of the village now, so they turn right past the cave, which is under the crown of the hill. Here Papa keeps their cheeses cool. They work their way around the hill, Toni resting frequently which makes progress slow. Yet this works in their favour too. They are able to wait and see if they are being followed, and while they do they observe the movement of troops in the valley below. There are endless lines of infantry retreating towards the northwest, interspersed with mules which drag artillery and provision carts. They look like processions of ants, dragging their prizes back to the nest. They can hear on the breeze the thunderous rumbling and squeaking of tanks and troop carriers as they make their way up to the village of Croce on the opposite ridge. From their higher position they can make out, between the few trees, more tanks parked in Croce and along the ridge at Menghino. Soldiers pull camouflaged nets over them.

Francesca says, 'Why are they putting all those tanks over there?'

'I heard Papa tell the priest they want to overlook the valley for when the British arrive. I wonder if they'll come here.'

'No, Mama said they wouldn't come all the way up to Gemmano. We are safe here.'

They look around them carefully, but of Di Stefano there is no sign. They contour round until they arrive at the road, winding down the eastern side of the hill from Gemmano to Villa, and then running north, down to the Conca. The flow of Germans getting out of Gemmano has eased and there is time and space to use the road between trucks. In any case nobody gives them more than a glance. They are just two more refugees upon the road, looking for shelter. Approaching the Villa hamlet they stop again, hidden behind a tree, keeping the road in view. Francesca says, 'Toni, sit and eat something.'

'We can't eat that. It's for Lorenzo.'

'Look in the bag. Mama has put in enough to feed the entire

village, as usual. Here, take a fig, and a tomato.'

He bites into the tomato and lets its sweet flavour fill his mouth. Francesca says, 'Where now?'

Toni points, fig in hand, 'We'll take the right hand fork in the road below. Soon after there's a scrubby hedge which runs almost all the way down to the stream.'

'Toni, it's still such a long way. Why don't we just follow the track after we turn right, to Il Tribbio? Then we are close and I don't think anybody will see us. There are trees above the road to protect us from the eyes in the village.'

It is a tempting thought particularly as it is evident nobody is following them. The cries in his head echo and resound around his skull. It is rarely this bad. Indeed, sometimes the entity doesn't evince more than discomfort, or confusion, and such emotions will leave less residue. He rests his head against her shoulder and she puts her arm around his head and strokes his hair.

While they have been talking, two figures have shuffled into view, climbing up the Morciano road towards them. They are hard to see beneath the mottled shadows of the plane trees. They are women, or girls, wearing skirts down below their knees, their hair tied up, their clothes and hair rendered grey-white by a thick layer of dust that covers them from head to foot. Each carries a bag, and the second, smaller figure looks barely able to drag hers any further. The taller one takes her hand and pulls her a few steps more. They stop and talk, and then stagger forward again, step by wavering step.

They stumble to a halt by the side of the road about forty metres from Toni and the younger one simply collapses in a heap beside the road. The other sits beside her, puts her arm around her and helps her to sit up. Then she gets out a flask, unscrews it and offers it to the younger girl.

'Come,' says Toni.

They walk down to the two girls, who are white with dust, faces like clowns with make up smeared across their mouths where water from the flask has run.

Francesca kneels before the older of the two and looks in her bag. She produces two peaches and hands one to Toni. She smiles to the girl and places the peach in her hand, telling her to eat. The girl gives a little gasp of surprise and appreciation and bites into it as if she hasn't eaten for a week.

Toni has put his arm around the younger girl who, having drunk from the flask, slumps against him with her eyes closed. He tries to place the peach in her hand but the girl's arm rests limply in her lap. He strokes her hair a little and speaks quietly to her, trying to get her attention, but she doesn't respond. He takes the peach and using his thumb he gouges a chunk of the soft flesh out of it. Holding the piece between his finger and thumb he wafts it under the girl's nose, and then he gently rubs it along her lips. Suddenly her mouth opens slightly and he is able to slip the piece between her teeth. She gives a little moan and begins to chew and before long he is able to push another piece in. Little by little he feeds her the whole peach. When he stops she opens her eyes and looks up at him.

'Do you want another one?'

She nods and so he reaches into the bag and hands her a fig.

'Thank you, Toni,' she says.

He is so surprised he almost drops the fruit. 'But how do you know my name?'

She shrugs, 'Well you're my cousin, of course.'

She doesn't appear at all surprised to see him. Toni looks at Francesca and the older girl says, 'It's us. Don't you know us? We are Floriana and Letizia.'

Toni gets the flask and pours water over the face of each of them, much to their discomfort, and as the dust and grime washes off he can see that they are indeed the cousins from Cattolica, down on the coast.

'My God,' cries Francesca and gives Floriana a hug, 'but what are you doing here?'

'We're coming to find you. We have nowhere else to go. Our house has been bombed and destroyed. We've been walking for two days. When I saw you coming down the hill I thought God had sent you to us.'

They laugh and hug again, and Letizia smiles wanly at Toni before she tucks into the fig. Francesca gets some bread out, carefully leaving some aside for Lorenzo, and makes sure they eat properly. The girls are desperately hungry saying they have eaten nothing on the road, and so Toni waits until they are calmer before he puts his question.

'And Zia Evelina? Where is your Mama?'

Floriana immediately bursts into tears and it is Letizia who answers in a small voice, 'Mama died. She died yesterday, beside the road. We had to leave her there. Germans came along and made us move away. They stole our food and then they threw her body in the ditch. I saw them do it.'

Toni and Francesca are shocked into silence. Then Francesca says in disbelief, 'Why would they kill her?'

Floriana sniffs, 'No, she was giving birth. I was helping her but the baby was dead. We shouldn't have left the house, but everybody was getting out of Cattolica, and then they bombed us and we had to do the same. Before she died Mama told me everybody is coming to the hilltops to places like Gemmano which are safe, so we came here.'

'And Zio Mario?'

'He's away, in Sardinia, with other soldiers. We've heard nothing for eight months.'

Letizia and Floriana huddle together while Toni and Francesca stand and talk.

'What shall we do?'

Francesca says, 'I must take them back to the house.'

'What about Lorenzo?'

'Do you feel all right?'

'Yes, perfect.'

She looks at him dubiously, 'You still look tired to me.'

'I have no choice, Francesca. I must release him,' he glances around them, 'and soon. He must be starving. What if the British don't come for days, and we can't get him out of that hole?'

Taking what is left of the food, Toni follows the track towards Poggio as Francesca advised. He walks slowly, Remo at his side, while Romolo investigates the row of trees above the road. It is now mid-afternoon and the heat saps him further. He glances across the valley to the southeast where Montefiore perches on the hill, its towering castle standing watch over him. From time to time he hears the low rumble of heavy artillery pound out from somewhere beyond the Montefiore ridge.

His attention is attracted to some activity at the bottom of the field below. He can see German soldiers digging trenches and piling up sandbags in front of them, so they are protected from

Montefiore above. From there they can train their guns on the Ventena stream at the bottom of the valley. Toni backs up and keeps over to the right hand side of the road, so that they cannot see him. If he gets stopped Lorenzo may never get out.

Now he is alone the wailing inside his head reasserts itself, lessened but clinging on. It is as if a small shadow, an echo of the entity, is twisting around in his head, emitting cry after cry. His head aches and he squeezes his temples, though he is consoled that there are no entities around now. He isn't surprised by this. After an encounter they tend to leave him alone. Perhaps, he has speculated in the past, they feel he is of no use to them in this state. He wishes he could get to Lorenzo for the sake of distraction, and he quickens his pace.

He gets to the fork by Il Tribbio, just below his pigeon trap. Hidden from Gemmano, he veers up to the right, and then pauses as a German truck roars along the Zollara-Gemmano track above, leaving a trail of dust in its wake. Then he climbs into the field and retraces his steps from the previous night.

He walks into the ruin, calling Romolo to heel and grumbling at him for his tardiness, and immediately starts shifting stones off the hiding place. Just as he reveals the final layer of planks, one of them is pushed roughly aside from below and the muzzle of a gun emerges and points straight at him.

'Madonna, but must you point that at me every time you see me?'

Lorenzo is in no mood to share the humour. 'Get me out of here.'

Toni grasps his hand and drags him out. Instantly on his feet he takes a deep breath and stretches, his eyes closed. Then he groans and bends to hold his leg.

'Here, let me take a look at it.'

Toni hands him the bag and Lorenzo sits to eat. Toni notices again how he takes small pieces of food and chews carefully, though he doesn't stop until the bag is empty. While he eats Toni checks the leg and brings him up to date with the situation.

'You say the Germans are heading for San Marino?'

'Well, in that direction but they are not going away. We saw tanks on the ridge opposite. And they are digging in down the hill, and also I saw some going to Zollara.'

'But how then am I to get to Gemmano? I cannot stay in that hole another night. I cannot!'

Remo comes up and rubs his head against Lorenzo who caresses him distractedly, much to Remo's delight.

Toni doesn't much like the look of the wound. He says, 'There are many caves underneath the crown of the hill. Papa and I will have to sleep there tonight, to avoid the fascists. Perhaps you can stay there with us.'

'Well, a cave I can survive.'

'Then we'll go there, but not until after dark.'

Lorenzo lies on the ground talking to Remo who rolls over on his back to get his tummy rubbed. Everybody is Remo's friend if they will just rub his tummy. Romolo as always keeps his distance. Lorenzo laughs and says, 'This one makes me think of a dog we had when I was a boy. Such a softy!'

Toni watches him, smiling. 'Why did you join the army?'

Lorenzo looks over his shoulder and replies, 'You are wondering how somebody who loves animals can kill humans so easily?'

Toni makes a depreciating gesture, 'No, just that you are a kind man, I think. I knew you wouldn't shoot that gun at me yesterday.'

'Once you are a soldier you are put in certain positions – you are given no choice,' Lorenzo sighs.

'But why a soldier?'

'You've grown up with both your Mama and your Papa. When you don't have a Papa you feel different. Everybody else at the local school has a Papa, and sometimes you get teased. It's like you aren't quite one of them. You feel like you come from somewhere else. Then you wonder what your Papa was like, but even if you ask your Mama she can't tell you very much, because although they fell in love they didn't spend very much time together. They didn't get to know much about each other before he was healed and had to go back to the front. I remember Mama told me that she offered to cut open his wound so it would take longer to heal, but he wouldn't agree to that so he went back, and that was the last she heard from him. She supposed he was killed.

'The only thing I knew about him was that he was a soldier. So when Mussolini declared war I became a soldier! Silly, isn't it? Probably he was only a soldier because of the White War and the rest of the time he was a smallholder or something. That's how fate leads us by the nose as it wishes.'

'And your Mama?'

'She didn't know she was pregnant until after he left. Her parents consulted the priest who told her to have the baby. She lived with them and then a few years later she met another man called Berto. This man had only one leg, from the war, but he was a good man and didn't mind that she had a child out of wedlock and she loved him for that. I think I was about three when he came along. He was always nice to me but I knew he wasn't my Papa, and I wasn't given his surname. I had to declare Bergamas at school. But he was decent to me, and when other children came they were like my brothers and sisters.'

'So you have a family.'

'Yes, but my grandpa was going to leave the farm to my Mama and Berto, who in turn would have left it to his oldest son. Not to me. So I didn't have a future there. But I was happy enough, and I want to go back and see they are all right.'

'Have you killed men with that gun?'

Lorenzo nods, 'Want me to show you how to use it?'

Toni shakes his head.

'Go ahead, hold it. Just try holding it. Nothing more.'

'I cannot.'

Lorenzo takes his hand and presses the gun into it. Toni leaps back, snatching his hand away, and the gun goes flying. 'Don't make me! I cannot. I know what it has done. I can feel what it has done.'

Lorenzo holds up a hand, 'Okay, okay…easy. It doesn't matter.'

He picks up the gun with his forefinger and thumb, holds it up for Toni to see and deposits it in his pack once more. Toni settles down beside Romolo who offers him a rare lick on his face.

Lorenzo says, 'What did you mean, you can feel what it has done?'

Toni rests his head against Romolo's flank. 'I am tired now. I am going to sleep for a while.'

When it gets dark Toni leads the way up to the track and over it. The wails continue to assail him, if less frequently, and he still feels a sense of utter desperation from the entity. Lorenzo has assured him that his leg is up to the trip and they slip quietly between houses, the dogs on their best behaviour. The sound of distant, heavy artillery is now a low, constant thunder to the southeast as Toni edges down a path towards the cave. He lets out a low call but gets no response, repeats himself, and then creeps down. To his surprise the cave is empty. Telling Lorenzo to wait he goes up the field to the house. In the kitchen Floriana is helping Mama with some cooking but of Letizia and Francesca, there is no sign.

'Papa, I thought we were going to sleep down in the cave tonight?'

Papa gives a little chuckle, 'We don't have to, my boy. Those fascists have done a runner. Scarpered after lunch when they thought everybody was hiding from the heat. Paisani saw them throw a suitcase into the back of a German car and they were out of here in a cloud of dust. Sitting up straight in the back as if they were going somewhere important. They'll be lucky if the Germans don't ditch them half way down the hill. Anyway, good riddance.'

'OK so can I bring Lorenzo up here?'

Papa frowns, 'He isn't still at the hole?'

Toni explains and adds, 'I thought the cave would be safe if we were also going to sleep there.'

Mama says sharply, 'Yes, it is safe, so leave him there. I don't want him in here with all these girls around. Anyway, he will bring trouble with the Germans about.'

Papa says, 'I will come down and talk to him. We can bring some more food and blankets.'

'Papa, he is still in his uniform. I think most of all that's what makes him a danger – you know, if the Germans see it.'

Papa nods, 'You are right. I will find some clothes for him. I think he is roughly the same size as me.'

They see Lorenzo safely installed in the cave, shifting the cheeses to one side so he has space to sleep. Back in the house Toni moves into the small bedroom so that Francesca and the girls can share his larger bed. Sleep brings with it a welcome relief from the noise in his head.

Chapter 9
September 2nd 1944

Toni is digging potatoes, his favourite job. Placing his foot on the spade, shoving it in near the plant and then levering it up, feels like uncovering a hidden cache. The clump of earth-coated treasure huddled on his spade is like the land revealing a secret, offering up a bounty he can always count on. Letizia has come out to help him and crouches beside the hole he has dug, picking out the potatoes. She counts them into the sack that Mama thrust into her hand. They are trying to break their record of nineteen potatoes from a plant. Letizia seems to be enjoying herself, pleased to be doing something useful and grateful for the distraction.

Toni glances up. 'There's a vehicle coming.'

They back up quickly against the stall until it has passed, not wishing to be observed in the vegetable patch. It is possible for greedy eyes to catch a glimpse of them from the road between the houses. People who steal cows won't hesitate to snatch an easy sack of potatoes.

'Okay, back to work. Look, you missed one there.'

'Only because you pulled me away,' she pouts.

Earlier Toni took food down to the cave, and he and Lorenzo sat watching a dog fight in the sky above, the planes tracing tangled artwork across the blue. Below, the tanks he had seen in Croce were no longer in sight, but there was still plenty of activity. Mules were dragging artillery up towards the village, and to their left a column was heading in the direction of San Marino. He was struck by the calm and organization of the movements.

'That's the Germans,' said Lorenzo.

Picking up the two cheeses from the cave he brought them up to the house, for Mama wanted them in the cellar for easy access. At the stall he pushed aside the straw hiding the trapdoor down to the cellar, and descended the wooden steps. He looked around, deciding on the coolest place, and in the gloom he banged his face on a ham hanging from the low ceiling. The cellar was wide at the front where the trapdoor was, and tapered to a dark narrow angle near the back, where Papa had burrowed into the hill. There was an unused bread oven that Papa had built, and broad, cement shelves on which he often placed demi-johns of wine. A small wine press and other equipment for wine making were stored here.

Toni laid the cheeses on a shelf by the oven and, carefully covering the trapdoor with straw once more, he returned to the cave and brought the pig and the sheep back up to the stall. There he was able to feed them easily, and he planned to take them down to the cave again later.

Letizia looks up at him. 'See, the bag is full.'

There are still a few plants but he decides to leave them in the ground for now. 'OK, let's show Mama how many we've dug up.'

They go back into the kitchen and are joined almost immediately by Francesca and Floriana who are carrying bags of fruit.

'Look, figs and peaches. We had to climb right to the top of the fig tree to get any. Lots of people have the same idea now.'

Mama nods briefly, 'Now go out and pick what you can from the garden. Toni, you fill the water tank. I want Letizia to help me here with the food.'

Toni goes out to the well, which is just on the other side of the vegetable garden fence. He has to draw the water up to ground level first and then transfer it to another bucket attached to a pulley, and that gets hauled up to the roof. Then he ties it off, goes upstairs, reaches for the bucket over the edge of the house and pours it into the tank. This doesn't usually take long, because he only puts in sufficient for the day. Now he has to fill the tank. He calls to Floriana, 'Leave the fruit and come and help me. You go upstairs and I'll send the water up to you.'

He lowers the bucket into the well. It is familiar, rhythmic work and his mind, his wonderfully empty mind, wanders free. He woke this morning with no noise in his head and now he feels clear and strong. He is happy to be working together with the family and as the food amasses in the kitchen he joins in their growing sense of hope. They will get enough food for a few days and here, safe on top of the hillside they will lie low, huddled in their house. Lorenzo and the girls can hide out too, without cause for worry, and then the British will come and liberate them. The Germans are going backwards and it is only a matter of time before the front passes over them. It is a wonderful thought. He doesn't really understand why Papa is so glad to see the back of the fascists, but he has never liked Ugalotti and if it pleases Papa then they all feel better.

The tank filled, Toni makes sure Gerta has enough food and that the sheep are tethered fast. Inside, Mama is showing Letizia how to make gnocchi, having boiled up the potato and then passed it through a sieve to make a fine mash. There is flour all over the kitchen table and a growing pile of gnocchi at one side on a tray. Francesca is slicing up the few peppers and the aubergines she has found. Papa comes in.

'But why are you making gnocchi now? We have no time for this.'

'And what am I going to do? Of course I must prepare the food. This is such a small thing. I don't even have time to make passata from all these tomatoes.'

'We need clothes and blankets packed, in case we have to get out.'

'I have to get the peppers under oil. At least that way they will last a time. Otherwise they will all be lost. There is no salt to be found in the village at all.'

Papa looks impatient. 'We should have bags packed just in case.'

Mama takes a pot off the stove. 'Look, food is ready for lunch. Tell everybody to come in and eat and then afterwards we'll prepare your bags for you.'

Francesca calls Floriana in and they pull chairs around the table. Mama says, 'Here, grate some cheese onto the gnocchi. Afterwards there are tomatoes, but no salt for them. Here's bread from this morning.'

Everybody is hungry. Letizia says, 'Are we safe here? I saw Germans around the village earlier.'

Mama glares at Papa. 'We're safe here, darling. Don't be afraid. Soon the British will be here, and then we'll be free. The British are good people and they'll chase the Germans up to San Marino, and then we'll be left in peace.'

'And then you can introduce me to the mysterious Lorenzo,' smiles Francesca to Toni.

'And me,' says Floriana.

Papa can't help a brief explosion of a laugh and Mama says, 'My God, even now all you can think of are boys.'

'I only want to meet him,' says Francesca. 'Toni told me about him. He sounds a very nice man.'

'Yes man, and not boy. That is a man who has been to war. He is much older than you. Don't be foolish. You're still a child.'

Floriana says, 'Toni, tell us about him again. Is he good looking?'

'Well, it isn't really for me to say if he's handsome or not,' says Toni, and the girls laugh.

Francesca persists, 'But come on, what's he like?'

Toni considers. 'He is careful, but passionate. He has suffered a lot in the war, I think. He doesn't like enclosed spaces and…'

'And what…Toni…and what?'

Toni glances at Papa, 'He eats very carefully, chewing slowly. A bit like Papa.'

'An educated man!' exclaims Floriana.

'A man in need of peace,' says Francesca.

Toni nods, 'He's both of these things. But most of all, right now, he needs care on his leg. It's worse than he thinks and he doesn't want to rest it.'

'And then maybe he will want to dance,' giggles Floriana.

Letizia bursts into tears. Through her sobs she says, 'Oh, dancing…it makes me think of Mama.'

Francesca puts an arm around her, 'There there, my darling.'

'It's wrong to be laughing so soon after she has died. I feel guilty.'

Floriana too breaks down and the two sisters hug each other, inconsolable. Storms of emotion sweep over them as if held back for many months and, now released, their tears are like a breached dam, which spews water down the valley. The tears mingle as the girls hug closely, their hands gripping each other's hair. Mama and Francesca put their arms around them and console them as best they can and Papa, perhaps feeling helpless, goes outside.

Toni finds himself watching this scene from a distance. He feels removed from the others, as if floating in the room looking down at them. He is unable to move or to speak and he grips his spoon tightly. The sensation is a bit like an impending spasm yet he does not fear it. He knows it is something else. This is more like something poised inside him waiting to happen.

Suddenly he finds himself standing and going over to the girls. He kneels down before them and takes Letizia's hand in his. With his other hand he cups her chin and makes her look at him. He speaks without thinking or preparation, conviction driving his words.

'Zia Evelina is all right now. She's not suffering any more. In fact she's in a happy place and at peace, and she looks over you both with all her love.'

Toni speaks with such calm and certainty that Letizia stops crying and looks at him. 'How do you know this?'

Toni shrugs, 'I don't know. I just know.'

'Oh,' says Floriana weakly.

There is silence at the table, and then Mama goes and gets two plates, which she places in front of them. 'Look, here's a little bit of lemon tart from yesterday. I've saved it for you two.'

Floriana looks up and gives Mama a wan smile but Letizia just stares at the tart. Then Papa comes back in. He has something hidden behind his back and it looks as if he is having trouble keeping it there. He comes round the table and crouches beside Letizia. Then he produces a little black and white kitten, not more than two weeks old, and he places it on Letizia's lap.

'Look who I found this morning in the village. In all the confusion she has lost her parents and now she needs somebody to take care of her. Can you do that, Letizia? Can you watch over her?'

In spite of herself Letizia gives a gasp and a little laugh, 'Aw, she is so sweet.'

Papa points, 'Look, she's going to grow up with a little star on her forehead, I think.'

'Oh, how sweet, how sweet,' coos Floriana.

'So you have to give her warm milk every day, Okay?'

Letizia nods, eyes wide. 'What's her name?'

'Well, she doesn't have a name. If you're going to take care of her then that's your job. What do you want to call her?'

Letizia looks around at the others, 'Oh, I don't know.'

The suggestions are not slow in coming. 'Call her Bella.'

'What about Piccola?'

'Call her Star.'

Letizia holds the kitten up to her face. The creature is quiet and gives her an uncertain lick. 'It looks like a thumbprint on her forehead. I will call her Thumb.'

She feeds Thumb a little of the lemon tart and she and Floriana crouch down watching the kitten eat. Francesca clears away the plates from the table and Mama looks at Toni.

'How do you know that?' she says quietly. 'How can you be sure?'

'I told you, I don't know. I just know it.'

The family gets to work again. Papa goes out with an axe to chop firewood, saying he must stockpile for the coming days. Floriana is sent for more fruit and Toni, on his father's instructions, gathers some essential tools in a kitbag.

He is just stowing these in the hallway when they hear the roaring of motor vehicles outside, followed by the sound of car doors slamming and shouted instructions in German. Toni goes up to the front door and opens it a crack. The Germans have parked three vehicles outside Casa Paisani on the opposite side of the road, and they are already carrying items of radio equipment inside. As Tony watches, one of the daughters is pushed out of the door, glancing anxiously around, clinging to a small bag and guiding a screaming youngster in front of her. Then comes her ageing grandmother waving her stick in fury, barely able to walk, and then the two other kids with their parents stumble into the road. The kids are gripping items of clothing and the mother clasps a loaf of bread and a bag from which falls a piece of fruit. Signori Paisani, frail and sick though he is, drops a small carafe of wine and turns to protest, but a German soldier punches him in the mouth so hard that he falls down.

The women help him to his feet and the family straggle up the road in Toni's direction, the Germans paying them no further attention. From an upstairs window not facing onto the road a head sticks out. It is Angela, the oldest daughter. In her hands she has a bundle tied with string and with a low call to the family she hurls it as far as she can in their direction. Then she throws out a couple of bed sheets tied together to form a kind of rope. She skims down these with an alacrity born of strength and fear, and runs over to the family who grasp and hug her.

Toni turns and calls, 'Papa, Mama, come and look.'

But his parents have already surmised the situation. Telling Toni to get back out of sight Mama opens the door a little more to show herself, raises her hand and calls to the Paisani family, gesturing them urgently to come over. One of the little girls sees, and tugging upon Angela's skirt she points. Angela gathers the family and they stumble over as best they can. Mama ushers them all inside, into the salon, where they collapse in a kind of promiscuous heap. Grandma Paisani is helped to one of the chairs where she sits with her hands shaking uncontrollably. Papa gets the last of their belongings inside and they shut their front door firmly but quietly.

A kind of shocked silence descends upon the room, and even the little girls are too numbed to cry. They lie where they have sat or fallen on the floor, still gripping whatever treasure they have come away with. Mama goes back to the kitchen and puts a pot of water over the fire to boil.

Papa nudges Toni, 'Bring me the bottle of grappa and some glasses.'

Papa pours glasses and hands them around, even to the little ones, though in these glasses he adds plenty of water from a jug that Toni has also brought. Paisani gulps his down and asks for another.

'They said they need the house for their headquarters! And where are we supposed to go? When I asked him he smacked me.'

Papa says, 'They're alpine troops. I know their uniforms. They are famed for being brave, but very tough.'

Papa and Toni go back to the kitchen where Mama and Francesca are preparing some food.

'Where will they sleep?'

'They can sleep in the salon, with Grandma on the sofa. Toni, later on you and the girls will bring in some straw from outside. Perhaps one or two of the small ones can come upstairs with us. Toni, the boy can go in with you.'

Papa says, 'We'd better butcher Gerta. With all these mouths to feed we'll need the meat. We'll eat it all before it goes bad.'

In the salon they can hear one of the little ones crying and then another, and soon this grows into a kind of general wailing which waxes and wanes like a howling wind.

Papa goes through. 'Listen to me. Don't despair. This won't last for long. The British are almost here, and once they arrive the Germans will leave and you will have your home back. Until then you'll stay here with us. We have food and a pig to butcher, so we won't starve. If we sit quietly nobody will bother us. The British and the Germans are going to be too busy killing each other. But kids,' he looks around at the little ones with a finger to his lips, 'Ssssshh, mm? Let nobody know we are here.'

The kids lapse into silence one by one and the parents smile at Papa. He comes back through to the kitchen and starts looking for his butchering knife.

Toni sighs, 'Here it is, in this drawer. The one with the good grip you like so much.'

Papa glances at him and cannot prevent the echo of a smile on his features. He is about to say something when a tremendous pounding starts up on the front door. It is far too heavy to be fists and although it is a strong door it cannot survive such an assault for long.

Angela's face appears at the door. 'It's them. It's the Germans. This is exactly what they did to us.'

'I should have known it,' growls Papa. 'Francesca, you and the girls grab some bags and get all the food you can.'

Mama staggers. 'But what? They are coming in here? They cannot. They have no right!'

'Toni, get that bag of tools.'

Mama turns back to the fire and begins to sprinkle cornmeal into the hot water. Papa grabs her by the arms and glares into her eyes, 'Donatella, they are here. Accept this. You must. Accept this and help me. Donatella!'

The Paisani family are already tumbling through from the salon, away from the front door, and Francesca starts ushering them out the back, through the stall and into the vegetable garden. Mama stares at the chaos around her and then looks up sharply as the pounding stops for a moment and a harsh voice shouts, in Italian, 'Open this door. If not we will blow it up, and kill anybody inside. You can save yourselves if you open the door.'

Realization sets in and Mama spins towards Toni, 'They will try and make you work for them. Get down to the cellar and hide. Hide yourself so that Jesus Christ himself couldn't find you.

Guido, you too.'

'I will not hide from anybody in my own house. Don't worry, with this leg they will not make me work. But Toni, you get down to the cellar.'

Toni stands rooted to the spot, his mind spinning. 'But...'

'Now, Toni, Now!'

Papa turns and strides into the salon. He shouts through the front door, 'Just a moment, I'm coming. I have to find the key.'

Toni turns and stumbles down the stairs into the stall, tripping over a small Paisani as he does. He pushes Gerta to one side to her immense indignation, sweeps away the straw, and pulls up the trapdoor. He almost dives into it and does not notice the blur beside him. Behind him the trapdoor smashes shut and he can hear Mama say, 'Floriana, cover the door with straw, and make Gerta stand on top of it.'

There is the sound of feet tripping over each other, up and down the steps from kitchen to stall and behind this, more muffled, there is still shouting and Papa's voice assuring the Germans he will soon have the key. In the kitchen it sounds like panic but Toni can't think about that now. Glancing around for the best hiding place he is confronted by Remo, sitting and grinning at him.

'Oh Remo, you're here.' He kneels and gives the dog a hug. 'Come, let's find somewhere safe.'

He goes round the bread oven to the cement shelves hidden on the far side from the trapdoor, where he sees some hessian sacks in a pile. He gets on the ground and slides under the bottom shelf, pulling Remo with him. Then he pulls the sacks over them both.

There is a crash upstairs as the front door is smashed open and heavy, booted footsteps tramp into the house and down to the kitchen. Tony hears screams and then Papa's voice demanding to know what they want.

A German answers, again in Italian, 'We are commandeering this house for billets. You must all get out. Right now. You... leave that food. We will need that.'

Mama says, 'But we must eat too.'

'Leave it! And you, you must come with us. We need every able bodied man.'

Papa says, 'I cannot work. My leg is damaged. Look here at the scar. I can barely walk.'

There is a silence and then a crash as the table is turned over and hurled to one side. Then there is a sharp report and Toni hears a thump above him and Mama cries out, 'Leave him be, leave him be.'

Another voice shouts in German, 'You are a liar. Get up. Show me you can walk. I know you can walk. How did you get to the door?'

It is a voice Toni knows. He knows it from a nearby field, kneeling over the prone, bleeding body of Remo, pigeons in his belt. It is Wolfgang, the squarehead. Toni can barely hear Papa mumbling, 'My walking stick, where is my walking stick?'

There is another thump above him and Papa cries out, 'Oh, my head,' and he hears one of the girls scream. There are more stomps and thumps, and the sound of somebody crawling across the floor and then being dragged back. There is a terrible bang and a deep groan from Papa.

'Now take him out, now that he truly is no use to us.'

Toni is so scattered that the spasm catches him by surprise, before he can spot it rising within him. His entire body doubles up like an embryo in a womb. A wave of black sweeps across his consciousness and he shakes his head, trying to stave it off. He goes to sit up and smashes his head on the cement shelf above him. The nausea surges up and he grabs a sack and vomits into it again and again and it is this that helps him stay conscious. Finally, panting, his body quiets and the retching stops. Pushing the sack away he waits until his equilibrium returns.

Above he can hear feet stumbling down the steps into the stall and the fading weeping of the girls as they pull each other through the vegetable patch and out to the field. Then there is a rifle shot and Mama cries, 'Not the pig!' followed by two more shots.

There is a command in German. 'You two, take these carcasses up to the field kitchen and see the meat is given to the chef. You, get that mule over to the artillery battalion.'

Beside him Remo is quivering at the terrible noises from above and Toni pulls them both in behind the bread oven, making them as small as he can. Boots march back and forth and another truck arrives outside. Somebody shouts, 'Look, here are bags with fruit and tomatoes, and this looks like pasta ready to eat.'

Sounds of furniture being shifted filter down to Toni for the next hour or so, as he hugs Remo in the near dark. As always after a spasm he falls asleep for a time, though he is disturbed by terrible dreams, and he awakes not knowing if he has ever been properly asleep at all. There is no light filtering into the cellar and he thinks dusk must have fallen. The dog's warmth and smell are comforting and he believes Remo gets the same comfort from him, and so he talks to him in a low voice, telling him everything will be all right. He tries not to think about Romolo and where he may be hiding. He knows Romolo won't have gone far and he fears Wolfgang will find him and shoot him too.

Nobody tries the trapdoor, which he has barred from inside, and this raises hope that the straw is doing its job as a disguise, at least for now. At a certain point there is a sharp command in German followed by the sound of many boots exiting the front door. He knows it is only a matter of time before they find the cellar – after all every house has one somewhere – and wonders if this is the moment to escape. But he can hear a couple of people moving in the kitchen, occasional comments passing between them, and he lies still. In order to pass the time he listens to see if they have orders to follow the others. For now they are discussing practical matters, with one of the men claiming a space by the door for his bed. It seems he always has to pee during the night, and doesn't want to stand on other sleeping bodies when he has to slip out.

The other voice says, 'This is a fine boning knife. It has a good grip. I will take it up to the kitchen later. Or maybe I will hang on to it. They probably have lots in any case.'

'You should hand it in.'

'So you haven't taken anything yet, I suppose? What did I see going into that little bag of yours yesterday, taken from the back pocket of that body down near Morciano?'

'You didn't see anything!'

'Right! And neither did you.'

There is another silence.

'This is a comfortable house. How long do you think we will be here?'

'I heard the *leutnant* say we are digging in here. We have already fallen back from the first defences, and the orders say that is enough. We are to halt the allies here before they get to San Marino and the Po valley.'

'But on this hilltop?'

'It is good strategically. We can see all around, and across to the other ridge – you know, the Croce ridge. We can shell them from here in safety, if they come up the Conca valley to attack Croce and Coriano.'

'Shell them with what? We're all out!'

'They're bringing up more troops and artillery. We aren't the only ones you know. What about the Alpines that have joined us?'

'Those guys...they make me...well, to tell you the truth they make me nervous. All they talk about is the next battle. It's as if they think of nothing else.'

'I tried to get into them once.'

'Yeah? What happened?'

'They wouldn't have me. Oh, I was efficient enough, I believe. But they said I wasn't of a...certain disposition.'

'What kind of disposition?'

There is a silence for a moment, 'I suppose I am not quick enough to kill.'

'Yes but...'

'Enough! We've some unloading to do. Come on, let's get to it.'

Once the front door closes there is silence, punctuated only by the sound of vehicles arriving and departing on the road outside. Toni waits a while before disentangling himself from Remo. He creeps over to the steps and removes the beam that was barring the trapdoor. He jams his ear up against the trapdoor and stands still for a full two minutes, but there is nothing to suggest movement or threat on the other side. Slowly he pushes it up.

Straw slides off the trapdoor which he catches before it can fall open with its usual bang. He raises his head cautiously until he can look around the dark and empty stall. Then he climbs out, his hand slipping in a sticky pool of Gerta's blood. Peering over the vegetable patch towards the field, he can see the first stars are showing. He turns and pads up the steps so he can look into the kitchen. There are two candles sitting on the table, replaced at the centre of the room, and by their light he can see bedding has been laid all over the floor. He is about to turn away when he spots a bag sitting on a chair. He creeps through the area where their coats hang and into the kitchen itself. He hardly has to step in to be able to reach the bag, which he does with one sweeping movement. Its weight is encouraging and he retreats down to the stall once more. In the vegetable patch he hunkers down and puts an arm around Remo to keep him quiet.

Not daring to believe his luck he remains still for several minutes, and his prudence is rewarded when up ahead, near the rickety gate, there is a movement. A match is struck and somebody lights up a cigarette. Now that the figure has shifted Toni can see the silhouette of a German helmet. The soldier is standing by the fence, apparently facing over to the Croce ridge. Toni's heart is pounding and he has no idea what to do. He cannot go back to the cellar for they will surely find him in the morning. There is still far too much activity to go out on the main road either. He remains frozen, arm around Remo, a mere twenty yards away from the German guard.

Perhaps half an hour passes and Toni can feel his left leg beginning to cramp. He watches it carefully, watches the pain, and like this he is able to ease it and calm it. But the sweat runs off his forehead and he knows he cannot keep still for much longer.

There is a...movement?...a sound?...to his left and he closes his eyes and allows his other senses full rein. He knows it is the kind of sound Romolo would make when licking his chops after eating, and he clamps his hand over Remo's nose. At that moment the guard steps outside the gate and a moment later Toni can hear urine splashing on the ground. Pulling Remo with him he crawls towards where he and Letizia had been digging potatoes that morning. Romolo finds him with a brief lick on his face, though when Remo tries to greet him Romolo dissuades him with the faintest rumble from the bottom of his lungs.

The German picks up his rifle and between drags of his cigarette he begins, rather tunelessly, to hum a melody. Toni has one hand on Romolo's back. He can feel the dog is crouched low and now begins to crawl along the wall with the tomato plants against it, and suddenly Toni understands where he is going. The dog flap is up ahead. This is the hole in the fence that he cut for them, for when they return from hunting and the gate has been latched for the night.

Hidden at the base of the wall he knows they are hard to see, though he fears Remo's rust-coloured fur may be visible. There is no choice but to keep crawling and it takes them, centimetre by centimetre, another fifteen minutes to arrive at the flap. It is only covered with a piece of heavy hessian and Romolo brushes this aside with familiarity. Toni follows, guiding Remo and making sure he stays silent as they get through. In theory they are coming into the soldier's range of view but, crawling up against the hedgerow they merge into the deeper blackness. Even Remo has got the idea now and stays hunkered down, scraping along on his belly.

They crawl like this until the hedge dips over the edge of the hill and Toni turns to see the houses of Borgo are out of sight. He utters a low rumble of greeting in his throat, and now Romolo and Remo rub muzzles together and lick him properly.

Once Toni gets his bearings it is a relatively simple matter to slip down towards the cave where his parents are hiding. But when he walks into camp he is shocked to find thirty or forty people sitting around a couple of fires at the mouth of the cave and Papa, unconscious, lying on a makeshift bed.

Chapter 10
September 3rd 1944

Toni contemplates a bed of nettles. He has brushed past it on many occasions, making his way along this path, part of a network through which he has roamed the countryside unseen for years. It is not that others don't know of the network's existence, but that they find little use for it. This path appears to peter out on the side of the hill, and only Toni knows that if you contour another thirty metres you'll find an overgrown pig track following the circumference of the hill, out of sight of the town walls.

The nettles are not ideal. Mama has asked for the tender ones so she can make a soup. She obviously doesn't remember that by this time of year they are big and aggressive, standing tall and determined to defend themselves. Their stings run down the stems as well as the leaves. They won't be good eating unless he can break off the greener tops, or find younger shoots near the ground that are pushing up through the tangle of dying stems. Easier said than done, when you don't have any gloves.

He removes his shirt and, bare to the waist, he wraps it round one hand and approaches the nettles. Selecting a stem he eases it loose of the others and bends it towards him. With the forefinger and thumb of his unprotected hand he grips it well up the stem, firmly in order to negate the sting, and then snaps the top off. He tosses it to one side and repeats the action until he has a good pile lying around him. He uses dock leaves to cool the odd sting, and then as gloves to pick up the tops and gather them in his shirt, spread on the ground.

When he finishes he dumps himself on the ground for he is very tired. Stumbling into the cave last night, fending off the hugs and kisses of his family, it had been almost impossible to sleep. He'd sat beside Papa at first, observing the heavy bruising down one side of his face and the cut on his temple. Papa's right hand was bandaged and the arm was up in a makeshift sling. Mama said, 'They beat him so hard, with their fists and their gun butts. I think his hand is broken. He was still conscious when we got out of the house, but Angela and I were almost carrying him down the field while all he could do was mumble about his walking stick. Just as we arrived at the end of the field he collapsed completely. The others had to come and help carry him in. Now he just lies there, not saying a word.'

She dabbed her eyes. Tony took Papa's hand and stroked it until Don Morelli arrived. The priest said he had nothing to bring them but two canteens of water for there were many villagers hidden in the various caves under the hill. He prayed beside Papa for a time and then said he must move on.

'Montefiore Conca is ablaze,' he told them as he left. 'I am conducting mass beneath the abattoir tomorrow. Come if you can.'

Tony sat with Papa until his head dropped and his eyes drooped. The cave was lit only by candles, which were balanced in crannies, leaving large jagged areas in darkness. Being taller, Toni had to stoop to avoid banging his head on the bare, sharp outcrops of ceiling. The cave was narrow and split into three still narrower dead ends, obscured by the dark, where people squeezed beside each other to sleep. The musty atmosphere was the least of their problems. It was impossible for Toni to find anywhere to lie down between so many sleeping bodies, and he finished up sitting on a ledge near the entrance, squeezed between Francesca and the wall. They put their arms around each other but his head kept dropping down, and then he would jerk upright at the sound of the guns firing, waking her too. Eventually Lorenzo had the idea of stringing a rope in front of them as a support over which they could hang their arms and heads, and they slept that way. The packed cave was filled with groans and weeping, a child asking a piercing question or complaining she was hungry. But as the night wore on people calmed and settled a little, though nobody slept deeply.

This morning he stumbled out at first light and went to urinate out of sight of the cave. Looking over the valley as the light came up he was aware of being hungry, but it was mild and didn't trouble him greatly. When he returned, people were emerging from the cave into the warm air, like arrivals in a new world. The sound of troop carriers rose distantly from the valley floor, while behind Gemmano to the south the British guns blazed away, much closer than yesterday. He sought out Lorenzo and made him sit while he examined the wound – 'much improved,' Lorenzo was quick to assure him.

'Don't walk on it if you don't have to,' he warned and went in search of his family. He found Mama with Letizia.

'Zia Donatella, I need to pee. Where can I go?'

Mama called Francesca and Floriana. 'Find Angela and the young Paisani girls. Get Toni to show you a private place and then you all stand guard over each other to make sure nobody comes. Understand?'

As Toni guided them over Francesca said, 'You're lucky, you don't have this problem – at least not like us!'

Outside the cave the women were talking to each other in low tones, discussing what food there was. One woman had come away with a pan full of beans that she had been about to cook. There were one or two baskets of fruit, and loaves of bread, and the bag Toni had reacquired the previous night turned out to be full of tomatoes. Yet it was little enough for some thirty-five people and Mama sent Toni off for the nettles as a supplement to the beans.

'If only there was some salt.'

One man, Carlo, managed to start a fire with a glass he always had about him. He kept it small and would allow no green shoots to go on it. Speaking for him Paisani told the others, 'We can't be showing any smoke.'

'It takes so long the way he does it. We must cook.'

'Have a little patience. The fire will be big enough in due course.'

Amazingly Toni falls asleep beside his haul of nettle tops, the warmth of the morning sun caressing him. He is awoken by a particularly loud artillery bang and feels instantly guilty, thinking of everybody waiting for the food, but when he returns they haven't even begun cooking. Mama takes the nettles and says, 'Now we need water.'

Toni blows out his cheeks, 'Where are we going to get water? The streams up here are dry now. The only one still trickling is in Zollara but we can't get to it.'

Mama says, 'So, it must be the well.'

Toni winces, but he can see they are desperate. 'OK, I'll go up and get some.'

'Not you! Are you mad? Didn't I tell you they'll take you away?'

Lorenzo calls over, 'I can go.'

Toni says, 'You can't carry anything. Water is heavy.'

Signora Paisani says, 'Send some of the girls. Angela is strong. They can bring some.'

Lorenzo says, gently, 'Signora, you do not know what you are saying. There are soldiers there. Many of them. German soldiers. They haven't seen a woman for weeks. Maybe months. What do you think will happen if they catch pretty young women like Angela and Francesca? And they won't release them afterwards, you know.'

Mama spits and looks at Signora Paisani. 'So it is you and I. We are too old to be of interest.'

Francesca puts her arms around Mama, 'No Mama, it's too dangerous.'

Toni says, 'I'll go tonight, when it's dark. Then they won't see me.'

Signora Paisani says, 'We cannot wait until then. The children are hungry.'

Mama says, 'They can eat some fruit and – look – tomatoes. Toni's right. We can go up tonight.'

'And what do we drink today?'

Angela says, 'I heard a cow mooing down the hill. Maybe we could...'

There is general enthusiasm at the prospect of milk to drink and a frenetic search of the cave for a bucket to put it in. This gets wiped out with grass and Angela and Francesca are sent to find the cow.

Toni goes back into the cave to the prone body of his father. As he gets closer he sees that Papa's eyes are open, staring straight up at the roof of the cave. He kneels beside him and takes his hand, 'Papa, can you hear me?'

Only his eyes moving, Papa looks at Toni. He whispers, 'Am I alive?'

'Yes Papa, in the cave. This is our house, for now.'

'Is everybody here?'

'Everybody.' Toni is smiling through tears.

'And you?'

Toni tells him briefly of how he escaped and then checks Papa's pulse. Satisfied, he turns and calls Mama, and the family rushes over. They help Papa to sit up and to drink a little milk that the girls have brought. As he recovers himself and looks around, the family takes turns to kiss him and Mama holds his face. He closes his hand around her wrist.

'So what will we do now?' he asks weakly.

Mama pats his face firmly and says, 'We will wait. We are alive. That's the first thing. We'll hide here until the British come and we will find food. You'll see. They'll liberate us and then we can go back to our homes.'

Papa speaks a little more strongly, 'If Toni escaped that means the Germans didn't find the cellar. And did you cover the door with straw when you left?'

Toni nods, grateful that habit took over, even in such a moment of crisis.

Papa looks at Mama, 'There are bottles of passata in that cellar, and a ham I was hanging.'

Toni chips in, 'And two cheeses I brought there.'

'And soon we will be liberated and the British will provide food,' says Angela, clapping her hands.

Lorenzo has hobbled in and perched himself on the ledge where Toni slept, using his crutch for support. Papa's clothes fit him well and he now looks like one of the villagers. He says, 'I wouldn't be too sure. I've been watching the movement of the troops below. It seems to me they are keeping a lot of infantry and tanks around. That indicates they're digging in.'

Mama glares at him, 'And what do you know about it?'

'I know enough to recognize a defensive line being manned.'

Mama says, 'They cannot stop the British. They're on the retreat.'

Toni butts in, 'I overheard the Germans talking about bringing more troops and guns, and I saw them digging holes to the southeast, facing Montefiore Conca.'

Paisani says, 'So what does that mean?'

Lorenzo says, 'They're going to stand and fight, and they're going to do it here. You should see the hardware that's been stockpiled in Croce.'

'But then are we safe, up here? In these caves?'

Paisani says, 'If all their strength is concentrated in Croce then that is where the trouble will be. We have no fear up here.'

Lorenzo says, 'I have my doubts. This is a perfect position to look down on the Conca valley and over to the hillside leading up to Croce. If I was German I would set up covering fire from here, and that means the British may have to come up and take control of this hilltop.'

Mama says, 'You're too gloomy. Anyway, what do you know?'

Lorenzo rolls his eyes and says nothing and now Papa, with some effort, makes himself heard, 'We must ask the British.'

Mama sits back and looks at him. 'Oh, you have one of those telephones, perhaps?'

Papa waves a hand, 'Don't be a fool. We must go down to meet them. We must find their commander and tell them about the tanks, and ask what is going on, and we must tell him that there are people sheltering here, and they must take care if they come up.'

Mama cries, 'Are you mad? Who is to go down there, with all those Germans running around? How are they to get through the lines to talk to the British, and in any case how are they to get back?'

Lorenzo says, 'It's the right plan if it can be done, but it is difficult. I would go but...'

He gestures in frustration at his leg. Francesca hands him a fig and smiles at him, putting her hand on his arm by way of sympathy.

Paisani says, 'I cannot go. I am too weak, and there are no other men here except Carlo at the fire. He is good at fires but none too bright. He cannot speak to anybody, especially not in English.'

'I speak English,' says Toni reluctantly.

Mama swats at him as though there was a wasp on his shoulder, 'My God, always you. Always you.' She turns to Papa, 'He cannot go. He must not go. Guido, tell him. This is crazy.'

'I don't want to go, Mama,' says Toni, 'but if it's necessary...'

Papa scratches his face. 'It's not so stupid. He's overheard them speaking. He's seen them digging. This is important information for the British. He speaks good English. Between us we could make them understand, and believe.'

Mama utters a cry of frustration, 'You too! How can you go? Look at you. Just look at you. Who is the fool, I ask you!'

'He's too young for them to take him seriously. I must be there too.'

Mama turns and points at Lorenzo, 'You started this. You go. You cannot sit there on your arse like a coward.'

'Mama, that's too much. He can barely walk. I've seen his wound.'

Papa is pulling himself up on the ledge. 'Come Toni, help me to my feet. I'm sure I can walk.'

Mama raises her hands above her head with a great cry, bursts into tears and slumps to the ground at the bottom of the cave, 'Oh yes, that is perfect. Leave the family without any man to take care of things. Take your only son and walk off into the war.'

Francesca and Signora Paisani crouch down beside her and comfort her while Papa, arm around Toni, glances at Lorenzo. 'Come outside and we'll make a plan.'

Overlooking the valley, Lorenzo indicates with one hand to their right, 'They have been retreating up the valley from the east, but the flow is much lessened now and pretty soon it will stop. They won't try and hold the valley. They are too exposed to attack on both sides. It is logical that the British will use that road too. So I think there must be a town of some kind down there through the haze, yes?'

'There is Morciano.'

'So I do not think the Germans will defend Morciano. They will leave it empty. Perhaps you can meet the British there.'

'If we travel by night we can get there by tomorrow morning, all being well.' Papa glances at Toni, 'I'm sorry you have to come on this with me, but I don't think I'll manage the trip alone.'

'We can bring the dogs, Papa, right?'

They return to the cave where Mama has recovered herself. She is talking to Francesca and Angela.

'So, it is up to us to get into the cellar tonight.'

'And I will come too,' says Lorenzo from behind Toni.

'You! I thought you couldn't walk.'

'I can walk, or crawl, that far. I can help carry the food if the girls can get the water. But somebody needs to show me this cellar.'

'Somebody will show you,' says Mama, and she says it slightly more cordially.

Because darkness is needed to cover movement, both expeditions will set off after nightfall, and so the company subsides into afternoon slumber as best it can. Nobody gets much rest, for the booms from the guns keep jolting them awake.

Chapter 11
September 3rd – 5th 1944

By the evening, Papa is hobbling about the hillside, peering into the gloom below and assessing troop movements. Earlier Toni forced him to sit while he revised the sling for his shoulder, and some colour returned to his face. Toni could do nothing for the hand but he cleaned the cut on Papa's head. He has nothing to cover this but Papa says it will be fine.

'I only have a bit of a headache from it.'

Now he admits to Toni that his leg still hurts, for as they staggered out of the house yesterday he fell on the steps and banged his leg on the skull of the pig before her body was dragged away.

Toni sighs, 'What a mess you are.'

Papa has found himself a staff, which he clasps using his good hand with a grip that is white-knuckled. By good fortune he answered his front door to the Germans in his walking boots, and so it is these he has come away in. He tells Toni this is a good omen as he climbs above the cave entrance for a better view. But Toni can see he is labored, leaning heavily on the staff.

It is dusk and Papa is impatient to be off. Toni laces up his string and canvas shoes, the only footwear he ever puts on. Mama gives them a little bread, but they refuse the fruit and Papa says,

'It'll be easier for us to search for food on the journey than for you to find it here.'

Lorenzo comes over with his pack and pulls his gun out of it. 'I think this will be of more use to you than me.'

Papa shakes his head, pats Lorenzo on the shoulder and says a little gruffly, 'No, you're closer to the Germans. We don't plan to let them even see us.'

Lorenzo grins, 'What am I going to do? Hold off the German battalion with one pistol? Take it.'

He thrusts it into Papa's hand. Papa hands it back reluctantly and smiles. 'You're a good lad,' he says, his voice still thick.

'Well then, listen,' says Lorenzo, 'When you get to Morciano be careful of booby-traps, hm? If, as we suspect, it has been deserted then they'll have filled it with terrible things. I've seen thick beds of straw just inviting you to throw yourself down and rest your tired legs. Boom! Filled with mines. There will be mines on the roads. There will be mines *beside* the roads in case you think to avoid the danger by walking to the side. I've seen mines attached to bedsprings, and to doors. If you see a dead animal, like a mule or something, then look to see if it's been exploded. That means you're in a minefield. Even in the fruit trees you will...'

Papa pats him on the cheek, 'Lorenzo, I know you wish you could come with us. We'll be all right, hm?'

Lorenzo lapses into silence with an embarrassed smile, then embraces them both and steps back.

Mama comes and gives each one of them a huge hug, to show that her earlier despair is over. 'Take the Collision Brothers with you. We cannot feed them here.'

Francesca clings to Toni tightly, and then she goes and stands beside Lorenzo.

Toni is asked to lead the way, for Papa knows he is at home on the hill, and in this light. He is careful to keep the dogs close. They will be crossing fields to begin with, so he doesn't want them to bolt after a rabbit. He contours for a while, following the route he and Francesca took yesterday towards Villa. Beyond that he sticks to the hedgerows, so in the dark there is no easy walking, each step needing their full attention. The Germans are still about, so at least they needn't worry about mines at this stage. He finds a pig track to ease their way but it is unreliable, with offshoots that end for no reason and force them to backtrack. Each time they do, he can hear Papa mutter under his breath and eventually, when they come to another dead end, he just forges on by the light of the stars. After a time Papa's breathing gets too heavy for Toni's liking and he stops and sits.

Papa lowers himself to the ground. 'Don't stop on my behalf.'

'I have to rest Remo, he's not himself.'

There has been a steady rumbling of heavy guns all day. Now father and son jump for without warning there are sharp, hard reports, far closer than before. They hear whistles overhead, and suddenly there is a mighty explosion just short of the eastern wall of Gemmano. A second one follows, landing beside it, and then two more go off to the west near Monte Gardo.

'Careless fools,' growls Papa, 'they almost hit the village.'

The next shell hits the village. It explodes against a house on the north side near the church and part of the external town wall collapses.

Toni cries, 'My God! We must go back.'

Papa puts a hand on his shoulder. 'Wait.'

After two or three more explosions on the north side, the shelling stops, leaving only the sound of the distant guns, with broad, dull flashes illuminating the horizon.

Papa says, 'We need to get down to the British quickly and tell them how many people are hiding up here.'

'But Mama! Francesca!'

'They are safe in the caves for now. Those shells were targeted at the village itself.'

Papa goes slower and slower, as they work their way down off the hill. Alone with the dogs, Toni would have been there in half the time. He can hear Papa stumbling in the dark as they descend, cursing as he steps in a rabbit hole and, on one occasion, emitting a grunt of pain when he goes sprawling.

When they get to the valley floor the ground evens out and they step onto the road. Toni stands with his hands on his hips, looking at a ploughed field beyond which lies the river Conca. He listens carefully and although he can't hear a vehicle he feels uncomfortable with the idea of taking the road to Morciano, given Lorenzo's warnings. He chooses the field.

He finds a gap in the hedgerow and helps Papa through. He shudders at how naked he feels crossing the field but there is no moon and he trusts to luck, forcing the dogs to walk into heel for fear that the field is mined. From time to time he glances around and up at the silhouette of Gemmano, dreading the sudden eruption of another shell. Ahead there are vehicles to be heard on the other side of the river, moving up the road, but there are no soldiers in evidence on this side and before long they reach the cover of the trees by the river. Toni realizes that the well-worn path by the Conca may also be a risk, but clearly Papa cannot manage any more rough ground, and they want to reach Morciano before first light. He loses track of time as they creep alongside the Conca, for they pause often. Finally, although it is still dark, Toni recognizes a bend in the river beyond which will be the first outhouses of the town of Morciano di Romagna.

Toni turns to see if Papa is following. He has to wait a while, and when Papa comes up his breath is rasping and he is mumbling to himself. Toni asks him if he wants to rest and Papa blunders into him without looking up.

What? What did you say? Did you say something, boy?'

'Papa, let's sit here and eat a piece of bread. Look, the dogs have found a dip near the river. It's almost like a hole. We'll be hard to see.'

Toni glances over to the east. The guns have fallen silent for the present, and there is a pale smear across the horizon as dawn creeps into the sky.

Papa groans as he sits. Toni says, 'Tell me where the pain is.'

'It's my head and my hand. And my leg. The head is worst.'

Toni gives him a piece of bread, which Papa chews even more slowly and rhythmically than usual. Romolo seems to sense they are going to be here for some time for he takes Remo off with him, and Toni mentally wishes them good hunting. He fears for mines but they must eat and he has nothing to give them. Then he says, 'Papa, lie back for a little while. Look the grass is quite thick and flat here. You'll be more comfortable.'

'But we must get into the town.'

'We can rest a little here. We don't know if there are still Germans in any case. Come, I need to rest too.'

'Well then, if you are also tired…'

Papa lies back and then groans again, 'I cannot lie down, my shoulder is too sore.'

It is unbearable to listen to Papa suffering such pain and, remembering Lorenzo, he takes a deep breath. 'Papa, listen to me. I'm going to do something to help you. You must trust me.'

'What thing?'

'Lie back, and don't move. It will help you.'

Papa eases back gingerly and Toni kneels beside him. It is three days since he tried this on Lorenzo and he feels he has regained some of his strength, at least the kind of strength he needs for this work. He places one hand on his father's head, and another on his shoulder.

107

'What are you doing?'

'Be quiet now.'

He feels the energy rise within him easily and is surprised at the power. It is as if, by removing the limits with Lorenzo, he has accessed a deeper level, and the energy flows into Papa more like treacle and less like a blast. He is even able to control it a bit. He lowers his head until his forehead is almost brushing the back of his hands and holds it there as long as he can. Papa does not gasp the way Lorenzo did, his body gradually relaxing as the energy plays on the pain and he finally lets out a long sigh of relief.

'I feel…well, there is less pain. Much less!' He looks over at Toni. 'How did you do that? What was that you did?'

Toni lies down on the ground, aware of Papa's eyes upon him. 'I will tell you after, but now I must sleep.'

And he does.

When he awakes it is day, but he judges the sun hasn't been up for more than an hour. He is not rested for he has been disturbed by vehicles across the river. Impossible to identify as British or German, they have been passing down the road, always heading west out of Morciano. Papa still sleeps and there is no sign of the dogs. This doesn't concern Toni for he knows their hunting expeditions can take hours, and in any case he has no plans to move on yet. This hollow provides them with good cover and looking up, Toni can't even see Gemmano for the contours of a rise in front of them.

He listens for evidence of troops in Morciano. A distant lorry starts up and heads along the road, and then there is silence. He stands and stretches, and looks around. There are a few ragged olive trees, like scarecrows in a row, and there is usually a fruit tree or two to be found on the end of such a row. These ones, surprisingly, are unharvested and he gratefully collects some apricots and pears. He sits to eat, gorging himself to the point where he knows he must stop or his body will void it all without absorbing the goodness. Then he walks the last half kilometer to Morciano, which turns out to be deserted.

When he gets back the Collision Brothers have returned. They grin at him and lick their chops. They have eaten something it seems, and this is confirmed when they both curl up and sleep beside him. One of them nudges Papa causing him to stir, and his eyes flicker open. Toni helps him to sit up which he does without too much trouble.

'How do you feel?'

'I feel quite well,' Papa says, watching him.

Toni doesn't return his gaze, 'Here, have some fruit.'

Papa eats slowly and they finish the leftover bread together. 'We have slept a while.'

Toni nods, 'It was necessary. Now we can look for the British.'

Papa rhythmically chomps through a pear, 'Toni, what did you do to me earlier?'

In a way it is a relief that he stands revealed. Papa's questions are similar to Lorenzo's of course, and Toni can only give him the same responses. 'When I tried it on Lorenzo, it was the first time ever with a person.'

'But how long…?'

'Since I was a child.'

'Nobody knows? Mama?'

'Not Mama. Fra' suspects something.'

'This is a gift!'

'You are not healed. It is merely the pain that is gone for a while.'

'Nonetheless, you have a gift! You are blessed.'

Toni is surprised by Papa's vehemence and unburdened by his reaction. For years he's feared it might make him an outcast, and he feels his eyes sharp with moisture.

He whispers, 'It's not…it's not a sin? Like copying the son of God?'

Papa Says, 'Pftt! A sin! Course not! Well…it might be if you saved it for animals. You should be using it on people.'

Toni considers the idea that he has been given a gift and that the power need not be a source of fear for him. In fact, here he is being applauded for it. His whole perspective changes as he realises that he will not have to hide anymore, and it is like someone has pulled a great thorn from his chest. Not hiding. Think of that! Without viewing the power through a lens of fear, knowing that instead of applying it surreptitiously he will be welcome, presents the whole thing in a different light. He feels different. Special even.

They are silent for a time and then Toni says,

'Papa, when I watch Lorenzo eat, I see you. Also his eyes are yours.'

Papa has pulled out his pipe and is packing tobacco from his little leather pouch, sewn together by Mama. He glances at Toni and sighs, 'Well, if Morciano is deserted it would be foolish to move from this safe spot for the present. We'll use our ears for when the British arrive. Do you have anything I can light this with?'

Toni shakes his head and so Papa shrugs and puts the pipe away again. 'I told you I stayed in that farmer's house while my leg got better during that terrible war. His name was Bergamas.'

'Yes.'

'And it's true there was a daughter called Stefania, for it was she who nursed me. Until I could walk she brought me food every day in bed, and sometimes when she had time she would sit and talk to me. I told her about the war and about my life here, in Gemmano, and she said it sounded like her life there. The truth is we fell in love, very passionately.'

Papa glances up, 'This was before I ever knew your Mama, okay?'

Toni nods and Papa continues, 'When it came time for me to go back to the front she didn't want me to go. But although I wanted to stay I knew my comrades were suffering back there and I felt I must return. She told me we could make the wound look worse and it would take longer to heal, and I really thought a lot about that. But in the end I just couldn't do it.

'She wept all night on our last night, and I was very sad too, and I held her in my arms for hours. All I wanted to do was keep her safe. She looked up at me with shining eyes and gave me a little piece of her embroidery to keep. I still have it hidden away in the house somewhere. When I got back to the front I always knew I would return for her, and as the end of the war approached I was more and more excited about seeing her again. I didn't write and neither did she. We both knew our letters would never be delivered, such was our army's organization, but we each believed we would see the other again.

'We were pulled back from the front in those final months so we were relatively safe. Then, with only three days to the end of the war (I learnt this later), I was driving a truck, which was picking up rifles from the ammunition dump. Not explosives, for my good fortune. I drove away and had gone about a kilometer, when there was an unbelievable explosion behind me. Some idiot had lit a cigarette or some such thing, and the whole dump blew up! Can you believe it?'

Papa gives a short laugh, leans over and spits. 'The blast caught up to our truck immediately and hurled us off the road. I was knocked unconscious, and I didn't come round. Because the end of the war came, my friends commandeered an army ambulance and shipped me back to Gemmano. I can tell you I'm glad I wasn't conscious for that trip!'

Toni is distracted as considerable firing starts up, with smoke rising from where Montefiore Conca must be. They look at each other and fall silent, listening to what they suppose is a British attack. After a time the firing stops and then, a little later, it recommences, although it appears to have moved west. The sun has risen indicating mid-morning, and Toni can't bear it any more. He climbs out of their hollow and up the rise to look back to Gemmano. It looks like a toy from here. As Papa joins him there is a huge explosion on the hill near Villa.

'Perhaps they're aiming at those dugouts I saw,' says Toni.

He is wrong. In fact it is a signal for the start of an enormous bombardment. The whistles overhead intensify and the explosions are so numerous that they almost merge into one noise. Toni and Papa hold onto the dogs so that they will not run in panic. Shell after shell crashes onto the hill, and then onto the village of Gemmano. Those that hit the ground hurl great chunks of earth and vegetation about the place, and from the village pieces of masonry large enough for them to see, shoot out and down the hillsides. Now aircraft come flying in from the east, over their heads, and when they get near Gemmano they swoop, their bombs crashing into the village. The pounding goes on and on and they can see clouds of smoke boiling up into the air and falling down the Ventena valley, presumably covering those dugouts with dust and rubble. Other monstrous shells whistle in from the coast and join the assault.

'Oh God help us! They are firing from ships as well,' cries Papa.

The smoke and dust cloud grows in size and density so that it becomes almost impossible to see Gemmano. The shelling intensifies and the planes swoop in and out of the cloud, or shoot low over the rooftops. The flashes of the explosions are out of synch with the sounds, giving the whole scene a surreal aspect. The planes begin to machine gun the ground around the village, chewing up the ground in trails of spurting dust that Toni can still make out in spite of the distance.

At a certain point Papa unwittingly releases Remo and sinks to the ground. Toni joins him and they don't say anything for there is nothing to say. They just look at each other in horror and then Papa drops his head in his hands and weeps.

Finally the bombardment ceases but they cannot see what has happened, for the cloud hanging over Gemmano shows no signs of dispersing. Toni and Papa hug and grip each other as if to convince themselves that they, at least, are still alive. Papa mutters into Toni's shoulder, 'Our home, our home.'

They are unable to move. In the end it is Romolo who comes and nudges Papa's elbow. He looks up and says with an effort,

'Come, we must start back. We must find out who is alive.'

'We have no food or water and the river is no good. It's so nearly dry that the pools are stagnant. Come, let us check the town for a well and some food, and then we'll go back.'

Throwing caution to the wind, for they cannot be sure if the last Germans have finally left, they hurry into the town. There is nobody around and they hunt through the streets and lanes. It takes some time before they come to a little piazza and in the open Toni glances back to see if the cloud has lifted off Gemmano. But the haze makes it hard to see.

The piazza has a well in the middle of it. They hurry over and Papa grabs the end of the rope. He starts to pull on it and then stops for a second to get a better grip. Just as he begins to lean his weight into it again there is a click.

There is a click from the pulley where the rope goes through. They both hear it.

Papa doesn't let go of the rope. He turns his head slowly towards Toni, 'What was that?'

The well is a semi circle of stone wall, which backs onto a stand, a place where somebody can address a crowd. There is a wooden frame above the well, cemented into the walls, and a strong crossbeam from which hangs the pulley. Toni climbs onto the stand and bends around to look at the pulley.

'What can you see?'

'There is something. Something like a wire attached to the rope. If you pull the rope the wire comes too…oh! On the end of the wire there is a grenade.'

'Just one?' asks Papa quietly.

Toni peers round further, 'It is bound onto some others too.'

'Look very carefully. Does the wire come from the grenade?'

'Yes, I think so. It comes out of the bottom of the grenade handle.'

'But it is still attached?'

Toni feels nausea move in his gut, 'Yes.'

Papa takes a breath, 'Listen carefully, Toni. It's a booby trap. Can you see how it would be activated? It would be necessary to give the wire a firm tug so that it would pull free from the grenade.'

'That's easy. If you pull on the rope now you will pull the wire free.'

'What if I let the rope go?'

Toni is forced to stand still for a moment, waiting for the world to stop weaving in front of him. 'Well, I don't think anything will happen because the rope won't move. The bucket is sitting on the bottom of the well now.'

Papa speaks as if he is reluctant to believe himself, 'No, I don't think it is. I believe I raised it a little before I heard the click. If I let go now the rope will definitely be pulled down a little way, perhaps half a metre. Can you see?'

Toni looks even more closely, hanging over the well until he is almost touching the bomb. 'Oh, Papa, I don't know. It's too much to think about. I feel dizzy.'

'Sweet Christ, Toni, please just…' Papa catches himself. 'It's okay. Toni, just listen. I want you to get down from there and sit on the ground for a moment. It's all right. I have it by the rope. I won't let it go. Just rest yourself.'

Toni climbs down, aware of Papa's agitation, and angry with himself for his lack of self-control. Sitting quietly he watches his breathing as it come into his nostrils, feeling the cool down the back of his throat, and noticing how it is no longer cool when he releases it. He counts during his in-breath, to four, and repeats this again and again. Then he begins to count the out-breath, and once that too has settled he feels the release of tension at the end of the breath as it slips out of his body through his feet. He lets go of the trap, and of Gemmano, and even of Papa. He knows Papa is waiting for him but he maintains his rhythm until he is steady. Then he stands.

Papa nods, 'Okay, so come around the other side of me and take hold of the rope, just here above my hands. Then I'll let go and you hold it in place while I take a look.'

Toni gets into position and takes the rope in his hands.

'Good. Now grip it firmly and slowly take the weight of it. Feel the weight – you mustn't suddenly pull too hard, or too little. There, can you feel?'

Toni nods and stands calmly as Papa releases the rope and steps slowly back. Papa struggles to get onto the stand for his leg is troubling him again, and then he cranes his neck around and examines the grenades. After a time he climbs down.

'There is nothing I can do about that. If we release the rope they will explode and there are about six grenades so it will make a terrible mess. I cannot tie off the rope on the supports – it's too short. I think they've cut it deliberately. So listen. I'll take the rope again and you go and find help. We need somebody to bring something tall and heavy, like a car, that we can place here beside the well and tie off the rope.'

As carefully as a cat stalking a dormouse they make the exchange again and Toni steps back.

'Search, but remember you can't shout. If there are Germans they'll just shoot us. We are ruining their trap.'

As Toni sets off he catches sight of Gemmano out of the corner of his eye. But he knows he cannot spend time staring at it and hurries out of the piazza, dogs at his heels.

It is as if a virus has spread through the village and wiped out the population. He feels like he's in the eye of a storm, the Germans departing west, the British arriving from the east. Getting desperate he starts knocking on the doors of houses that are still standing, of which there are many, but if anybody is inside, hiding in a cellar, they are not answering.

He sees a cart in the street leaning forward on its shafts. It has a number of barrels on it, and laboriously he unloads it, counting every second. Unconsciously he is listening out for a bang, but he cannot dwell on that or his skin crawls. It takes him fully ten minutes to unload the cart and then he goes round to the front and tries to raise it. But it is well made and heavy, and it is all he can do to lift the shafts to horizontal. Putting his back into it, he hauls it forward a couple of metres then slumps, defeated. He surveys the road ahead, but he's over a kilometer from Papa and the slight rise will make the task impossible. If only he had a mule now.

Dumping the cart down with a groan he hurries back towards the piazza, for Papa has warned him they must take frequent turns holding the rope. When he arrives Papa makes him rest and get his breath back before they exchange places.

'So where did you say this cart is?'

After Papa has set off Toni has all the time he needs to look back at Gemmano. The pall has drifted away and the village, on its hilltop, looks lopsided. The church spire is still standing but this is the only thing Toni can make out, distance pulling a haze over the grizzly details. Two thin trickles of smoke climb into the blue.

Absurdly he starts thinking about food. He finds himself imagining a piece of focaccia fresh from Mama's oven, perhaps a little goats cheese spread half-melted upon it. He can almost smell a tomato sauce bubbling in the pot, ready for a pan of squid, rolled in flour and frying in oil with parsley. Then the rope shifts slightly under his weight and he jerks back to reality, panting and wild-eyed as he glances around.

Papa returns, cartless, and says they have no option but to wait for the British to arrive, so they spend the rest of the afternoon taking turns to hang off the rope. Toni finds another well, so that they have water, but there isn't enough time to hunt for food between their ever-shorter shifts. Toni must grasp the rope at face level and the ache in his shoulders comes back sooner each time. In order to distract himself he says,

'Papa, you didn't finish the story about Stefania.'

Papa says, 'Okay, give me the rope again.'

When the exchange is done, and never taking his eyes off the rope, Papa says, 'Back in Gemmano, when I came around, they told me I had been in a coma for a month. Think about that! I had no idea where I was or who I was talking to. All these faces around my bed, and I didn't know who they were. Then, little by little, over the coming days and weeks, things started to come back to me. First I recognized the faces, and as weeks passed I remembered whether they were important to me or not. To begin with I didn't know my own house, but walking around the village I found my way without difficulty. I knew all the places I would go for work and even, with help, how to do the work. But people would tell me about certain events like an outing that we went on before the war, or an incident during an olive harvest, and I wouldn't be able to remember those at all.

'The war was completely blanked out for me. It came back in dreams like clouds across the sky, and then later when I was awake too. But I was never able to remember the explosion. That is a memory I have acquired from others in the telling of it.

'One day, after about a year, I was sitting and rubbing my injured leg, and the twinges of pain were like a message from the past. I remembered I had been in hospital and then how I'd learnt to walk on crutches. Finally memories of my recuperation returned. I saw the farmhouse, and even Stefania, though I didn't remember her name to begin with. I knew better what she had done for me and then, in time, what we became to each other. But you must understand, Toni, this was more than a year after the war, and at that point it still seemed like a dream. I didn't really believe that I had been the lover of a wonderful girl in a distant village, just that I had dreamed it.'

They change places and Papa swings his arms and rubs his shoulders. 'I cannot tell you why I suddenly knew it wasn't a dream, and that these events really happened, and that somewhere was this girl who loved me, and who I loved. That is the strangest feeling, Toni, the strangest feeling. A love that exists in both hearts, but with the connection completely severed. Then it took the longest time to get in touch with the army and for them to check back on records showing where I had been billeted. I didn't remember, you see.'

Papa carefully begins to rub Toni's shoulders. 'I believe it was over three years after the war that I got off that train in Spinea. I recognized nothing, but I had the address and I asked a local. As I got closer I felt I knew the track I was walking along, and when I saw the farmhouse I was certain.

'I stopped there on the track, not knowing if I should go on.

Sometimes I still had doubts that it had ever happened. As I hesitated the door opened – and Stephania came out. I was a bit distant so I couldn't see her closely, but I knew her hair and the way she walked. She held the hand of a little boy, maybe three or four years old. She bent down and kissed him on the forehead and then pointed over to the chicken run at the other side of the farmyard. The little boy scuttled over and began picking eggs out, putting them in a little peaked cap he was wearing.

'I was about to step forward when from the house now came a man, and he was holding a baby. I remember him because he limped, like me, even the same leg. She turned to him and kissed him, caressing his hair. Then the little boy came running back with the eggs and they all went inside.'

Papa stopped for a second, looked away and then swallowed before he went on, 'I didn't know what to do. I imagined them sitting down at the kitchen table I knew so well and…the little boy counting the eggs out and showing them to the man. Stefania would take the baby and feed it, and her mother would be cooking dinner for them. I recall it was a Sunday and I remembered how the whole family would sit around the table, offering a prayer before eating, and later…going to evening mass together.'

Toni waits while his father composes himself. 'They looked happy?'

'I walked away, and I have never been back,' says Papa. 'I still have that piece of embroidery, you know. She gave me it before I went back to the front. Her work was wonderful, and her mother had put pieces in frames on the wall all over that house. Mine is a little scene of that house with the pond in front of it. There were even little ducks on the pond, and her initials, SB, sewed into the bottom left-hand corner.'

'Where is it?'

'You know the old bread oven in the cellar, the one we never use? There is a cavity with two loose bricks, and I hid it in there with one or two other things from my youth. I didn't think I should shove them under Mama's nose, you know?'

It is time to change places again and then Toni says, 'She didn't wait for you then?'

'She will have thought me dead. I doubt if our army had records of the last days of the war and probably nobody knew I had been transported back. It would have been months after the event before she investigated and it was such a big mess.'

'So you didn't know she was…expecting?' Papa shakes his head. 'The little boy – he might have been your son!'

Papa looks sideways at him, 'And your brother. Well, half-brother anyway.'

Night falls. There isn't enough time between shifts for sleep, and in the darkness another bombardment starts up. The whole of the Gemmano hilltop is ablaze. The flashing of guns and the explosions light the place up as if it was day. Papa grits his teeth as tears run down his face. 'We have to get back there. We have to!'

Eventually the bombardment stops and there is silence in their valley, magnified by the lack of the familiar cricket chorus. From time to time they hear other guns firing, though Toni cannot tell where from. There are the constant heavy guns to the south, and other smaller arms and artillery fire to the west. Papa says, 'You take the rope again Toni. My head is very sore now, and my shoulder.'

When Toni takes over, Papa slumps down against the wall, head on his chest, and he does not speak or move.

As dawn begins to break Toni says, 'Papa, I just can't do it any more.'

'Me neither. Come, we'll hold it together for a little longer.'

As they grasp it Toni says, 'What happens when we can't go on?'

Papa doesn't respond immediately, and when he does his voice is deadened by despair.

'That time has come, Toni, so listen to me. When I tell you, I want you to let of the rope. Take the dogs and get behind a building, and shout to me when you're safe.'

'And what about you?'

'I'll be all right. I will drop the rope and the bomb will fall into the well. I'll lie behind the wall here.'

Toni is shocked, 'No, Papa. It won't drop. You will die. You will die.'

'I'll be all right. We can't hang on any longer. You must go. You must!'

Toni is weeping, 'I will not. I will not.'

Papa is weeping too, 'You are a good boy, Toni, and you are young. You know what to do. Let go now. You know this is right.'

Toni stands back. It is light enough for them to look into each other's eyes, and he kisses Papa and holds his face. 'I will come back and find you filling your pipe. You'll see.'

A soldier dressed in khaki marches into the piazza, rifle at the ready in front of him. He sees them immediately and approaches cautiously.

Papa's voice breaks, 'Oh thank God, he is British.'

The soldier comes up to them and Toni points dumbly up at the grenades. The soldier assesses the situation briefly and then gets on the radio. He nudges Papa and indicates that he will take the rope, but Papa doesn't seem to hear him. He clings on grimly and will not let go. The soldier turns to Toni.

'Make 'im let go, will you? He's out on his feet! Going to drop the whole bloody thing any minute and blow us all up, isn't he? Look at him! There's bomb disposal coming up in a minute.'

Toni prises Papa's fingers loose and they make the exchange, and then, sure enough, a jeep thunders into the piazza and grinds to a halt in a cloud of dust, some fifty metres away. Two more soldiers come over, also dressed in khaki, with heavy-looking belts in which they carry a selection of tools. One of them studies the bomb while the other tells Toni and Papa to get behind the jeep.

As Toni helps Papa away he hears the soldier say, 'I'm going to loosen the bindings here. We'll drop the whole bloody lot down the well and let it detonate in there.'

Crouched behind the jeep they are joined by the first soldier who has left the experts to their task. There is a muffled blast and they stand in time to see a cloud of rubble blast out of the well. The bomb disposal boys stand and dust themselves down.

''Aven't seen one like that before, 'ave we?'

''Allo, look at this nice beastie,' says the other, crouching down to greet Remo who has trotted over to say hello.

Toni and Papa lean against each other and the soldier comes up to them, ''Ow long you been there, then?'

Toni says, 'Yesterday, last night. I don't know. We are very tired.'

The soldier grins and slaps his arm, apparently unsurprised that Toni responds in English, 'You're very 'tai-red' are you? Well come on, we'll get you some grub.'

'What are you going to do with them?' asks another.

'Take 'em up to H.Q. They said they've been looking for some local guides lately.'

Toni says, 'We cannot come. We mus' go to our 'ouse.'

'Your house, mate? Where's that then?'

Toni turns and points at the smoking ruin that was once Gemmano.

'Sorry son. Got orders to bring all locals to the commanding officer. Besides, there's nothing for you up there, is there?'

Chapter 12
September 5th 1944

The jeep leaps about like a recalcitrant goat being dragged in for milking. The roads in the town are not that bad if only the driver were less enthusiastic. Papa leans against Toni in the back seat, exhausted by the night and groaning in pain. Toni glances back to see the dogs racing behind at full speed, skidding round corners, never losing sight of the jeep.

A cloud of dust erupts around them as the jeep slides to a halt. Two guards stand outside a house with a kicked-in door. They are dressed like the rest of their regiment, in baggy, khaki shirts and trousers, which are tucked into gaiters above heavy-duty black boots. They have various pouches hanging off their belts and straps, front and back, but they have dumped their packs, which lie propped against the wall of the house. Their helmets sit on the packs.

Toni helps Papa down from the jeep and they are ushered inside. There are three officers standing at a table poring over a map, and in the corner is a radio operator plying his trade. Beside him is a cap with a badge and the words 'London Scottish' on it. Nobody looks up and they are hurried through into a kitchen very much like their own, except that nothing is cooking and nobody is tending a fire. They are told to sit on chairs at a little table, and one soldier gives them biscuits and a tin of processed meat, which Toni passes to Papa. Another soldier pulls a bar of chocolate from a pouch. 'Try that.'

In a corner the first soldier has a little solid-fuel Tommy cooker, on which he is boiling water. From somewhere he produces mugs, and Toni gets a whiff of what might be tea brewing.

The soldier gives the liquid a stir with his finger, and as he grabs three mugs he winks at Toni. 'Officers first, you know how it goes,' and takes them through next door.

'Oh, well done, Higgins,' says one of the officers. 'Now, you'd better get everything packed again. We're moving out shortly.'

'Yessir.' Higgins returns and puts two mugs of hot water onto the table between Toni and Papa. He drops in two cubes, which begin to dissolve, and Toni sniffs suspiciously.

'Don't worry, son. That's a combo. You've got everything in there. Tea, milk, sugar, the lot!'

Toni understands the soldier is trying to be kind and he nods, though he doesn't believe it will be drinkable. But once he tries it he finds the warmth and sweetness are comforting, and ignoring the taste he sips it down. Glancing over he sees a change in Papa's appearance. One eye appears to have slipped a little down his face. He places Papa's hands on the other mug and forces it up to his mouth. As he tips it, sip by sip, into Papa's mouth, he talks to him quietly, soothingly, and realises he is trying to soothe himself too. Then voices from next door impose themselves.

'I do wish they'd settle on one plan or another, up at H.Q.'

'Be that as it may, we must prepare ourselves as best we can. For a start, where is Croce?'

'Here sir, about three and a half miles to the west of us, atop this ridge by the Conca valley – the one we're travelling up now.'

'What do we know about the German defences?'

'We haven't got much information at present, sir. We know the Royal Fusiliers are in the area, but we don't know what resistance they've encountered.'

'H.Q. doesn't seem to think there'll be too much trouble. The Hun is backpedalling as hard as he can and the sooner we get after him the better.'

'We have these two local chappies, sir.'

'Local? Right, bring 'em in.'

'Higgins, bring those two local chappies in, will you?'

Higgins indicates to Toni and Papa that they are to go through. Toni assists Papa who is merely shuffling. They stand before the three officers who Papa identifies, *sotto voce*, as a major, a captain and a lieutenant. The three continue to talk as if Toni and Papa aren't there, though the lieutenant glances over, once. Toni feels as if he is back in school, waiting to see the headmistress.

'They look at us as if we were insects,' mutters Papa. When he speaks his voice is so faint it is like the softest breath of wind.

'Right, stop talking there,' says the lieutenant. 'Do you speak English?'

Toni is overawed and struggles for words. Papa nudges him.

'You must answer.'

Toni nods reluctantly and gives their names, which the major notes down.

The lieutenant says, 'And you are from?'

'We are from...we are from Gemmano.'

The captain turns to the major, 'Sounds familiar, sir. Isn't that the place we pasted yesterday?'

The major nods and motions the lieutenant to continue.

'So what are you doing here, in Morciano?'

'We 'ave come to find you.'

'Find us? Who, Major Findlay? What are you talking about?'

'To find you. You. British army.' He is flustered by the lieutenant.

'And why would you want to find us, laddie?' interrupts the major quietly, with a smile.

Toni takes time to compose his words, 'We are in Gemmano. Many Germans come and put us from the 'ouse. Then we see British coming, so we think you come up to Gemmano. So we want to tell you we are there, in the caves. We many people of Gemmano.'

Papa nudges him and says, 'Tell them we have information about the Germans.'

'What's he saying?' asks the lieutenant sharply.

'We 'ave saw many tanks, German tanks.'

'Where, precisely?' asks the captain.

'Hm, we saw many in Croce, also on that hill. And big guns pulled by...little horses...donkeys!'

The officers look at each other, a little incredulous. 'In Croce?'

'*Si, Capitano.*'

'I'm a lieutenant. Now what about Gemmano?'

'Yes, Tenente, many Germans. Also holes. They dig holes and put in guns.'

The captain says to the major, 'Doesn't sound very likely, sir. We've pasted that place.'

The soldier who brought them in speaks up from behind Toni.

'Excuse me, sir.'

'Burnett?'

'They were found in the town hanging onto a rope over a well. It was a booby trap. But I don't know why one of them didn't

123

come and get us before. It's possible that the Germans left them there, like that, with false information to feed us. Just saying, sir, they might be spies.'

The major nods, 'Thank you, Burnett. I'm sure that'll become apparent if such is the case.'

Toni conveys this exchange to Papa who grips his arm. 'You must be very careful now, Toni. They shoot spies.'

The major turns to Toni, 'Now, laddie, when was it you saw all these Germans in Gemmano?'

Toni considers. It is so hard to think backwards now and everything is confused. They spent last night – on the rope! And the night before? Yes, the night before they were coming down. So that means he was in Gemmano…'Two days ago, *Capitano*.'

The major and the captain exchange glances.

Tony says, '*Capitano*, my Papa is very ill. You can look 'im.'

The major leans forward, 'Yes, I can see. We'll help your Papa. But first you must tell us everything you can about these troops and tanks you say you've seen.'

Papa is taken next door again and a medic called. While he is tended the captain shows Toni the maps and explains what it all means. Toni finds it easy to understand, in fact he likes spotting places he knows, like Zollara and Onferno. Then the captain asks Toni a series of detailed questions, which Toni answers as best he can from memory. When he has finished he is sent back to the kitchen to finish his tea. As he goes the major says, 'Laddie, do you know this area well? Croce, Cevolabbate, San Savino and so forth?'

'Croce, *Capitano*. I know Croce.'

The major nods, dismissing him, but as Toni sits down again he can hear them through the door.

The captain says, 'I don't believe he's a spy, sir. It's just that his information is out-of-date.'

Outside there is an unfamiliar noise and Higgins goes and looks out. 'Column arriving, sir.'

The soldiers are gathering their stuff together and getting out into the street, and Toni and Papa are bundled out too. Coming along the road towards them marches a column of soldiers, kicking up dust into the still morning air. There are two men playing musical instruments at their head. They have bags tucked under their left arms with pipes sticking out of them, and they are blowing into a tube. From the pipes comes the sound of pigs shrieking, and Toni clasps his hands over his ears.

'What's the matter, son? Don't like the bagpipes?' laughs one of the soldiers.

The music and the column come to a halt and shortly afterwards a number of lorries, whining and jolting, shudder into silence beside them. Many have canvas covering their backs and spare tyres hanging off the front, and there is a jeep or two dotted between them.

The major says, 'Finally, transport! Get as many men as possible into the T.C.V.s, Lieutenant. The rest will have to walk alongside. Make sure it's the fresher ones who are doing the walking. Depart in five minutes. That's 7.15am sharp.' He turns and points at Toni, 'And don't forget to bring him.'

The lieutenant opens the passenger door of the lorry that has pulled up beside them, 'Right, lad. Up you go.'

As he understands what is happening Toni cries out, 'But I cannot go. I must go back our 'ouse!'

The lieutenant shakes his head. 'You're needed here as a guide. Your father will have to go back himself.'

Toni says, 'But my Papa – 'e is not well. I mus' care for 'im.'

'We've fixed him up. He'll be all right.' The lieutenant glances away uncomfortably as he says this.

Toni feels hot tears spring to his eyes, 'But I cannot go. My family is bad. I 'ave my dogs.'

Papa appears to wake up to the situation and starts tugging at the lieutenant's sleeve, mumbling, 'You cannot take him. He is needed with me, to help the family when we return to Gemmano.'

He takes Toni by the shoulder and begins to walk him away from the lorry, and beside them Romolo sets up a ferocious noise. Suddenly the lieutenant loses his patience and pulls out his pistol. He points it at Papa.

'Tell your father there is a war on, and he should remember that. If we recruit you, it's not an invitation. It's an order. If you refuse to obey it you will be considered the enemy. Remember, until a year ago, that's exactly what you were in any case. You are not in uniform so you will be shot as spies.'

Romolo is crouched, ears back and snarling, readying himself to spring. The lieutenant turns his gun on this sudden threat and Toni cries,

'No, no, I will come, I will come.'

He jumps between the soldier and Romolo, wrapping his arms around the dog so that Romolo cannot launch himself. He talks quietly to him, keeping his mouth close to the dog's ear, settling him. He embraces Papa, placing Romolo in his care, and then climbs up the step into the lorry. Looking out of the door he shouts to Papa, 'Hold the dogs, hold the dogs, or they will try to accompany me.'

Papa is pushed out of the way as soldiers begin to march alongside the lorries, and he stumbles back from the edge of the road. Beside a dusty orange tree he kneels down and gets a better hold of Romolo and Remo, who are struggling to get free. He is almost pulled into the dust by them, and this is the last Toni sees of him as the lieutenant jumps into the lorry and instructs the driver to get moving.

The lorry pulls away with the rest of the convoy with much crunching of gears. The driver beside Toni winces, 'Sorry sir, this thing's ready for the scrapheap.'

'Just do your best, Corporal, and mind you keep your distance from the vehicle in front. You know the rule.'

The column moves slowly towards the bridge crossing the Conca, and follows the road along its northern bank. Though early, there is some heat in the sun, and the dust infiltrates the cabin in spite of the windows being wound up. The lorries are doing no more than twenty miles per hour, bouncing about in potholes and kicking up more dust. Toni sits wedged between the lieutenant and the driver, wondering how Papa will get back to Gemmano safely with the dogs. The lieutenant ignores him and studies the map he holds, looking out for landmarks and periodically marking their position. He glances up.

'Hold your position, driver. You're getting too close. Come on man, fifty yards is the rule and you ought to know that. Pay attention!'

The driver does as he is told, taking his foot off the accelerator until the gap in front has grown to the lieutenant's satisfaction. Surreptitiously he glances at Toni and rolls his eyes.

To their left Toni can see the stony bed of the Conca through a line of ragged trees, and on the other side is the path he and Papa crept along. He looks up reluctantly, for beyond the treetops is the Gemmano ridge, the neat fields along its slopes smudged and disheveled where shells have spattered them. Monte Gardo marks the high point at the western end. Slightly lower, and to the east in the clear morning light, sits the ruin of Gemmano herself.

Toni was once shown a photo of a town near the Somme after the First World War, and this is what he remembers now. There is almost no vegetation left around the village, the ground stark and bald on the slopes leading up to it. The trees have been splintered and destroyed and so nothing impedes his view of the remains. He cannot make out individual buildings any more, not even the church. There is just a low, uneven silhouette of grey, with one or two towers of bricks still standing: corners of houses that have not yet fallen. The silhouette has dips where a roof is gone and parts of window frames now form the roofline. There is no movement of any kind that he can see.

Toni is jolted forward in his seat as their driver jams on his brakes, following the lead of the lorry in front. The lieutenant grabs Toni by the shoulder and hauls him back, then cranes his neck out of the window to take a look. Unable to see anything he dismounts and takes a few paces up the road.

On the Gemmano ridge, under the village, Toni notices some flashes and then they hear distant reports of artillery. As whistles come overhead the lieutenant leaps back into the truck and has just the time to shout 'Incoming!' before the truck in front of them explodes in an eruption of fire from a direct hit.

'Jesus Christ!' yells the corporal.

'Get this thing off the road,' instructs the lieutenant. He jumps down from the lorry again and begins to run back along the column shouting, 'Get off the road. Get these T.C.V.s off the road now!'

It is the last Toni sees of him. The driver revs the engine, and just as he does two more explosions erupt to the right of the road, just in front of them. 'Bloody mortars,' cries the driver, turning the wheel hard left and driving the lorry off the edge of the road and almost into the Conca. The dip is such that the lorry tips over onto its side with a crash, lying on the slope with its wheels higher than its cabin roof. Toni is hurled against the passenger door and the driver crashes on top of him with a gasp.

There are explosions all around them and the sound of vehicles revving and reversing. Toni is crunched up under the driver who is doubled up, inert, his shoulder jammed into Toni's face. He nudges the soldier's ribs as best he can, and after a moment the driver stirs and comes to himself. With a long groan he grabs the steering wheel and drags himself up towards his own door. The door handle is broken off but he manages to push the door up and open, much like opening a hatch in a submarine. He has hurt an arm but he pulls himself out of the vehicle just the same, and Toni has the presence of mind to push him from behind. He gets out, stands astride the open door and reaches in to offer Toni a hand. Toni grasps it and feels a firm grip hauling him upward. As he climbs out of the cabin the driver is propelled backwards by a blow of such force that he is knocked off the lorry, almost as far as the road. He lies there, unmoving.

Toni stares at him for a moment but rapidly becomes aware of the *tchin*, *tchin* of bullets peppering the cabin. He hurls himself off it, landing on the ground below with a thump that knocks the air out of him. There is so much noise and confusion that all he can do is crawl up to the stricken lorry, get underneath as best he can, cover his head with his hands and lie there quivering with fear. He can hear shouting from the rear of the truck.

'Get across the road. The fire's coming from that ridge up on the left. We're sitting ducks here. Get over on the other side and find some cover.'

'Got injured here, Sarge.'

'Get them over as best you can, Dalglish.'

Toni can hear people crawling out of the lorry but he dare not move, much as he wishes to join them. The noise and the fire intensify, and the explosions get closer. There are more bullets hitting the lorry, people cry in pain, and he waits for the end.

He does not know how long he lies like that, accepting that he will die here on the road between Morciano and Taverna. The confusion seems to go on for hours before the explosions ease and calm returns, and he remains too afraid to move. In this new, unsteady silence, all he can hear are groans of pain from an injured man, which gradually subside.

Eventually he hears the crunch of footsteps, one person, walking beside the lorry. They come to a stop beside him, a pair of hands grasp his ankles, and he is hauled out from under the lorry. It is a British officer and Toni knows, because Papa has explained about the pips on the shoulders, that this is a captain.

'Are you Mazzanti? Antonio Mazzanti?' Toni just nods open-mouthed and then, as another explosion hits nearby, he tries to scramble back under the lorry.

'No you don't,' says the captain, grabbing him by the scruff of the neck and dragging him out again, 'You can't stay here. You'll get your arse shot off. Come with me.'

Toni is forced around the lorry and up to the side of the road. The captain pulls him down and crouching together they run across the road, Toni struggling to make his legs move. They tumble into a ditch, and then the captain begins to climb the rise before them, dragging Toni with him. They stumble on for a couple of minutes until they arrive at a farmhouse. The captain pushes Toni inside, to find various officers and men hunkered down away from the windows.

The captain, still crouching, goes over to the other side of the room, where the major that Toni met this morning is sitting on the floor holding a bloodied rag to his side. There is a medic working on him.

'Lieutenant Marsden is dead, sir, but this lad claims to be Mazzanti.'

The major nods weakly, 'That's him. Thank you, Jock. Keep him alive will you? We'll need him if we attack Croce.'

Toni is given a place to sit in another room where soldiers have set up a machine gun on legs at the window. He sits there completely scattered, trying to get his breath and to calm himself. The soldiers pay him no attention, muttering amongst themselves and taking it in turns to watch out of the window. From another room Toni can hear groans of pain, and at one point somebody starts screaming. Toni sees a figure dash by the doorway with what looks like a syringe in his hand, and shortly afterwards the screaming stops.

After about half an hour the captain who rescued him comes into the room and crouches by the soldier at the window. Toni observes him. He has short, ginger hair, a young, kind face and a soft mouth. His blue eyes are steady. He is not a big man but he carries himself with quiet assurance. He touches the soldier on the shoulder.

'All quiet?'

'Yessir, nothing but the occasional shell. No movement close by that we can see.'

'Right, carry on.' He makes to leave.

'Er, Captain Will, sir?'

'What is it, Burnett?'

'Don't want to make a fuss, sir, but I got a splinter. Might the medic have time a little later?'

'Let me see.' Burnett holds up his shirt for the captain to get a look. 'Yes, you have caught one, haven't you? You'd better come along with me now.'

Not really knowing why, Toni gets up and follows them out. Burnett notices him, 'Sir, this young lad…'

The captain turns and snaps, in the way Mama does to the dogs, 'Go back. Go back and sit down. Keep down! Understand?'

Toni only wanted to be near a familiar face. '*Capitano* I want to say…I want to say thank you.'

Captain Will's face softens slightly, 'Oh that. Well, we need you in one piece, don't we? Look, do as you're told and go back in there, understand? Can't have you getting shot now. And don't bother me any more.'

Realizing he is holding the captain back Toni nods and returns to his place on the floor.

Chapter 13
September 3rd 1944, evening

Lorenzo watches as Toni and Papa disappear down the hill into the gloom. He feels something is lost to him that he may never get back, and he wants privacy to pray. He turns to climb above the entrance of the cave, asking Francesca to wait for him. She smiles, touches his arm, and goes back into the cave.

Leaning heavily on his crutch, he finds a space to sit and closes his eyes. He never prayed regularly like this before the war and he feels a little hypocritical doing it now, in times of need. He doesn't even know precisely why he prays. He was always taught to, of course, but he doubts his prayers make any difference. After all he has no evidence to that effect. Still, there's no harm in trying, and perhaps he's notching up points in the ledger for when he stands before his maker. One thing is for sure: he feels better after he's done it.

Today he rather flits through his regular prayers. He prays for his family as always, and for two or three friends from whom he has been separated. He prays for the dead he can remember although this list has grown too lengthy to mention each individually. He only names the last five or so and the rest he commends to the Father's hands, in the knowledge that God knows and cares for them just the same.

Vito, fallen in Russia, is top of the list. It seems unfair that Lorenzo, by contrast, should have escaped so miraculously. Why wasn't it the other way around? He wonders if in death Vito was able to look into the hearts of those left behind, and to understand how a person truly felt about him. Observing the love, the hatred, the envy, the comradeship to be found there, does he then put in a good word, or otherwise, with the God who awaits them all? Or doesn't it work like that? Either way, he feels Vito must have seen the love Lorenzo felt for him, and perhaps that eased his passing a little.

Now Lorenzo adds the people in the cave to his prayers. He asks that Mama will see him clearly and understand him for who he is, and that she may be less hostile. He prays for the Paisanis, sitting with their arms around each other as they await the outcome of events they cannot predict. He cannot help a smile as he prays for Francesca who he suspects carries a little torch for him, and vows to do what he can to let her down gently. Antonia remains in his heart, and Francesca must be allowed to see this. Above all he finds himself praying for Toni and Papa with whom he now feels a powerful bond. Their journey is perilous, though necessary, and he asks fervently for their safe return.

There is even a prayer for his people and his country. He has seen such pain and so many ructions during his travels north that it seems as if the whole country has been scarred deeply, permanently. A shame hangs over her so heavily that she cannot raise her battered head. He prays for right thinking people to step up and be heard, and for families to be given the time and peace to return to their lives. He prays for Antonia, and her kin, that they be left alone to rebuild their lives, that her brother will return safely from the war and, yes, that she should not forget him.

At the end he prays for his unknown father. He doesn't know if he still lives here, in Gemmano, or indeed if he is alive. He finds it difficult to pray for somebody he cannot visualize.

He raises his head and reflects how his daily prayer is growing longer, and then he thinks of the priest in his church back home. He likes to do this. It gives him a sense of peace and confidence that the Catholic church, which has survived so many wars, will survive this one too. It will persist as the point of continuity for them as they return to rebuild their smashed lives. There will be mass on Sundays, their priest will still nod off in the vestry, and the Virgin Mary will look down upon them with the same love and mercy she has always shown.

He always feels better having prayed. He doubts it will change his current circumstances, but it seems important that somebody recognizes the world is not right, and at least makes a mental note of it. This mayhem, this butchery, must not go unnoticed, unmentioned. It must not become the norm so that nobody sees it anymore. If they all pray then perhaps, in time, the Spirit may know where to begin when it comes, in order to set things right.

He sighs, for it is time to go back down. They will be planning the raid on their own cellar, and he doesn't want Mama to have another excuse to accuse him of malingering. At the cave entrance Francesca comes over to him, standing close, looking up into his eyes.

'Lorenzo, what do you think about the cellar? It will be safe for me and Angela to go too, won't it? You know, now it is dark?'

She puts her hand on his arm and he pats it reassuringly. He is still deeply reluctant to have the girls on this trip, but sees that there's little choice. 'We cannot take too many. It will just become noisy. And we absolutely must not be seen.'

Mama looks up. 'But *you* will be with us?'

Lorenzo gives a little bow. 'I will, Signora, but who else?'

Mama says, 'I'm coming and...' she nods at Francesca and Angela. 'They know the way to the well, and the cellar.'

'Well that is quite enough. Now listen, the most important thing is silence. We mustn't talk when we are close, so let's decide now who'll do what.'

Francesca says, 'I know the way to the cellar. But Toni told me there was a guard standing on our gate.'

'Let's wait and see if he's still there. Even if he is...well, it may still be possible to slip past.'

'So Angela and I will get the water from the well,' says Mama.

They agree that Lorenzo will be the point of contact for them all, at the top of the field, and that they can leave things with him when they go back on a second journey.

'No more than two journeys,' insists Lorenzo.

It is almost completely dark when they set out. To begin with they are able to walk, but as they approach the brow that will bring them in view of Gemmano, they crouch down beside the hedgerow and crawl. This proves a relief for Lorenzo who is on his belly, for the wound is at the back of the leg. With no weight upon it the pain eases, pain that is otherwise constant and nagging. In spite of Toni's ministrations it does not ache less, and sometimes he thinks he feels a sharpness to it that wasn't there before.

He insists on taking the lead, saying he has the experience, and the women seem content to accept this. In fact it is because he'll be the slowest and doesn't wish to be left behind. They may not understand as well as he does the importance of sticking together. It is hard to crawl, burdened as they are with buckets and bottles.

They crawl up the dry grass, strands of it tickling their ears, and all the time the continuous background rumble of artillery punctuates the air with muffled reports. From time to time they are forced to stop and disentangle themselves from bramble tendrils that snake out from the hedgerow, almost as if they were working in league with the Germans.

As they get closer Lorenzo stops. There is a rustling behind and Francesca settles beside him, her arm brushing against his.

He says, 'Show me.'

'That's our house,' Francesca points, 'so I have to crawl through the dogs' flap at the end of the hedge here. Angela has to climb over a gate in the hedgerow and the well is on the other side. But Lorenzo, what if they have guards on it?'

'Then thank God for that cow,' says Lorenzo drily. 'But I can't see anybody by your house. Let's crawl up to that gate, and I'll wait there.'

At the gate Lorenzo makes them sit silently while they listen for evidence of guards. Then Angela and Mama climb the gate and head for the well with their buckets. Francesca is so close to him that her hair is tickling his nose and he feels her softness, is affected by it, feels his senses heightened throughout his body. It reminds him of sitting close to Antonia and he does not want this. He sits back against the hedge.

'You'd better not waste too much time.'

He can sense Francesca sit back too, and then she says, 'See you soon.'

Alone he tries again to listen. He relies so much upon sound at night that he'll sometimes shut his eyes when crawling during an advance. But now the firing in the distance is too loud to catch subtle noises so Lorenzo is reduced to peering through the gate, and at Mazzanti's house.

It is about ten minutes before he sees a shape in the gloom and Francesca arrives, rolling a cheese before her as she crawls.

'It was easy. There's nobody there. I can just walk in. Look, I have two bottles of passata here in my dress. Back there is another cheese, a ham, and two more bottles.'

She is too overconfident for his liking. 'You can only risk one more trip. If you have to choose, then bring the ham. We'll need some meat.'

'Don't worry, I can make all the trips I want.'

Francesca produces a little penknife from the depths of a pocket, and cuts off a good sliver of cheese. 'Here, taste this. Papa made it. It's good.'

'Francesca! When we get down to the cave I will try a piece. Now you need to move quickly.'

Francesca sighs, '*Si, signore.*' She gives a mock salute and crawls back towards the house.

Angela returns with two buckets brimming with water. 'Signora Mazzanti is waiting for me at the well. She is hidden behind a hay stack.'

Lorenzo is so busy fetching the empty ones to pass to her, that he is only half aware that a light has gone on in the Mazzanti house. At the same time he hears the familiar whistle of an approaching shell. 'Angela, get down!'

They lie flat, on either side of the gate, and the shell erupts on the eastern side of the hill, towards Villa. Seconds later another explodes and this is followed by two more on the western side by Monte Gardo.

'*Porca miseria*! They are shelling the town. Go and get Signora Mazzanti and bring her back. We can get the rest of the water later. We have to get out of here.'

Crouching low Angela disappears, and Lorenzo crawls quickly, using his elbows, towards the dog gate. There is a lull in the shelling and he thinks he hears a cry from the vegetable patch, though he cannot be sure. He finds the dog gate, pulls aside the hessian and drags himself through what, for him, is a very tight fit.

There is something going on nearer the house, in the stall. As he gets closer he hears more cries and soon he can see by the light from the kitchen that Francesca is being held down by two German soldiers. They have dragged her out beyond the stall into the open air and forced her to the ground, face in the dirt. One German lies on her head, and the other has thrown her dress up over her back, and now grips her hips and rams himself into her. Her muffled cries can barely be heard for the first soldier has his whole weight crushing her head.

Lorenzo reaches for the gun, though he knows it is probable suicide to use it here. He has subdued the wave of disgust and fury that first swept over him and his mind is very cold and clear.

Then he remembers the bayonet he keeps in the boot of his good leg and silently draws the long blade out. He knows he cannot take both soldiers. Not with this leg. But if he gets one then, perhaps, Francesca can escape while he holds off the other, and that is all that matters.

He pulls his good leg up under him, getting ready to leap as best he can, when a whistling noise tells him more shells are arriving. He flattens himself as there is a tremendous explosion in the field close to where he was lying seconds earlier. There is a shattering, tearing sound as shrapnel rips through the plants in the garden like a wave. Tops of beans and tomato plants are sliced off and shredded. In front of him the soldier assaulting Francesca goes rigid and then his hands go up to his neck. Lorenzo can hear him choking, and in the light from the kitchen he can see blood spurting from a shrapnel wound in his neck. His comrade looks up and loosens his hold on Francesca who begins to kick and struggle again. The guard, distracted by her, doesn't hear Lorenzo until it is too late and the bayonet is thrust through his ribs and into his heart. He topples into the straw of the stall and the two soldiers lie there side by side, their blood spilling into Coco's old shit.

Lorenzo grips the weapon but it will not easily pull out. He twists and turns it, eventually putting his foot onto the body and yanking it. The bayonet comes away, catching something that wraps around its tip. In the poor light he cannot see what it is, but for some reason he grabs it and thrusts it deep into his pocket. He takes Francesca by the hand. She is weeping and spitting at the same time and she aims a kick at the corpse before he can drag her away.

'We have to get out of here. More shells will come.'

The nearby guns go quiet and relative silence descends as they crawl back to the gate. Aware of her distress, Lorenzo has his arm around Francesca. He knows they must get away from the corpses which, once discovered, may well cause terrible repercussions. There is no way the Germans will believe both soldiers died of shrapnel wounds, and they must not be seen here no matter what.

At the gate Lorenzo entrusts Francesca to her Mother's care with a muttered, 'Two soldiers got hold of her.' He and Angela grab what little water and food they have managed to gather.

Metre by metre they crawl away from the village and down the hill, and Lorenzo is relieved to find the shelling has stopped. It is hard not to slop water from the buckets with his leg making him so unstable and he swaps with Angela, taking the cheese from her. When they get back Mama comes up to him.

'Make me a fire, over there.'

He is tired and puzzled. 'You have the fire here, in front of the cave. We don't want more light than necessary in case...'

She tuts, 'Somewhere private, you understand?'

He gets it, and taking a couple of burning brands he starts a new fire just out of sight of the cave. He calls Mama who goes off with Francesca, carrying one of the buckets of water.

They are gone for about half an hour and when they come back Mama tells the community that Francesca was knocked over by a shell and one of her legs was cut. When nobody is looking she takes Lorenzo's arm and pulls him outside.

'You tell nobody. Understand? You say nothing about this. It is a terrible thing for her, but ten times worse if others know.'

'Of course I will not say anything. But will she be all right?'

'She will, she will – ' Mama hesitates, ' – the bastard didn't finish. You understand? Just keep quiet about it. And especially you don't say anything to Toni. He loves her so much, but he is delicate.'

Perhaps not as delicate as he seems, Lorenzo thinks, but he keeps it to himself. He nods, and is about to go back down to the cave when she says, 'Hey, Lorenzo. She is not for you. You know that. Right?'

'You need not fear, Signora. My heart is elsewhere, held by another. At least I hope, and believe in that! In any case I would never betray it.'

Mama looks him up and down. 'Hm. Yes. Well, I think you must stay with us for now. We will need you.'

Over the horizon to the southeast Lorenzo can still see flashes illuminating the night sky, and the thunder of guns rolls on.

Chapter 14
5th – 7th September 1944

Toni is awoken by a crash, and the floor shakes beneath him. A curtain of dust detaches itself from the ceiling and floats down over his hair and face, causing him to sneeze and spit. From next door he hears a voice speak with authority.

'S'ant major, see about that, will you?'

A rigid figure marches past the doorway and he can hear chunks of material falling before the figure returns.

'Direct hit on the farmhouse, sir. Small hole, but no structural damage.'

'Casualties?'

'None, sir. The room isn't in use.'

Nobody seems unduly concerned so smacking the dust out of his hair, Toni rises from a mattress and stretches. Furniture in the room amounts to a sideboard and a bed that has been shoved up against the wall on its end to make space. There is one soldier at the window by the Bren gun, hunched on a low stool and peering over the windowsill, and Toni stands beside him to look out of the window. As the soldier becomes aware of his presence he puts a hand on Toni's shoulder and firmly pushes him down.

'Ye'll get yer heid shot off like that, son.'

Toni kneels, and sees they are overlooking the road where they were attacked. It is maybe a hundred and fifty metres below them, and beyond that is the Conca. Although a relatively calm scene now, there are five burnt out vehicles strewn along the road. They are just heaps of blackened metal and shreds of canvas, and he can see one lying on its side, wheels and axles exposed. There are several bodies along the side of the road, not yet collected for burial, and Toni is struck by how far Captain Will must have come, under deadly fire, in order to find him.

From time to time a shell explodes nearby and he ducks down. But glancing across he sees the soldier doesn't move from his post unless there is a clear whistling noise first, in which case he too takes cover.

Toni feels a lump in his pocket and finds some of the biscuit he was given in Morciano. He was saving it for Remo but now he takes it out, breaks it in half and offers some to the soldier, who glances down. His craggy features soften into a smile.

'Naw, you're aw right, son. You eat it.' The soldier sticks out a hand, 'Bill Dalglish. Fae Govan. That's near Glasgow. Ken? Scotland!'

Toni nods in understanding. 'You come from Scotzia.'

Dalglish smiles again, 'Aye, Scotzia. Somethin like that. An you?'

Toni turns to the window. He points across the Conca and up to the top of the ridge. 'I live there.'

'Oh, Christ almighty,' sighs Dalglish. 'Then ye'll probably be better off wi us.'

Toni eats the biscuit in silence. Everything has happened so quickly since the cave, and he has not the space in his head for it all. He fears for Papa, utterly exhausted – infinitely worse than exhausted. The dogs will lead him back to Gemmano, but it is a long climb up the hill. And now some serious shooting has started on that hillside as, Dalglish explains, the Germans and the British go toe to toe. There are tanks rumbling along the Conca and beyond it all kinds of machine gun fire, punctuated with a smattering of smaller shells.

'Mortars', says Dalglish.

Toni cannot bear to watch. From nearby he can hear constant groaning, and going next door he finds five men, three on beds and two on the floor, in what is a temporary infirmary. There is one medic who is wrapping a bandage around the thigh of a soldier, and it is the man on the bed opposite them who is groaning so loudly. He is stripped to the waist with a bloodstained bandage around his abdomen, and he has been tied to the bed. His body arches in pain as he groans, grinds his teeth and groans again. A lieutenant puts his head around the door.

'Can't you do something for that man, Docherty?'

The medic turns his head from his work, 'I'll get to him next, sir, but I must stem the bleeding of this artery first, or he'll be dead in a few minutes. That boy's got internal bleeding I think, but I've no more morphine to give him for the pain. And I've only got the one pair of hands.'

'All right, Docherty. Do the best you can. We've sent for more medical supplies and a proper doctor. Can you use Dalglish here in the meantime?'

'Thanks sir, and another...hi, what do you think you're doing?'

Tony has acted instinctively. He has gone over to the soldier and placed his hands on the bloodied abdomen. He doesn't hear the question because all he knows is the warmth rushing up through his arms. Almost immediately the soldier quietens as the pain drains out of his body and Docherty, intrigued, stays back and observes. Tony senses deep injury beneath his hands and, working without fear, he finds he is able to distinguish between the pain and the wound. He plays his heat on the damaged tissue and feels the edges of it beginning to heal. There is some form of regeneration going on here as if the flesh, at a cellular level, is revising itself. He has no space to be startled, but this ability to direct the heat in different ways is new. He stays with the soldier as long as consciousness permits him, controlling the speed at which it flows through him, delaying the moment when it is exhausted. Finally he is spent, the black sweeps over him, and he slides off the soldier and onto the floor by the bed.

When he comes round he has been put back in the other room, but they have pulled down the bed and placed him on it. It feels like he's coming from a deep place, and his rise to consciousness is gradual. He becomes aware of voices in another room, not speaking Italian, and then he understands it is English and remembers where he is. He looks up to the irregular wooden ceiling and counts the beams holding up the floor above. Outside he can hear the squeaking and roaring of what he now recognizes as tanks going past. Through the cacophony he starts to tune in to disjointed bits of conversations.

'Pass that to Major Robertson, would you?'

'We need the adjacent map.'

'Captain Pugh just arrived, sir. Says there's stonking everywhere.'

'Thank heavens. Has he got medical supplies with him?'

'Yessir.'

'Right show him through to the sick bay straightaway.'

The rumbling outside stops suddenly and the discussion becomes clear, though punctuated by the occasional explosion.

'Now then, what about this local lad who can show us the way into Croce? Can we trust him?'

'Before he was evacuated Major Findlay mentioned him, sir. Said he claimed to know his way around the village.'

'I wouldn't trust any of them, sir. Look the other way and they'll swipe the wheels off your jeep before you can blink.'

'Or he could easily be leading us into a trap. Jock, you found him.'

Toni recognizes the voice of Captain Will. 'Yes, I pulled him out of the convoy, sir, on Major Findlay's orders. The major felt he could help us, though he's just a boy. I'm no lover of Eyeties as you know. Remember how they stole my horse last month? He must have made a bloody marvelous casserole. But I must say, the lad was right about the Bosche being in Gemmano. If we'd listened we'd have avoided that bloody shambles with the convoy.'

Another voice speaks out, 'There's something else you ought to know about the young fellow, sir.'

'Speak up, Lieutenant.'

'I'd be reluctant to bring this up if I hadn't seen it with my own eyes, and Docherty saw it too. The boy wandered into the sick bay and...'

But the officer's voice drops at the same time as more tanks rumble past and Toni can't hear any more. Then more shells crash around the farmhouse, closer than before and Dalglish, manning the Bren, growls, 'Those bloody tanks. Every time the London Irish go past they attract more unwanted attention our way.'

Toni sits up and Dalglish glances round. He watches Toni for a moment and then gets up and goes out. He returns shortly with a large tin cup filled with the suspect tea. This he hands to Toni, watching him carefully the while. Toni cups it in his hands and sips, ignoring the taste.

Dalglish says, 'That boy next door. It's no the first time you've done that, right?'

'Not exactly the first time,' says Toni quietly.

'Docherty says that boy might even recover. Says he's actually healing. We thought he wis a goner.'

Toni looks away uncomfortably. This doesn't sound right. There is something almost blasphemous about the idea of resurrecting a person. Supposing the British think so too?'

Dalglish leans forward and ruffles his hair reassuringly. 'You're a guid lad. You did a guid thing. You take it easy now.'

Toni looks up and smiles, 'I am 'ungry.'

'Aye, join the club, son. We've not eaten all fucking day.'

It is another hour or so before a lieutenant makes an appearance, and Toni is brought before several officers who surround a map. Once again he is shown the details of where they are and then quizzed on the terrain, the nature of various buildings shown, and about vegetation. Keeping as calm as he can, he answers to the best of his ability, and when he is finished he is brought before the commanding officer.

'What's your name? Toni? Right, well we have to move out of here, Toni. Too dangerous, see? Now, you'll be coming with us on this show, understand? We need a guide.'

Toni nods, though the thought terrifies him.

'This is Captain Will. You already know him. I want you to stick to him like glue. Like glue? Oh…never let him out of your sight. Got it?'

'*Si, Capitano.*'

Captain Will says, 'Zero hour, sir?'

'17.30. Better get your men ready.'

As the time approaches, things quieten down in the farmhouse. Even the wounded are silent. Toni sits huddled behind Captain Will and his men in the farmyard, hidden from the 'stonking' as the captain calls the shellfire. If a soldier speaks to another it is in muttered tones, but for the most part each is absorbed in his own thoughts. There is a young soldier with blonde hair sitting nearby, no older than he is, a sheen of sweat lying across his brow. His wild eyes flicker from the captain to the back of his hands, and to the gap between the buildings that leads out of the farmyard. Another man looks like he is writing a letter home, leaning on the back of the soldier in front of him, licking his pencil, gazing into the sky for a moment. A couple of others are whispering to each other.

'How long do we have to bloody sit here?'

Dalglish says, 'Get used to it, Jimmy. It's been like this since we came out to Persia. Mostly you're waiting, or cleaning, or waiting, or digging, or waiting or fuckin marching.' Dalglish gives a sour laugh, 'Though I widnae complain if that wis all we had to do.'

'Christ, I'd give anything for one sandwich. I've had nothing since last night.'

Captain Will ignores Toni completely. He too is writing but it doesn't look like a letter. Toni notices the captain holds the little notebook awkwardly, and this is because his left hand is damaged. There is a dip in the back of the hand, and the middle finger is sunken, out of line with the others, creating the effect of a claw. Toni catches a glimpse of what he is writing.

1530hrs: It is a beauty. B Coy to attack Serra Fabri. C & D Coys also up. Looks a trifle fraught! At present p

As if he realizes he's been observed Captain Will puts the diary away, stands and approaches the ranks. He makes a couple of quiet jokes with the men and then looks down at the blonde-haired soldier.

'All right, Watson?'

'All right, sir.' Watson's voice is shaking badly.

'You'll do fine, Watson. Just remember, the Ted in front of you is as nervous of you as you are of him. And you are a good soldier. Now, double check your kit.'

For a time Captain Will paces restlessly around the farmyard. Suddenly he glances at his troops and, as if aware he needs to set an example, he sits and resumes his writing activities. Nearby a couple of infantrymen argue over a cigarette.

'Belt up, the pair of you,' snaps the captain.

Around five in the afternoon a soldier comes out of the farmhouse and approaches Captain Will.

'They want you inside, sir.'

As soon as the captain goes, the murmuring grows louder and speculation spreads like disease through the ranks.

'Called off?'

'New orders!'

'Bit of grub?'

'Naw,' says Dalglish, 'it'll just be another postponement. You watch.'

Captain Will returns. 'Attack postponed indefinitely. All right now, I want no comments. Dawson, break out whatever you've got in the way of tea rations and let's have a brew up.'

At 18.30 they receive revised orders. Assembling again in the farmyard they wait for a lull in the shelling and then move out. Toni sticks close behind the captain who has still not said a word to him, and by staying close to hedgerows they avoid being seen. There are constant sounds of battle around them from across the valley by the Ventena torrent, and up behind on the ridge near Croce. They creep down the hill, under strict orders for silence, until they are close to the road. Here, they find a series of trenches and dugouts carefully constructed along the roadside. They are so well camouflaged that Toni didn't even notice them from the window this morning.

'These are old Bosche placements,' says Captain Will to Sergeant -major Thom, 'Good ones too. We'll be much safer here. Post some guards, and get the rest of the men underground, will you?'

At about nine o'clock there is a call from one of the guards.

'Vehicles approaching, sir.'

'What are they?'

'Food trucks, sir!'

There is a cheer through the dugout. Thom shouts, 'Right, leave it out. Want the Hun to know we're here, do we? Shall I organize rations for the men, sir?'

'Yes indeed, S'ant-major. Take all the help you need.'

Packs and parcels are handed down into the dugout and Toni tucks himself out of the way behind Captain Will. Presently the smell of cooking emerges from further down the trench and Toni finds that he is salivating, even if the smells are unfamiliar and not altogether good. There is certainly meat in there. Soon a private makes his way towards them, bent low, clutching a mess tin for the captain.

'Best I can do under the circumstances, sir.'

The captain gives him a quick nod, 'Well done, Dawson.'

As Dawson turns away the captain adds, with a thumb in Toni's direction, 'Get this boy something, will you?'

While the captain is eating, a runner arrives from the farmhouse and hands him an envelope. 'Orders, sir. Major sends his compliments and says we'll have a radio link established as soon as we can, sir.' The runner takes a few breaths and turns away, 'Can't say I'll be sorry when they do.'

Toni is presented with a mess tin. There are thick slices of corned beef and a mound of what looks like, but doesn't much taste like, pureed potato. There is a green, slimy mass, which he eventually identifies as *fagiolini*, but they have been boiled until they have no flavor at all. There are great slices of bread with layers of – again who knows, it doesn't taste like butter – all over it. He gets a big mug of tea, and he scoffs the lot, beef and all.

The captain folds the orders and slips them into his inside pocket. He and Sergeant-major Thom talk in quiet tones for a while and then Thom is to be heard moving through the dugout telling people to eat up and get their heads down for a spot of shut-eye. They don't know when they'll get another chance to rest. Nobody says anything to Toni but he finds, with his belly full, his eyes get heavy. He leans his head against somebody's pack, and in spite of the sound of constant shelling and machine gun fire coming across the valley, he falls soundly asleep.

The following day is perhaps the dullest Toni can ever remember. He has nothing to do, no dogs to talk to, and nowhere that he is allowed to go. None of the men seem inclined to talk to him and Captain Will has too many responsibilities to pay him any attention. They won't even let him go above ground for fear of snipers and stray shells. At a certain point Major Robertson, who is in command, slips into the dugout and chats to the captain for a spell. Toni observes his ruddy features and clipped moustache until the major glances at him, and he quickly busies himself with tying a shoelace. Later he is presented with another mess tin; this time it is eggs that have been fried with *pancetta*, but great thick chunks of it, cooked to a crisp so that they disintegrate into salty flakes in his mouth. More slices of bread and tea and again he finds himself devouring it all.

When nobody is watching, he slips up to the edge of the parapet and looks across the valley. Gemmano is quiet for once, for there is a lull in the battle and the smoke has cleared. He looks to where the caves are, hoping against hope that he will spot some movement, and his heart lifts a little as he catches sight of a thin trickle of smoke emerging, going straight up into the morning air. He imagines Mama squatting by the fire, and he thinks of her preparing spaghetti for lunch. Francesca is beside her, taking some boiling water off the stove, and giggling with Floriana when

Lorenzo walks by. Little Letizia sits holding the kitten, Thumb, rolling it over on its back, letting the kitten try to catch one of her fingers. Papa sits not far away, smoking his pipe, and the Collision Brothers are calm at his feet. He has recovered from his climb back up the hill, safe and home amongst his own. He talks to Paisani occasionally.

There is a hand on his shoulder. It is the captain. 'Get back down below, you bloody fool. Any sniper for miles could get you here.'

It is evening and quite dark, when the company packs for battle and moves up the hill. Toni leads them past the farmhouse and onto the ridge, to a spot somewhere to the east of Croce, perhaps a kilometer away. He can see men creeping off into the dark on either side of him, and then the captain gives the signal and they wait again.

The captain leans towards him. 'When we start I want you to stay close behind me. I may need you. I mean *close*.'

Toni needs no urging on this matter. He has no idea what the next few hours will be like but he doesn't think it will be good. After another long wait a message comes along the line from Major Robertson. 'Advance.'

The captain glances at his watch, 'Advance now? Where's that bloody barrage?'

Watson whispers to Thom, 'What's the barrage for, Sarge?'

'Clears the way, doesn't it? Quiet now.'

They move forward in a silence emphasized by the non-appearance of the barrage. They creep across a ploughed field, through a dry gully, and up the other side. They have covered about two hundred yards when another message comes through.

'Advance postponed until 03.30, sir.'

'Of all the bits of bloody, cock-eyed staff work,' swears the captain.

They happen to be next to a house and so the soldiers nearby make themselves comfortable inside and have a smoke, the captain joining them.

'Nae barrage tonight then, sir?' asks Dalglish.

'Don't get me started,' says the captain through gritted teeth.

All too soon for Toni, 03.30 arrives and the much anticipated barrage commences. Shortly afterwards they resume the advance, and then they are forced to fling themselves to the ground as a pair of shells explode behind them.

'For God's sake,' mutters the captain to Thom, 'I do wish they'd get their range right, back there. Bad enough having to deal with the Bosche stonking without our own boys joining...'

There is a cry of pain and Dalglish shouts, 'Watson's hit, sir.'

Firing has broken out ahead of them and the company breaks into smaller squads commanded by the sergeants. They begin firing back, advancing on the enemy and covering each other. They seem to be making quick progress for as Toni and the captain kneel beside Watson, the company is already moving rapidly across the next field.

Dalglish shines a torch onto the prone body of the soldier. They can see blood splattered all over his face and his blonde hair, and it seems to be spurting from a wound in his chest, a jagged gash that must have been made by shrapnel. Watson's eyes are staring and he is making choking noises. They are plaintive gurgles, almost as if he is begging his blood and his life to depart as painlessly as possible.

Dalglish says, 'There's nae hope, sir. I'll stay wi' him a minute until it's over.'

The captain nods, 'Good man.'

At that moment firing opens up on their left and they hear the *tchin tchin* of bullets ricocheting off stones on the ground. The captain and Dalglish return fire with their machine guns as they advance upon the enemy, flinging themselves flat, shooting in bursts and then advancing again.

Remembering his instructions Toni is about to go after them, although every instinct in his body is urging him to turn and run the other way. Then he notices something about Watson's body. It has gone completely still and Watson is no longer making any noise at all. The flow of the blood has eased, his muscles have relaxed, and his chest no longer struggles to contain his life.

What catches Toni's attention is a sheen that appears on Watson's cheek. It is pale, and shimmers just off the edge of the soldier's skin. As he watches, the sheen extends, creeping across his nose and mouth, his ears and then over his head. It grows down over his uniform, covering the belt and trousers, arriving at his hands and feet, until the entire body glows with an unearthly light.

Toni sits back oblivious to the battle ahead of him. His attention is completely focused on this strengthening glow and a familiar tension arises in his breast.

Imperceptibly the glow strengthens and becomes more than just a sheen. It is growing out of the soldier, rising above him, and Toni recognizes the gradually-forming cloud of an entity like the ones he sees in the church. The cloud is untypical for he can sense no emotion from it, and indeed feels no connection to it. This is not his breath pulling it from the body. It is emerging of its own accord. Nevertheless he remains totally focused upon it, not wishing to be interrupted as he was in the church.

Once the cloud is hovering above the body it begins to alter, turning in on itself as if finding a shape that is comfortable. Toni waits for the sense of despair to assail him, but there is nothing. He doesn't know how long he sits and watches the entity. After a time it settles on a shape and, in some subtle way that Toni feels but cannot see, its focus changes. It becomes aware of its surroundings and begins to look around. Toni prepares himself. He watches his breath carefully and keeps his emotions in check as he awaits the first tendril. It won't be long now before they snake out towards him, and he finds he is afraid; he has never been so close to an entity and it seems entirely possible that the tendrils will reach him. And then what?

None of this comes to pass. The entity hovers silently, and now he does get a light sense of confusion, though not fear, from it. It is lost. The entity gives no impression of being aware of Toni's presence, at times appearing to look right through him. No tendrils of any kind emerge, and Toni holds his watching brief, profoundly aware of his breathing.

Of his own accord he stands and makes contact. He can see the entity doesn't know what has happened to it, or where it is supposed to go, and he feels great compassion in his breast for it. To be so ripped from its body must be a terrible thing. In the absence of a better idea, he points in the direction of the Croce church. Perhaps it may find an answer there.

Finally he senses another shift of focus and the entity begins to rise. It goes straight up, climbing to more than double the height of a man before changing direction and drifting off towards Croce. Though it is moving away, Toni finds he can see it quite clearly in the dark, although not with his eyes. He can see with his mind that the entity is drifting towards the local church. Eventually it goes over the brow of a rise and he can't perceive it any more.

He is left feeling at peace as he allows his focus to return to his surroundings. There is no sense of having been ripped away from the entity. On the contrary, he feels he has fulfilled an unknown purpose, simply by being present to observe its flight. He doesn't understand the purpose, but it feels like waiting for the departure was the right thing to do.

He crawls over to the inert body that is no longer Watson. He rests his hand on the face for a moment and makes sure the eyes are closed. As he stands to go and look for the captain, he feels a couple of raindrops land on his forehead and nose. Within a few minutes the first rains of the autumn have begun in earnest, and he is soaked through.

Chapter 15
7th – 9th September 1944

The early light is unfamiliar. The long days of summer have come to an end, as if scurrying away before the advancing armies. Dawn is nothing more than a gradual lightening of the black to grey, though the rain has stopped, and eventually Toni can see where they are. This is not Croce itself, which they have fought their way through. This is Casa Menghino, out on the left of the ridge looking straight over the valley to Gemmano. There is no better viewpoint on the ridge for covering the Morciano road.

There is plenty of evidence that the Germans left in a hurry. Knapsacks, rations, and a few machine guns lie around the floor.

'They haven't even had time to leave booby traps,' says Captain Will, breaking off a piece of German chocolate.

He wasn't too cordial last night when forced to come back through the rain in order to find Toni who had hidden himself from the shooting at the bottom of the gully in a bed of nettles. Toni heard his calls and answered, and soon the captain arrived, slipping and sliding down the gully on his backside until his feet were planted in the rising stream. Grabbing Toni by the scruff of the neck he dragged him back to the top.

'When I say stay close, I bloody well mean close! Understand?'

Knowing he couldn't explain, Toni nodded miserably and then spent the next couple of hours dogging the captain's footsteps by the simple method of putting his own feet into the captain's footprints. They had lost contact with the company, and to Toni it seemed the captain was following the sounds of the machine guns. This meant their progress was of a zigzag nature, and at times they had to throw themselves down on their bellies as enemy fire whizzed past.

At one point they burst into a house, the main room of which was lit only by candles. In the gloom they could make out perhaps twenty men, lying on the floor, or on tables, bandaged and bloody. Some were groaning in pain, and the flickering light seemed to raise macabre ghosts above them which danced as if waiting upon their souls.

'*Kamerad, kamerad,*' they cried.

'Bloody hell!' said the captain and then, pointing his weapon, 'We are not your bloody friends.'

'*Wir verwundet sind. Wir ergeben uns!*'

The captain raised the muzzle of his gun towards the ceiling. 'I don't know what the hell you're talking about, Fritz.'

Toni nudged the captain. 'He says they are the wounded. They surrender.'

The captain glanced down at him. 'You speak German?'

Toni shrugged. 'I understand it more.'

'And how am I supposed to accept their surrender just now? The hell with them!'

They ducked outside again and forged on. The captain muttered, 'Full of surprises, aren't you?'

'Is this a good surprise, *Capitano*?'

'We'll see about that.'

Later they could hear a tank trundling about in the dark. The captain whispered, 'That's not a Sherman engine. Come on, this way.'

Eventually they rejoined the fighting and at that point events got so confused that Toni couldn't say with any certainty how they had arrived here in Casa Menghino. There was a great deal of shooting, and endless explosions, and he spent his time either cowering behind a wall or crawling through mud and rubble. In spite of this he was aware of other entities, all heading for the church in Croce, and they absorbed his attention so that the captain was constantly nudging him back to vigilance, asking for directions. He only knows they've arrived when the captain points at a corner in the farmhouse and tells him to rest.

At present Major Robertson and Captain Will are setting up B Company HQ, organizing the radio operator and getting the sergeants to identify a perimeter.

'This is the best overview of the valley,' says Robertson. 'The Bosche will counterattack for sure.'

At about half past six in the morning they do. Mortar shells start exploding all around them and a cry comes from the perimeter.

'Enemy advancing, sir. I can see three groups crawling towards us.'

Bullets start whining past, and *tchining* off the walls of the farmhouse. From a window Toni can make out one or two soldiers worming their way around the farmhouse on their bellies. Then a bullet ricochets off the windowsill, spattering his cheek with wooden splinters, one of which digs in just below his ear. He hurls himself to the ground and crawls into a corner and there he cowers, curled up in a ball, his hands over his ears as the firing intensifies.

Each time there is a pause he hopes it is over, but the firing resumes as fiercely as before. The door bursts open and Dalglish drags another soldier into the room and lays him out against a wall near Toni. There is blood coming from the man's thigh and Dalglish gropes around in his pack until he pulls out a first aid kit. Ripping it open the contents spill all over the floor and a phial of morphine rolls over to where Toni crouches. Dalglish notices him.

'Here, pass us that over, would ye?' he says.

Toni obeys and Dalglish begins to work. With a small surgical knife he cuts the trouser leg off so they can clearly see the wound. There is plenty of blood but it is not pumping out and Dalglish says he doesn't think an artery is hit.

'Am I gonnae be aw right?' says the soldier.

'Aye, son. You'll be fine. We just need to get you bandaged up here.' Dalglish cleans around the wound as best as he can, whispering to Toni as he does, 'Mind you, what the fuck do I know?'

As he starts to apply the bandage he gets Toni to hold it in place while he wraps. The blood is still oozing, making the bandage sticky, and harder to put on effectively. Suddenly Toni says, 'Not like that.'

He makes Dalglish change places with him. Then he removes the bandage and looks inside the kit again. He finds a wad of padding and applies it to the wound, having cleaned it again so the padding will absorb the worst of the bleeding until they get the bandage in place. Then, getting Dalglish to hold down one end, he applies the bandage quickly and efficiently. Glancing down at the soldier he can see he is calm.

Dalglish looks at him with his eyebrows raised. 'Well, well. Guid lad.'

With that he disappears outside again and Toni is left to look after the soldier. He holds up the phial of morphine.

'Do you wan' some?'

'You a medic or somethin?'

Toni shakes his head. 'No, I am not. But I think is easy. I just,' he holds up a syringe, 'put in your arm, no?'

The soldier gives him a sickly smile. 'Why d'ye no just see if there are a couple o' pills in that there first aid kit?'

Toni does as he is told, and having taken them the soldier sits himself up against the wall and produces a cigarette out of his top pocket.

'I'll hae a quick drag before I go back oot there.'

Another soldier comes into the room. 'You the medic?'

'The what? No, I am not medic.'

The soldier looks impatient. 'Dalglish said there was somebody here who could put on a bandage.'

Toni shrugs, 'I can do it.'

The soldier thrusts out a hand and Toni can see that a bullet has passed right through the palm. He cleans and prods, trying to understand the wound, glancing anxiously at the soldier for a reaction. But the private is fuelled by adrenaline, and just watches on. Toni tends and bandages him and the soldier goes straight out, giving his comrade on the ground a dirty look as he does.

So Toni does what he can for each injured man until Docherty, the medic, appears. They work side by side and Docherty shows him how to administer morphine. As Toni thought, you just stick it in, although not in the arm.

'Don't spend too much time on each one,' says Docherty. 'All we can do is patch them up as best we can. Then we send them back to the field hospital.'

Toni considers using his hands on some of the worst cases, but he is still very tired from the previous day and he knows if he helps one then he'll be unable to work on any of the others.

Eventually the firing becomes sporadic and then ceases altogether. Major Robertson reappears together with a couple of NCO's. He tells the radio officer to communicate news of events through to Battalion HQ, and then gets his sergeants to check the men for injuries and ammunition. He assigns a corporal to gather up the dead and to lay them in a row outside, against a wall of the barn. At that moment Captain Will comes in, flushed and breathing hard, pushing a German prisoner in front of him. 'This one has been shot in the backside.'

They shove him in Toni's direction. Toni makes him lie on his front and begins to cut his trousers off him. As he gets down to the boot he finds a knife hidden inside it. He pulls it out and calls the captain.

'It was in 'is shoe.'

Captain Will snatches the knife, looking as if he'd expected Toni to keep it for himself. He thrusts the knife under the German's nose, and Toni gets the feeling he is holding himself back. 'Forget to mention this did you, Fritz?'

Never taking his eyes off the German he says to Toni,

'Right, patch him up as quickly as possible, will you? We need to get him over to Battalion HQ for the translator to question.'

Somebody gets a fire going and both the major and the captain go bare-chested as they hang their shirts to dry. Cigarettes are lit and passed around and even he is offered one, raising eyebrows as he declines. The captain sits himself in a corner and after a moment he pulls out his diary and begins writing in it.

After a time the radio operator turns to the major. 'Orders to withdraw to C company positions, sir.'

'What? Now?'

'Yessir.'

The major and the captain turn and look at each other with puzzled frowns.

'Thompson, ask for that order to be confirmed, will you?'

But the order proves correct and so they get out of their farmhouse and move a couple of hundred yards across the ridge to another, which Toni knows is called *Il Palazzo*. It is not so different from the farmhouse they have just left, with a scattering of outhouses and covered areas in which to keep carts. There they settle in while the major watches in amazement as the Royal Artillery bombards the positions they have just vacated, shells throwing up chunks of earth and pieces of rubble where they blow a section off an out-house. Incredibly, the main structure still stands.

'Well, what's the bloody point of that?' asks Sergeant-major Thom.

Later in the afternoon the radio operator says, 'Orders to

re-occupy the position at Casa Menghino, sir.'

Major Robertson rolls his eyes and B company prepares to move again. As they creep across to their former positions they are met with a hail of fire.

'The bloody Germans have re-occupied the position,' roars the major.

The captain sends Toni back to Il Palazzo and from there he watches the battle to take back Casa Menghino. Once again injured soldiers start to be brought in, so he does what he can together with Docherty and Captain Pugh, the medical officer who is based here. Pugh is able to perform minor surgery and Toni watches carefully as he administers local anesthetic to a hand or a foot. Pugh sees him observing.

'Stick your finger there, son. Now, we'll take this splinter out before we send this one back. That way his chances of survival are much higher. Reduced risk of infection, you see?'

Eventually B company retreats into C company's perimeter, and the firing stutters and stops. The Germans have won that round. Somebody sets up a stove and starts brewing endless pots of tea. Major Robertson and Captain Will receive mugs as they come in, and the two of them stand by the wooden table in silence, sipping and smoking. Finally the major turns to the captain and finds the energy to speak.

'Better count the casualties, Jock, now people are stationary. Also we've asked for some food to be sent up.'

Captain Will can barely raise his head. 'I'll see to it.'

Even Toni is puzzled when later in the evening a recce report informs the major that the Germans have evacuated Casa Menghino. So B company moves forward and takes control of it again, unopposed. Hot food is brought up on mules together with ammunition, (trucks being unable to handle the newly formed mud), and they settle themselves in for the night.

Toni cannot help himself. '*Capitano*, why 'ave we…er…move away over there, an' then come back 'ere?'

Captain Will puts down his plate and glances across at the sleeping body of the major. He contemplates Toni as if trying to work out whether he is to be trusted, but eventually he shrugs and says, wryly, 'It's known in soldiering as 'the fog of war'. Remember that. It's how wars are run.'

Toni might have asked more, but he barely rested the night before and sleep sweeps over him. The night is relatively undisturbed but at first light he is rudely awoken by another counter-attack. He drags himself from his slumber and does what he can for the injured. Both Captain Pugh and Docherty are over at Il Palazzo and so he is left to his own devices. As he works he finds himself uttering prayers in his mother tongue. He has not spent much time in church but has heard both his parents praying, and some of these prayers have stuck. When the prayer doesn't seem to fit he adapts it, asking for a return to health of the soldier in his care, and safe passage for his family.

Eventually the attack is driven back and the soldiers return to rest and regroup. The major and the captain move among them, offering a quiet word of advice or encouragement, sharing a cigarette or an anecdote. From time to time everybody ducks down as a mortar explodes or a sniper's bullet bounces off the stonework. Toni looks up from applying a bandage to find Captain Will looking at him. When their eyes meet the captain nods in approval, once, and goes on his way. Toni feels he has been seen by him for the first time.

There is a tapping noise. Toni's ears are still ringing from the shelling and he is not sure he's heard anything at all. He is about to inject morphine into a soldier with a gut wound when he hears the tapping again. It is low but urgent. He gives the shot to relieve the soldier's agony and then sits very still, waiting for a sufficient lull between shells. There it is again, just a couple of metres away. He kneels beside the table, and puts his ear to the floor. Yes, quite clear, and coming from under the floor. He rolls up a battered straw rug and underneath there is a trapdoor.

Without hesitation he opens it and an awful stench of human excrement arises from the cellar. About eight, dirty, staring faces peer out at him. There are at least three women, and four children and the last is just a hidden mask in the dark.

'*Aqua, aqua. Siamo disperati.*'

Toni takes a canteen of water from the prone soldier who is now under the caress of morphine, and hands it down.

'We heard your voice. Food. Do you have any food also?'

Major Robertson comes up behind him. 'For Heaven's sake, who are they?'

After a brief discussion it emerges they live in the farmhouse. When the Germans first arrived they ducked down into the cellar and, having managed to pull a rug over the trapdoor using a clever string and lever arrangement, they have hidden there ever since, listening to the battle rage over them. They have no food, water or toilet facilities.

Major Robertson rolls his eyes. 'Tell them they can't come out. It's far too dangerous and I can't have civilians in the middle of a pitched battle.'

'*Capitano*, they are desperate.'

'Give them a canteen and a little food. Ask Dalglish for it. Then cover them up again. They must understand,' he looks directly at Toni for the first time, 'there is no guarantee we can hold this place, and the Hun could be back here by evening.'

With a heavy heart Toni hands down what food Dalglish can give them. There is a girl of about sixteen staring up at him, and in her he can see Francesca. A tear slips down his cheek and falls like a glinting jewel, splashing upon her nose. She reaches up and touches it, and then stretches her hand towards him. Surreptitiously he slips them an extra canteen, and then closes the trapdoor over their tear-stained faces.

As he goes back to work a message comes through on the radio. Major Robertson calls to Captain Will. 'Jock, come over here a minute, will you?'

'What now?'

'Jock, it's your brother, Ian. He's been injured.'

'Did they say if it was serious?'

'I believe it's not. They said the 'nether regions'. I got the sense that if dealt with quickly it will be absolutely fine, so they've evacuated him back to the field hospital for attention.'

The captain nods, 'Thank you for letting me know, sir.'

'Yes, well there's rather more to it. What with all the injuries and a couple of mortalities I'm now senior officer on the ridge. That means I have to get back to Area H.Q., which leaves you in charge here.'

'I'll tell the men, sir.'

'Keep the radio operator on his toes, will you? And did you say that Italian lad speaks German?'

'He understood it well enough the other night.'

'Good. Our translator's been killed and we have some more prisoners to interrogate.' Robertson turns and points at Toni. 'You come with me.'

Captain Will says, 'Sir, he is rather handy with a bandage. We won't have anybody if you take him.'

'Can't be helped, Jock, but I'll try and send Docherty down.'

Toni peers through the drifting smoke at the blasted landscape as they crouch at the door of the building. Robertson says, 'Now when I say 'go' we run for it, got it? Keep your head down as low as you can, and if I hit the dirt you do the same.'

In the event their run back to C company goes almost unnoticed, and apart from one mortar shell is uneventful. There is a lull in the morning's activities, and Toni collapses in a corner for he has never felt so tired, both in mind and body. Major Robertson spends his time with the radio operator, trying to re-establish the broken link with B company.

Then there is a loud bang, and a corporal, on watch upstairs, shouts down, 'Panther tank approaching B company, sir. Just fired on them, but I think the shell went through the H.Q.'

'Where's our P.I.A.T.?'

'We lost that two days ago, sir,' says Sergeant Ramsey.

Major Robertson doesn't blink. 'Right, what've we got that can take on that tank?'

'Nothing now, sir. The biggest things we've got left are mortars and grenades. We can't touch it.'

The call comes from above, 'Hang on a minute, sir. The tank appears to have stopped firing. There's somebody getting out of it, and he's carrying a white flag!'

'What?'

'I can't see very well sir, but he appears to be approaching B company HQ. They've stopped shooting too.'

'Is he alone?'

'Yessir. And now he's gone up to the perimeter and a couple of our boys are bringing him inside.'

Major Roberson raises his eyebrows. 'Extraordinary! Keep a close eye on them, will you? How's that radio link coming?'

'Still trying, sir.'

After a few minutes the corporal calls down again. 'There's a party coming this way, sir. I think it's Captain Will with the

German – he's still clutching that flag.'

Sure enough the party arrives at Il Palazzo, and just as they do the radio operator gives a grunt of satisfaction. 'Working again, sir.'

Major Robertson bends and whispers to him, 'Right get onto Battalion HQ and tell them to get a couple of Shermans up here any way they can, pronto! We'll keep this blighter busy.'

The German is made to sit at the table. Toni sees that Captain Will's hand is covered in blood.

Major Robertson says, 'Are you all right, Jock?'

The captain is animated. 'Yes, it's not serious. This Ted sent a shell straight through the bloody farmhouse. Mercifully it didn't explode but I happened to be standing at the doorway as the shell came through and the damn thing grazed my hand as it did! Things looked pretty drab for a minute or two and then he emerged with a parley flag of all things. Well, as my German is a shade worse than my Hebrew the parley wasn't a howling success, so I thought I'd better bring him over here.'

'Well, we've got a couple of large friends coming up, if you take my meaning, so let's have a nice, long chat with our new chum here.'

Toni is called over to interpret. The German is breathless and nervous, and repeats himself a lot, and Toni, through a fog of weariness, has to ask him to clarify on a number of occasions. It transpires that the German, now he has a Panther tank covering both farmhouses, believes he is in a position to ask for a British surrender, and would like to avoid further bloodshed if possible.

Major Robertson touches Toni on the shoulder. 'Just take your time, laddie. We're in no hurry here. Ask him what provisions he has made for us under the Geneva Convention if we surrender to him now.'

The German begins to explain where they will be taken, and the kind of treatment they can expect for the wounded. The exchange goes on like this until the diversion is exhausted, and then Major Robertson says, a little desperately, 'Tell him we thought it was a Tiger tank.'

'Tiger, Panther, what's the bloody difference?' asks the German irritably. Toni has grasped the need for delay and begins to explain to the German tank commander the differences between

Tigers and Panthers as he sees them. For a moment the German seems to think it is this idiot of an Italian boy who is complicating matters, but he cottons on quickly enough.

'Don't you delay. If I am not back there in five minutes my tank will open fire again.'

At that moment they hear the welcome noise of a couple of heavy engines moving up from Croce. The German's eyes open wide.

'Those are Sherman tanks! *Schweinehund*!'

Major Robertson says, 'Inform this German, will you, that he's now officially a prisoner of war. Hobson, take one other man and get him back to battalion HQ, will you?'

The German explodes. He has come in under a parley flag and most clearly, most clearly, not a flag of surrender. The British are required by the code of war to let him return to his post. This is the most outrageous behavior. It is beneath the dignity of a British officer and they should be ashamed, no, mortified by their comportment.

He is still ranting as he is taken away, his expostulations growing louder as he sees the officers chuckling quietly.

'He must be joking,' says Captain Will.

Toni takes his hand and begins to examine it. The captain snatches it away irritably and Toni says, 'But I mend it, *Capitano*.'

'No time now. Another party about to start.'

'Take a moment, Jock,' says Major Robertson.

Captain Will reluctantly sits at the table and Toni cleans his hand up. It is heavily grazed but nothing more and the captain won't let him put a bandage on, saying it will restrict his movement. Toni rubs in some ointment and the captain stands.

'Right, better get over there. All hell will be let loose now.'

There is indeed another furious battle over at Casa Menghino before the corporal calls down to say that the Panther has withdrawn. With that comes relative calm for the rest of the day and later more mules come up with food.

The following morning it is C company's turn. The counter-attack comes in waves, each of which is beaten off, each of which means more casualties. Toni works with Captain Pugh as best he can, but they are no longer able to send people back to the field hospital because of the battle raging around them, and Toni is working through a constant headache. Major Robertson strides around issuing commands as the shells get closer, and at one point half the ceiling falls in on them. Toni is caught a glancing blow by a falling beam, but scrambles aside unhurt.

There is a shout from upstairs, 'Two tanks, and getting closer.'

The shelling intensifies and the men abandon the farmhouse, which is about to collapse, and hide behind the ruins. Toni sees Major Robertson pulling a prone soldier around the corner of a barn and runs over to help him. Together they are dragging the injured man to safety when there is the whistling of a large shell, very close.

'Get down!' cries the major.

There is a searing white light, and then nothing.

Chapter 16
4th – 5th September 1944

Lorenzo sits above the cave, lights a cigarette, and gazes across the valley. The weather remains warm and hazy, and the general movement of troops and armaments heading northwest has petered out. The main road by the river Conca for San Marino is deserted. Some vehicles have turned off side roads along the way, climbing up to vantage points on the ridges overlooking the valley.

Something is nagging at his mind, but he is reluctant to confront it. Instead he diverts his attention back to the events of the previous night. They returned with barely half the water they needed, and the cheese and the bottles of sauce will not last long. The children are all complaining of hunger and they need to go back tonight, but of course he cannot allow any of the women to come. He clenches his fists against his forehead as he remembers what he saw in the stall of Mazzanti's house. He has seen this in Russia, and often enough that he feared becoming immune to it, in a way he sometimes saw in others. He refused to protect himself with the callousness or the indifference he found in the enemy, or even amongst his comrades. He would not acclimatize himself to the brutality, and he pays for this now, as the injustice, the disrespect, the pain and the humiliation of Francesca overwhelm him. He feels nauseous. She is such a sweet girl. She will make somebody a wonderful wife one day. If she recovers.

He is feeling in his pocket for another cigarette when his hand closes on the alien object that he removed from his bayonet the previous evening. The object feels cool, metallic, with a little chain. Pulling it out he can see it is the dog tag of the soldier he stabbed. Stamped on the metal plate is a name, 'B. Hiller', his rank of Korp, a serial number and blood type.

The demoralizing part is that B. Hiller has a mother and father at home, waiting for him and praying for him. Who knows, perhaps there is a sweetheart; some stout Fräulein Frida or athletic Gerhilt whom he knew from his schooldays. Strolling with her down a valley near the Rhine, the vines running in rows up the hill, he gave her a ring and told her to wait for him.

Perhaps B. Hiller had never done violence to a woman in his life. Raised in a country town he knew how to respect girls, to honour and value them. At what point then, in his journey through the war, did those values slip away? The haranguing of politicians and senior officers might have aroused nationalistic tendencies as he pulled on his uniform. But did his training desensitize him to the things he would have to do? The maiming. The killing. And in deadening his emotional responses to these acts did other values, like protecting women, get thrown out too? How does that work? After all, certainly, B. Hiller was never specifically taught to assault a woman on his training courses.

Perhaps, in battle, he was indoctrinated by his field officers to believe that foreigners are of less value. Treating foreign women this way isn't the same thing. In fact rape is good, for it grinds the enemy down and demoralizes him, so undermining support for the war at home. Victory is everything. Was that sufficient cause to abandon any semblance of decency, or did it take more? Did he see friends butchered by the enemy and feel such a hatred in his breast as he has never encountered, a hatred that morphed into other forms?

Or was there some sinister gene, latent in him until released by war? When his society's values and laws no longer applied to him in this foreign land, did the beast within him expose itself without risk of identification, satisfying its rage and lust? And afterwards will it then return to Germany, to the fräulein, and become latent once more? Except it is no longer latent, not any more. It is dormant, waiting for the moment when it may safely satisfy itself again. After the marriage will it seek excuses to go out at night, to walk the streets?

Lorenzo snorts. Well maybe that is the case with others – it will not be so with last night's pair.

The women cannot go up again. He will not even contemplate debate about it. That leaves only him and old Paisani tonight. But this morning he isn't able to walk any better and Paisani is frail. What they can carry between them will be pitiful.

This thought shakes loose another, which has been nagging at his mind, and with a sigh he turns his attention to his leg. Glancing around to make sure nobody is watching he removes the bandage. There is a whiff of something foul that is swept away by the breeze. He has to strain around to see even part of the wound. His flesh is extremely swollen and shiny; red with creases that reach out from the wound towards the healthy flesh. He bends as close as he can get to it and sniffs, trying to catch another whiff, but there's too much breeze. He is slightly encouraged by this, until his eyes fall upon the stained bandage. He looks at where he has cast it down, and without realizing his lip curls up. Eventually, slowly, he reaches out and brings the bandage up to his nose. He makes a face and winces, throwing it down as the stench assails his nostrils. He has encountered that smell before. There is no spare water to wash anything, and the remains of Toni's poultice were ripped off in last night's struggle. He rearranges the bandage until the dirty part is on the outside and the rest of it, marginally less filthy, is against the wound. He doesn't want anybody else to know what is going on here. He refuses to become a liability.

He hobbles down to the front of the cave. Francesca is sitting on the ground outside the entrance, and Floriana is combing her hair with a broken comb. Paisani has got the young ones searching for wood in the undergrowth, but there is little enough.

'No, not green stuff like that,' he instructs them. 'Find old, dry twigs.'

Mama is at the fire with some of the women, discussing how they can make the food go round, and who can go out to collect nettles now Toni isn't here. A washing line has been strung up between a small tree and a pole rammed into the ground. Precious water has been allocated to vital items now hanging in the sun. He would ask for a little water for his bandage, but he doesn't want them to know.

One of the smaller Paisani kids plays with a spyglass that they use to light fires. He focuses it assiduously on various leaves to get them to smoke and then, when he bores of this, he starts finding insects to burn. Paisani is taking himself back and forth across the entrance of the cave, peering around the hillside, looking for potential danger, but he seems the only one concerned. For the present the firing has stopped and you might almost mistake it for any early September morning.

Lorenzo notices that Francesca has gone to stand on her own.

She is holding herself and looking around her in a distracted way. Like the rest of them she is wearing the same clothes as yesterday but she is barefoot. He goes over to her.

'Watch out for your feet. I saw an ants' nest yesterday, and what with all the vibrations in the earth those poor creatures were all over the place. Look, there they are, but they've settled down a bit more, around their nest.'

Francesca glances down absently and steps away. Knowing that to crouch will be too hard, Lorenzo lays down on his belly and peers at the ants.

'Come and look.'

Francesca is reluctant to observe.

'Come, it's interesting. You'll be surprised.'

Francesca sighs and lies down on her stomach beside him, and he begins to point.

'See, these ones here, they're scouts. They're watching out for trouble, and if anything comes they can send a message – I don't know how. Perhaps with their back legs drumming on the ground or something. Anyway, whatever they do, lots of others come running and they attack the intruder together.

'Now, this line here is a foraging party. You see these ones ahead? Well, they're looking for something to eat, and when they find it they'll send word to the others to come and help them carry it. You'd be astounded at what an ant can carry, and often they work in twos and threes or even larger groups. I tell you our Commune could learn a thing or two from them about working together.'

He pushes his finger into the ground and draws a furrow ahead of the leading ant. 'When I was a boy I used to watch ants for hours, and sometimes I'd make these little lanes for them to follow.'

'What happened to the ends of your fingers?' asks Francesca in spite of herself.

'Ah, that's a long story.'

'Did it work? I mean with the ants?'

'Mostly, but I always got the feeling that when the furrow didn't suit their purposes they would veer away and go across country. I was always trying to anticipate where they were going, because I wanted them to follow my paths. I suppose I wanted to be a soldier and give orders even then!'

He is encouraged as Francesca gives a wan smile. 'Your wife will have to be willing to put up with that.'

'I think she will. She and I have already talked about my tendency to issue instructions.'

She looks at him. 'Ah, you have a wife? I thought you weren't married?'

'Not married. But I have a kind of fiancé.' Lorenzo blushes. 'I must be honest. I think of her as my fiancé but I cannot say yet if she feels the same about me.'

Francesca watches him for a moment. 'What's her name?'

'Antonia.'

'And what's she like?'

'Well, she is quite tall, a little taller than you. Her hair is dark brown, but not black. She has a lovely singing voice and she sings to herself when she's working, as long as she doesn't think I'm listening.'

'How did you meet her?'

'She fed me when I was recuperating.'

Francesca pauses. 'Oh. I thought you were still free.'

He wipes away a couple of ants that have crawled over her hand.

'Perhaps in her heart, but not in my own.'

Francesca looks down at the ants and says, 'Oh, there are so many of them. They're all over the place. They're like the Germans.'

She shivers and a darkness crosses her brow. He sees the fear in her, and he loathes the war and the terror. A young girl has the right to grow up unhurt, until a gentle boy finds her and marries her. There is a churning ball inside him, and without realizing it he lowers his head to the ground and grits his teeth.

She says, 'Why does God let these things happen? Why is this war? All these people dying?'

He raises his head, shaking, wondering how he can answer her.

'I don't know. Nobody has ever explained it to me.'

'I want to ask Father Morelli. How can God be full of mercy and then look down on all of this without doing something to stop it?'

He searches for something, anything that will give her peace. Groping he says, 'Do not fear. I will never let any German come anywhere near you again.'

She glances at him sharply. 'And when you leave?'

'There will be no more Germans by then. I swear to you, Francesca, I will be here. I have a gun and nobody will bother you.'

It feels intensely important to him that she trusts his promise and takes some relief in it.

She scrutinizes his face, her eyes darting back and forth between his. Something in his face appears to satisfy her and she lowers her head.

'I feel so befouled. So dirty. So ashamed.'

He takes her hand. 'Look at me. Look in my eyes. The filth is not yours. The shame is not yours. They are his – that bastard's. You do not have to accept the filth. You can wash it off. It's easier for you to wash off than for him. Don't accept it in your mind. Don't accept it. It's not yours and you shouldn't carry it.'

'But…for getting married…a young man expects his future wife to be…well, you know…he expects her to…'

He interrupts, 'It doesn't count. I tell you it doesn't count if you don't participate in it. It's like it never happened. Only you can carry it around with you, and in time it is you who has the power to let it go. What matters is the soul, isn't it? We know this from church. What matters is inside and only you can take care of that. Nobody else can touch you there. And if you let this go, your soul remains pure. Yes, pure.'

'You really think it doesn't matter?'

'I tell you now, it wouldn't matter to me one iota. I promise you this, I would be proud to have you by my side in Father Morelli's church. Proud and honoured. And one day – one day sooner than you think – you will have a boy like that beside you, and none of this will matter. Not one tiny bit.'

She appears startled by his passion and is quiet for a while. Then she leans forward and picks at his forehead, 'Lorenzo, you have three ants crawling on your face. Be careful or they'll bite you.'

He gives a nervous laugh, relieved at her levity, and then glances up at the whistling of a shell coming overhead. It explodes just beyond Borgo, on the saddle leading up to Monte Gardo. Instinctively they duck down though it is a safe distance away. More whistles come over and shells start erupting all over the place, mostly in the town centre.

'My God, they're starting a bombardment,' says Lorenzo.

He catches Francesca by the hand and they hurry back to the cave mouth, the very ground shaking beneath their feet as the accumulating violence inflicts itself upon the village. The kids are swarming back too, and so there is a logjam as they scramble to get into the cave.

'Inside, inside!' cries Mama. 'Drop all your firewood.'

Lorenzo gives a strategic shove here and there and the heaving mass of bodies tumbles into the cave. People crush as far into the back as they can, fear of shrapnel driving them to huddle behind each other. The adults wrap their arms around the children to comfort them. Lorenzo and Francesca are last in, and he sets himself between her and the entrance, telling her they are perfectly safe here because the bombs are being aimed up at the town behind the cave. There is no chance of an explosion out front. She leans her head against his shoulder and clings tightly to him.

The ground continues to shake and a permanent film of dust hangs in curtains about the cave, shaken free from the roof and the walls. From time to time a small stone dislodges and drops onto somebody's head. Shell after shell rains down upon Gemmano, and the combined noise rises to a hellish crescendo, though it remains muffled inside their refuge.

Then they hear the planes coming in. First they are a distant drone, barely discernible above the shelling, but the tone of the engines changes as the planes go into a dive. A rising, tearing wail signals their approach and they whoosh suddenly overhead with a roar, the sound of missiles pounding into the village walls. Time after time the planes swoop over them, and then they begin strafing outside the walls, their machine guns tearing up the ground as they seek out anything that moves. One roars across the hillside so that its shadow actually shoots across the cave entrance. Then they hear it turn and come back, and machine gun bullets chew up the ground outside the cave, throwing the fire all about the hillside and sending a pan whizzing off into the distance. Lorenzo throws up his arm to ward off a burning branch that flies at him and then stamps on it until it can do no damage.

Eventually the last of the planes roars off into the distance and, quite suddenly, the guns fall silent. The company sits frozen, as if sedated, unable to believe they are alive, waiting for their ringing ears to clear. Eventually one of the boys asks his Mama if he can go outside. They all look at Lorenzo who crawls out and peers around.

'It's safe to come out.'

One by one, like mice emerging from their nest, parents and children creep into the light. A heavy pall of smoke hangs over the cave, so they can only see the sun as a stark, round disk that sheds little light or warmth. Together with Mama, and leaning heavily on his crutch, Lorenzo climbs the hill behind the cave. They cannot believe anybody will be alive after such an assault and they do not bother to hide.

As they crest the brow of the hill the awful truth confronts them. Gemmano is no more. The cloud of smoke and dust, thrown up by the bombs, floats down from the sky like a giant funeral shroud to be laid over the ruin. Its shadow merely accentuates the gloom. Parts of buildings still stand but the church is almost gone and so is the town hall. Pieces of the village wall including, oddly enough, the gate, stand shoulder to shoulder like a row of broken teeth, but there is not one building that remains entirely intact. Casa Mazzanti looks like a giant, misshapen 'U' where a missile has gone straight through the centre of the first floor, bringing the roof down and knocking a great hole through the front and the back. It has left untouched the entire ground floor, and the walls on either side.

Mama catches Lorenzo for a moment, and uses him to steady herself. He is forced to lean against her too, and they support each other like a rickety two-legged bean trellis that sways in the breeze. He can feel her shuddering. She rubs her face against his shoulder, shaking her head, muttering to herself. Then she takes a deep breath, and without a word she turns and goes back down to the cave.

'Kids, you kids! I want you to start looking for firewood again. Come on, we need to restart this fire. Paisani, get the fire going. Where is your wife? We need to find some wheat to make bread.'

Paisani looks at her. 'What did you see?'

She shakes her head, 'Don't ask me. Don't ask me. And don't go up,' she adds sharply, as Letizia begins to scramble up the side of the cave. 'It is gone. Our house is gone. The town is gone. Your house, I cannot say, I couldn't see. We must live here now.

Do you understand? This is all we have. We must find a way to live here. We are alive. This is the first thing. We must be grateful for this. We have the clothes we stand in and we have ourselves. Let us get to work.'

Mama speaks with such conviction that the community listens without interruption and, when she has finished, people set to their tasks without complaint. Lorenzo says he is good for nothing except keeping a lookout and climbs back up above the cave. He sees Mama glance at his leg, and then into his eyes as he goes by, but she says nothing.

By the time darkness falls they are mostly gathered around the fire outside. Somewhere a bag of flour has been scavenged and, with some of the precious water, Mama is baking bread in the embers of the fire. She digs a hole in the ground beside it, putting the dough in a baking tin and placing it in the ground, covering it with red hot embers. The children are hungry enough to eat anything and care not that the first batch is burnt on the outside and doughy in the centre. Most of the adults go hungry again, sipping water from a ladle that is passed around.

That evening, Lorenzo creeps back up the hedgerow accompanied by Paisani. He realizes he still doesn't know where the cellar is so he helps Paisani sneak up to the well, and between them they collect two more buckets of water. By the time they get back Lorenzo can scarcely speak for the pain. He crawls into the cave, the skin on his face feeling like it is stretched tightly over his skull, and he is instantly asleep. He barely notices when two of the children are forced to lean against his back and use him as a pillow. He doesn't even hear the second bombardment of Gemmano.

He is awoken at break of light by gunshots at the mouth of the cave. There is a shriek in his ear, which shocks and confuses him, unaware as he is that Francesca has been sleeping next to him. He sits up and peers out, but it is hard to see anything past people who are scurrying to get deeper into the cave. He can hear shouts and there are blurry figures moving about the cave entrance. Then more shots are fired, his focus comes into view, and he sees they are soldiers, and they are shouting instructions in German. The Italians stare without comprehension from the cave.

Francesca is clinging to him and he feels her pant with fear. She is building up to another shriek and he turns and puts his

170

hand over her mouth.

'Keep quiet. Don't draw attention to yourself. Stay below the radar, understand?'

She quivers, saying nothing.

'I'm here. I'm going to protect you. Didn't I promise? But you have to stay quiet now.'

He can feel a tiny nod, her head buried in his shoulder.

From outside there is a shout. '*Sofort raus!*'

'What are they saying?'

'*Schnell, schnell! Sofort raus!*'

One of the soldiers continues to shout, to no avail. Another comes to the entrance and grabs the first person he sees. He drags her out of the cave and gives her a kick down the hill.

'They want us out. They want us away from here,' Lorenzo shouts, 'Move together. Keep in groups and get out. As soon as you leave the cave don't hang around the entrance. Get away from it until you find a place where you feel safer. But stick together in a group.'

He grabs Francesca and Floriana, and holding them close to him they shuffle towards the entrance. There is a soldier yelling, gesturing with his gun and pointing down the hill.

'*Ja, ja, okay, andiamo,*' shouts Lorenzo, trying to get his acquiescence across in any language he can.

As they emerge he can see more soldiers arriving with boxes of ammunition and grenades. Others are assembling Spandau guns from their components. He ushers the girls out and to the left where there is a gap in the activity, and says, 'They're setting up a defense. They are working now. They will not be interested in us, so run.'

The girls scurry across the hillside for about a hundred yards, Lorenzo stumbling behind them as best he can, until the curve of the hill takes them out of sight of the cave entrance. They hurl themselves down and once they have got their breath back they turn to see who is following. Letizia arrives clutching Thumb and flings herself into Floriana's arms, and the two girls hug as if they will never be separated. Mama, panting, is close behind her, and shortly the Paisanis appear though there is one boy missing.

'Pietro, where is Pietro?' cries his mother.

Letizia looks up, 'I saw him go with the Massari family. They went the other way. They said they were going down the hill to Villa to try and find refuge there.'

'Villa! It will be full of Germans too!'

Angela adds, 'I heard others say they are going all the way down the hill to the Conca.'

Lorenzo winces for he doubts they will fare well as the British come up the slopes. They will be trying to pass through lines at the height of combat. Glancing around he is forced to admit their own position isn't much better. There is firing all about, particularly on the eastern side of the hill where Villa is. To the west, the high point of Monte Gardo is being constantly shelled. Mortars continue to explode sporadically in Gemmano itself and the bottom of the hill is literally a war zone. There are already many German defense positions being set up around them, aiming across the valley at Croce.

There has been so much shelling that most of the cover on the hillside has been blasted away, and the fields are all chewed up. Glancing up at the hedgerow he can see there is little enough of it left, and any small trees have had their leaves blown off and are completely bare, as if it were winter.

Mama looks at him, 'Where can we go? We cannot stay here.'

He forces his scattered mind to think. 'When we looked at your house yesterday the upstairs had been destroyed, by that missile. But the downstairs didn't look so bad.'

She looks at him. 'What, so we go and live in the ruin of our house? They are shelling the village.'

He gestures helplessly.

Francesca says, 'There is the cellar.'

Mama looks up. 'If we can get into it.'

Almost without another word, and with a common understanding forced upon them by their situation, they rise and crawl up the hill along the remains of the hedgerow.

'But Pietro. We cannot leave without him.'

Paisani says, 'We have no choice. We cannot go back to the cave now. The Massaris will take care of him, with their own children.'

They don't trouble to stay low as they hurry along, and soon Lorenzo is left behind. After a time he is aware that those ahead of him have stopped and he drags himself up level with them. They are looking at Casa Mazzanti, and Lorenzo feels a stirring of hope. The missile clearly entered from this side of the house and blew most of the rubble through and out onto the street. The lower level looks to have sustained relatively little damage and the stall is almost untouched. Even better, Lorenzo can't see any soldiers nearby. They must all be fighting down the hill.

Francesca leads the way through the rickety gate and over to the stall. A wooden beam has fallen over the trapdoor but with four of them working together they lift it off. The door opens easily and one by one they hurry down the steps. Lorenzo is last in. As he descends he glances around but nobody has seen them arrive. He pulls the trapdoor down and the dark falls over them like a comforting blanket.

Chapter 17
September 9th – 10th 1944

Consciousness returns in layers. First he feels. He is lying on hard ground with stones jutting into his buttocks and his legs. His head rests on something made of canvas. There are tiny specks of rain falling upon his face and chest, and the faintest breeze stirs over him. There is a throbbing in his right forearm, perhaps from a graze or a burn, and now he can smell burnt cordite in his nostrils.

He feels the numerous raindrops one by one. So sharp and expansive is his mind that he thinks he could identify every one as they land upon him. He can make out individual characteristics. Larger, smaller, the precise point one hits his skin, and when it becomes large enough to form a rivulet that trickles down his nose. He can feel the rivulet turned aside by the hairs on his chin. He can sense all these drops, a thousand times over.

Next he hears. There are groans near him, and somebody cries out in pain. A man close by swears in English and Toni can tell he is patting his uniform down for something, perhaps a cigarette. A match is struck. Beyond these sounds there are gunshots, not continuous, but more like holes punched through the dense fabric of the atmosphere that makes up the day. More distantly, a shell explodes.

Underneath this he can hear another level of sound. The raindrops patter upon stone, and into the mud. To him these are two separate, harmonised sounds. Beneath him, in the earth, worms are moving with a constant, grinding vibration, and amongst them a creature, perhaps a vole, quivers in fear and sends tremors sweeping across the paths of the worms. The senses of sound and feeling combine as the tremors enter his body and he wishes he could pull the little animal to him and comfort it. The ground itself rebels against the violence being inflicted upon it. Huge groans arise from the depths, escaping the surface in bubbles of air that burst and release a stench of anguish.

Now he opens his eyes and looks up at the sky, and he finds this sense too is sharpened. It is a strangely hued sky, the colour of birds' eggs in the nest, and he cannot tell where clouds and shell smoke end, and pale sky begins. Glancing around, he is lying in a ruin. There is a crispness to his vision that allows him to identify individual lichen on the stones that make up the walls. All four walls are broken down to less than waist height, and in this outhouse are the wounded. Turning his head carefully to the left he sees the face of Major Robertson. Dried blood from his nose has formed on his lip, and the major looks to be sleeping peacefully.

Toni knows this is not true. Something in his mind is clearer too, as if it's been rewired. There is no soul inside the major. It has passed on. He reaches over and touches the major on the face and wishes him a good journey.

'Jesus Christ, you're alive.'

It is a voice Toni knows. ''Allo Dalglish.'

His words ring in his voice box and glide from his lips. He can almost see them written on the air.

'How the fuck are ye no deid?' says Dalglish. 'I saw you. I know you were deid. Look, we even put you here, wi the deid.'

Tony struggles to sit up. 'I am wet.'

'Fucks sake, I put you here masel.'

''Ave you...er...'ave you a – camicha – a shirt?'

'It wisnae only me, ken? Three of us put you here. We all thought you were deid. Ye weren't even breathing.'

'Dalglish, I am a little wet.'

'Fucks sake. Ye havnae even a fucking shirt.' Dalglish goes off.

Toni sits up and looks around. Dalglish has gone over to a pile of garments and boots, perhaps stripped off the dead, and now he come back with some things for Toni.

'Here, try this. It's dry anyway.'

There are a pair of boots as well, which are incredibly uncomfortable and Toni refuses them. He asks Dalglish for his sandals but the soldier merely shrugs.

'Come over here, awa from the deid,' says Dalglish. 'Fucks sake!'

Dalglish gives him a cup of the famous tea, and Toni finds himself sipping and tasting every flavour in it; the overall tang, the essential oil and plant from which it was derived, a chemical used in its production. He smiles shyly at Dalglish, and at the day around him. Dalglish sits himself down on the low wall opposite and shakes his head.

'You should've seen the colour of your face, son. If we had the time we'd have buried you, I'm telling you.'

Toni can't stop smiling and he hopes Dalglish thinks it's because he's pleased to see him and to be alive. He feels so well that he cannot prevent a little laugh that bursts out of his chest, and then he looks down at his body in wonder. He begins to peruse it, the way he might an injured person, for it does not yet feel like it belongs to him. He can see his forearm is heavily grazed and holds it out to Dalglish. The soldier obliges with some ointment and a bandage.

'Look at that. You'll no find a better bandage job than that,' grins Dalglish.

'It is perfect,' says Toni.

Dalglish glances around. 'We're cut off, son. We're no in good shape. They Germans have got us on the run. The Welch are trying to come up to Casa Menghino to relieve us, but it's hard going. We'll know in an hour or so if we're going to get out o here.'

'So what 'appens? You just give up this position?'

'Whit? No way do we give it up. Somebody comes up and relieves us, ken – takes over from us. We get to go back for a bit of rest and recuperation. We've done our bit for now.'

'Is this normal? You fight for some days and then go back?'

'Aye, course. We rotate. Naebody would last long if they were in the front line the whole time, would they?'

Toni glances over at the body of Major Robertson. It seems strange to him that these men should give up so much of themselves for this piece of ground, for these two farmhouses, and then simply leave as if they were going home at the end of a day of work in the fields.

Captain Will and Sergeant-major Thom come into the ruin. They look haggard and grim. The captain has lost his cap and his short, ginger hair is tousled and matted. There are bloodstains down his arm but it does not appear to be his blood. At any rate he doesn't mention it, and Toni can sense that he's not hurt.

'How ready are the wounded to travel at short notice, Dalglish?'

'We'll be ready, sir.' He points at Toni. 'This one survived, don't ask me how.'

Captain Will glances at Toni, 'Thought you'd left us. Nice to have you back.'

Toni smiles shyly, 'Thank you, *Capitano*.'

Thom says, 'What now, sir? They've got us completely surrounded.'

'We're going to hold out, San't-major, until we're relieved. The London Welch, I am told, are trying to retake Casa Menghino, with an attack to begin shortly.'

Indeed at that moment a barrage of firing starts over to their left, and on the brow of the hill they can see infantry advancing towards their former positions.

Captain Will shouts, 'Come on, they'll need support.'

They leap over the wall and Toni can hear them rallying the men and shouting new orders. The fighting starts up as they re-engage the enemy and Toni can't help going over to watch. There is a perimeter running right around the ruined farmhouse, which has somehow remained in British hands. It is made up of outhouses, strategically manoeuvred carts and a burnt out jeep, and the British are defending their turf robustly. Captain Will is moving around the line, talking to soldiers and encouraging them, and engaging where the fighting is heaviest. Sergeant-major Thom follows his example in the opposite direction. At a certain point the two of them meet up, and then combine to lead a break out from the perimeter, taking the attack to the enemy who have got a Spandau far too close for comfort.

Even this scene cannot dispel his lightness of mood, though he feels great compassion for those caught up in the violence, and their potential fate if they are ripped from their bodies.

Dalglish comes up beside him, 'Get doon, you eejit,' he says, but at that moment there is a burst of machine gun fire and one of the soldiers with Captain Will collapses on the field of battle, both his legs shot out from under him. He lies there screaming while his mates are forced back. The counter-attack has failed and the injured man is stranded in no-man's land between the perimeter and the Germans.

Toni doesn't think about what he is doing. He acts entirely instinctively. He steps out of the ruin and walks towards the perimeter, the thought of danger never entering his head. He slips between the jeep and the corner of a barn, and without hesitation walks into no-man's land. The only thing he can see is the writhing soldier in front of him. Bullets whizz past him, pinging against the barn, and a Spandau chews the ground close to his feet. It all seems so far away to him, and so unimportant.

'Get back, you lunatic, get back!' cries Captain Will from behind a cart, but he pays no attention, walking up to the wounded soldier who stops screaming and stares at him. The British have ceased firing, not wishing to kill him and, astoundingly, the Germans now do the same. Toni scoops the soldier up in his arms, surprised at the ease with which he does it. As he walks back towards the perimeter his hands are already glowing warm and he allows the energy to pour from his chest, calming the soldier, relieving his pain. He steps through the space between the barn and the jeep and carries the soldier towards Dalglish.

Behind him the firing starts up again but he pays no attention to it. He lays the soldier down and begins to examine him. Dalglish is gawking at him and then, intent on being useful, he drops beside the wounded man and talks to him.

'Murdoch. Bobby Murdoch. Listen to me. You're gonnae be fine. Haud on, son. You're gonnae be fine.'

Both legs are badly shot up at the knee, but the left leg doesn't look so bad. Toni finds he is able to delve inside it with his mind, looking around the arteries and muscles, following the nervous and skeletal systems, assessing the damage. Slipping through torn tissue he finds a bullet lodged in the muscle above the knee, and he can see the hole where it entered. Looking up he asks Dalglish for pincers, which he works into the hole until he gets down to the bullet. He glances at the soldier who is conscious but still calm, apparently without pain. He gets a grip of the bullet and pulls it out, tossing it away. Then he leans over the wound and applies his thumbs to the hole. He lowers his head over his hands and he feels blistering heat come through his thumbs, cauterizing the wound and beginning the healing process.

Dalglish scratches his head. 'Christ almighty. I mean…Christ almighty!'

There isn't much he can do for the right leg because the bone is shattered, so he rests his hands upon it until the blood stops flowing. Then he checks the body for other injuries and turns to Dalglish.

'You 'ave morphine? The pain, it will come back.'

It is eighty thirty in the evening when they get the order to pull back. The Welch have fought their way through and there is an exit. Mules come and take away all the ammunition and firearms they can, and Captain Will insists that all the wounded are carried out. Somebody gets a captured German half-track up near the farmhouses, and onto this many of the wounded are loaded. Toni jumps up with them. As the vehicle bumps and slides its way back through Croce Toni is able to look out. It was dark on the way in, so he's not seen the destruction. There are smashed tanks, both Sherman and Panther, lying around like the corpses of cows. One of the Shermans has had its turret blown completely off. A Panther has shed one of its tracks and has the hatch on top thrown open, as if the crew were trying to get out and run for it. There are no bodies lying around to tell him if they made it or not.

The half-track rocks and slips its way down to the valley as darkness falls and when it gets to the road by the Conca it stops.

Thom says, 'Get the wounded down. We'll load them into T.C.V.s that are coming up shortly. The half-track's needed to get up and down the hill in the mud.'

As the vehicle grinds up the hill, merging into the dark, Toni starts to do the rounds of the wounded, lined along the side of the road. As he bends over each man he finds he has great control over his touch, and can limit precisely the amount of energy he infuses into a damaged limb. By doing so he preserves himself and has no need of sleep. Somebody gets a fire going and shortly thereafter he sees Captain Will sitting before it, head in hands. Toni has been passing mugs of tea around and he takes one over to the captain who looks up as he accepts it.

He frowns in puzzlement. 'What made you do that today? Walk out into the field of fire like that?'

Toni shrugs, 'That man, 'e was in pain. 'E needed 'elp.'

'You should've been killed. You're bloody lucky we all stopped firing!'

Toni turns away and the captain reaches out and catches his arm.

'Actually, you saved that man's life. It was incredibly brave. Thank you.'

'*Capitano*, I 'ave to go my family now.'

Captain Will shakes his head. 'Not yet. You have to come to Morciano with us first. We need you for the debriefing. Then we'll see.'

It is early morning by the time the T.C.V.s arrive and the wounded are loaded on board. The other troops have already moved off and Captain Will gets into the leading truck. Toni waits and then climbs into the last one beside Dalglish, and the two of them make the injured as comfortable as possible. The first strands of dawn are spreading across the sky and they bump slowly down the road towards Morciano. At the point they were ambushed, with the Conca now on their right, Toni moves right to the back of the truck and peers into the gloom. He can just make out the silhouette of the broken remains of Gemmano. He glances over his shoulder at Dalglish.

'I 'ave to go. My family – I don't know if they live or not.'

Dalglish looks up. 'Thought the captain telt ye to come wi' us.'

''E did, but I cannot.'

Dalglish hesitates, 'I cannae dae that, son. I'd like tae, but I cannae.'

'We 'ave not the relief, you know, Dalglish? Nobody come to take our place after four days. When you finish you can go away. But not me. Later go your 'ouse. For me, this place is my 'ouse.'

Dalglish is silent for a moment and then he nods. 'You're somethin else, son. You know that? I never seen anybody do whit you did wi' Murdoch here. He owes you his life. I'll make sure he kens about it.'

Toni smiles, slips over the back of the slow-moving truck and drops onto the road. As the vehicle fades into the gloom he hurries down to the Conca and eases himself into the river now swollen from the rains. He swims across letting the current carry him downstream to where some branches hang over the river. He pulls himself out, glances about him, and is gone.

Chapter 18
5th – 10th September 1944
Francesca

Francesca strategically places three stuttering candles for maximum light. They are the only ones left and they have burnt down to stubs, for this is the fifth morning the group has been marooned here in the cellar. She raises one of the candles and holds it over Floriana's head. She is sitting on a low stool and Floriana is on the floor between her knees. The others are spread about the floor on threadbare blankets or straw.

Bringing the candle close, Francesca peers into the remains of Floriana's hair, parting it with her fingers and feeling with her nails. Triumphantly she grips at something, pulls it out and stamps it underfoot. They are all infested with lice now, and have hacked their hair back with the kitchen scissors. This kind of baboon-like, rearguard action is all they can do to avoid being completely overrun.

They only emerge in the dark of the early morning, after the guns have fallen silent and the attacks have petered out, and soldiers are catching some much-needed respite. Around four a.m. they ease open the trapdoor and creep out, like dormice slipping into the territory of a bird of prey. Floriana pulls up the bucket that has been used as a toilet and drags it through several shell holes to the far side of the vegetable patch in order to empty it. Francesca and Angela crawl over to the well carrying the two wooden buckets because metal ones, as Lorenzo pointed out the first morning, would bang noisily against the sides of the well. Mama is very clear on bucket use.

'Do not put that toilet bucket in the well,' she instructs.

In the early daylight of the second day (the first was spent in virtual darkness) Francesca watched as a still coherent Lorenzo positioned himself under the hatch. When the firing finally stopped he listened at the trapdoor for any sign of movement in the ruins. Once he said it was safe Francesca, as the more agile, nipped up through the stall to the kitchen. She found no food of course, but a sideboard had miraculously survived, albeit collapsed at one end.

She heard something move in the street outside. She glanced up sharply, her heart pounding, and then she backed up to the wall to keep out of sight until the soldiers – three of them – stumbled past. A stark blast of terror rose up inside her and paralysed her. When it assaulted her like this she found she couldn't think straight, and lately the terror had become a constant acquaintance, perched on her shoulder like a crow. It gripped her like a vice and she needed a conscious effort of will to take back control of herself. With a moan she turned away and forced herself to check the sideboard. Inside she found a pile of Mama's homemade candles and her kitchen scissors. The familiar items, steeped in routine, helped her to push the fear away.

To begin with they talked. They speculated about what was going on above them, and how long it would take for the British to come up and liberate them. Floriana thought shells must have killed most of the Germans but Lorenzo knew better, saying they'd have got out during the bombardment and then re-manned the ruined town once it was over. Hadn't they seen with their own eyes the Germans setting up defensive positions? He had no doubt it was the same all around the crown of the hill. Furthermore, he'd heard the telltale squeaking of tracks and the rumbling of a panther tank. That wouldn't be an easy thing to dislodge once it was ensconced in these narrow streets and well supported by infantry. This, he advised them gravely, was not the time to go looking above.

Mama talked about Toni and Papa. Why had they not come back with news after they'd talked to the British? Had they even made it down the hill in the first place, or had they been arrested and shot by the Germans?

'I bet one of those Collision Brothers got itself into trouble,' she groaned. 'I know Toni. He'd do anything to save them – even risk his own skin.'

The others sought to comfort her as she rambled, but after a time they fell silent and let her mutter to herself, as if they knew there was nothing they could say. By the third day nobody was talking much anymore unless it was a practical matter such as cutting each other's hair, or sorting buckets.

Yesterday Francesca noticed Lorenzo's mind beginning to slip in and out of focus. He would babble warnings about things he must have encountered in Russia – the cold, or frozen corpses. It was his habit each morning to hobble over to the hatch and listen carefully. But when he tried to stand, he staggered and complained that the world was shifting from side to side. He sat down abruptly on the ledge, head in his hands. Sweat was pouring off him and he wiped it away with his sleeves. The back of his leg nudged the ledge, making him gasp. Any kind of touch to the wound appeared to trigger a flash of agony, as if the pent up ache exploded in one hellish moment of impact.

They placed him down at the narrow, darker end of the cellar beyond the useless bread oven. This was partly because of the smell from the wound, but mostly because yesterday afternoon Lorenzo descended into a fever in which he rolled and thrashed around, so that the younger ones were frightened.

Hearing him cry out Francesca went over to tend him. She ignored the smell as she removed the bandage, taking a little water and washing it as thoroughly as possible. It was still damp when she replaced it on the wound, in spite of her combined efforts with Floriana to wring it out. But Mama said this was better than leaving it and the wound dirty, even though the overused bandage was falling apart.

She held the candle over his face, for she'd never heard him groan before. She touched his forehead, pulling her hand away with an exclamation as if burnt. She collected another piece of cloth (Letizia was asked to sacrifice a length of skirt), dipped it in water and spent most of the afternoon mopping his brow and talking to him while he moaned. From time to time he would open his eyes, reaching to her for help. Once he called her Antonia. By early evening Francesca's constant ministrations were having some effect and he became more settled and calm. This morning he was half-lucid, if very weak.

They cannot give him any food for there is none. The ham, the cheese, and the two bottles of passata lasted three days, but there are ten mouths to feed and they didn't stretch as far as Mama hoped. They had no pasta to eat with the passata and so they drank it straight from the bottle. The ham bone is still there, wrapped in a piece of Mama's skirt, gnawed a hundred times over, but it cannot be used to make broth without a way to heat the water. They know that a fire would be seen from above and would, in any case, smoke them out.

Now Francesca helps Lorenzo take water from a dented ladle that she also collected from the kitchen. Then she passes it to the others and each takes a good draught of water before laying down again. The younger Paisani kids play little games in their heads, but Letizia looks as if she has no interest in anything. Francesca has to encourage her to take even a sip. They scarcely hear the battle above them any more, except to half-note that it has moved closer to them, or is in full cry above them, or that the firing has paused for a while.

During one such lull, yesterday morning, there was a scratching on the trapdoor above them. Francesca looked up first, and then over at Mama. There it was again. It became more frequent and urgent, intensifying to a scrabbling, as if a rabbit was digging above them. Francesca went over to the hatch, climbed onto the ladder and put her ear up to the trapdoor. The noise was directly above her, and then she heard a little whine.

Carefully she opened the trapdoor a touch and a nose pushed in, forcing the trapdoor up. She was confronted with a furry, rusty face with a black nose that licked her frantically.

'Remo!'

The dog dropped instantly into the cellar, going from one person to another and rubbing himself against them, grinning and groaning in pleasure. The kids laughed for joy and even the adults smiled. Francesca stepped up the ladder again and looked out, and there sat Romolo.

'Come,' she said. 'Come down.'

Romolo hobbled over to her and then whined and sat down again. His front leg had been blown off at the first joint so that the paw was gone, though most of the leg remained intact. Francesca gave a gasp and examined it. The wound was messy with bits of bone sticking out, and dried blood and matter forming a kind of seal. It didn't look like a fresh wound. Getting her arms around him she half carried and half fell with him back into the cellar. Then she climbed up and looked out again.

'Who is there?' asked Mama.

'Nobody. I can't see anybody at all.'

'So where are Papa, and Toni?'

Francesca closed the hatch above her and said, 'They will be coming, I'm sure.'

This, of course, was not enough for Mama. 'But they must be there. They must be. How can it be that the dogs come back without Toni? This can't be good. Look at the black one. We must go and look. Now!'

'We can't go out. It's too dangerous. There is fighting everywhere.'

'We *must* look! I will go.'

Francesca pointed over to the stricken figure of Lorenzo, moaning quietly on his bed. 'He would tell you no. He would tell you that it would only make things worse.'

'Francesca, get out of my way.'

'Francesca is right,' said Paisani. 'Listen above. They are shooting again.'

Mama dumped herself down on her log. 'What am I to do? What am I to do? I cannot even go and look for my own husband, for my son.'

Francesca crouched beside her. 'Listen, when the firing stops I will go. I will look.'

'No! I cannot lose you as well.'

'So instead we must lose you? We need you. We cannot manage without you.'

In the end the discussion was drowned out. The firing intensified to the point that they couldn't even hear each other speak. Shells rained down close to where they were, the ground shook, and the idea of raising the trapdoor even an inch was plainly insane. This went on until it was dark when the dogs insisted on being allowed out to hunt, even Romolo, who was better able to jump up than down.

Recently there has been a change in the noise above. There is still much firing but it feels as if the battle has passed over them and moved west, so that most of the noise comes from Zollara way, and from Monte Gardo. Lorenzo is sleeping, or in a coma, and unable to advise them, so they sit tight.

Later in the morning they hear footsteps overhead. Mama looks up and Floriana, nearest the hatch, pulls away from it, clutching her blanket to her. The trapdoor is thrown back – whoever it is knows what he is looking for. The person backs down the ladder and turns to face them. The light streams in on a face that is drawn and pale, blonde hair matted and messed beyond redemption. He wears a combat shirt that is clearly not his, worn trousers and his feet are bare. His eyes are still and calm, and he smiles gently.

Francesca bursts into tears and hurls herself at him.

'Oh, Toni, you look just terrible.'

Chapter 19
10th September 1944

Toni staggers backwards and clings to Francesca for balance. They clasp each other and he feels her trembling like she will never let him go. One by one the others get to their feet as if sleepwalking, rubbing their eyes and drifting towards him. Only Letizia remains on the ground staring up at him forlornly. They touch him to see if he is real and, more animated, they surround him in the centre of the cellar. There are gasps of wonder, and little sobs of relief as they hug and crowd him, so that Toni cannot see in front of him. Angela is holding his hand against her cheek. He caresses and kisses them, and eventually they part and before him stands Mama.

She is quite still and her face is grave. She has her feet together and her hands held in front of her, as if she were approaching Father Morelli's altar to receive bread and wine. She does not take her eyes off Toni. Now she reaches out and holds his face in her hands.

'So, my dear son, you are here. What can you tell me? What do you know about my husband?'

'He isn't here?'

It takes ten minutes for everyone to understand that the last time Toni saw Papa was five days ago, around the time the family moved to the cellar. Mama slumps upon her stool again, and he kneels beside her.

'It'll be all right. Soon I'll go and look for him. I think it's nearly safe to go outside.'

There is speculation about Papa throughout the cellar, and confusion is added when the Collision Brothers return and hurl themselves at Toni. He is bowled over onto the floor and they leap on him, licking his face and nudging their heads into his ribs and shoulders. Then he sees Romolo's paw and gives a little cry. Romolo sits quietly while he examines it and asks around for bandages.

Toni has had a good look at the town on the way in. Hauling himself out of the Conca that morning he made his way across the fields on the floodplain. In the dim light of the dawn it was easy to stay clear of the occasional tank heading west. Looking up at Gemmano as the light rose, there wasn't much fighting in the village itself. The noise and flashes had moved west in the direction of Monte Gardo, just beyond Borgo Mazzini. Hurrying to find the family he began to climb.

Half way up the hill he came across a deserted cottage and sat to catch his breath on the little veranda. Staring across the ridges to the glistening ribbon of sea, he examined the shading of clouds gathering over the water. Dark mountains and crevasses amassed, coated by lighter puffs, nudging and massaging each other like swaying crowds. He'd never noticed before the brilliant edge to each alpine meadow, as the sun sought to peek around them. He felt he could perceive the forces acting upon them; the gusts that shunted them about the sky, the heat that tore wisps from their tops, and the convection that thrust them ever higher. He could see these forces as clearly as the dragonfly that alighted on the veranda rail in front of him.

He knew there was a presence nearby, even before it slipped into his range of vision. The entity emerged from the wall, like the one in the church, and from it Toni felt great waves of confusion and fear. It made for him directly, and for a second he was frozen by the old terror, and the need to protect himself. He returned to his breath and focused inwardly, stilling his mind. He stood perfectly still as the entity approached, until he could have reached out and touched it. His eyes were wide, and his mind crackled and probed, observing. And then he opened his heart.

Its tendrils emerged and approached his head, and when they caressed him he found he had profound contact with it. The full force of its bewilderment and fright confronted him but he was not shaken by the emotions. Instead he found he knew what to say.

'Don't be afraid. There is nothing to fear. I will tell you where to go.'

The entity didn't respond but there was a shift in its attention and its focus fell upon him. Its fear remained, but was no longer dominant.

Together they turned and looked out from the hill towards the sea in the northeast. Towering cumulus clouds billowed upwards like gigantic eruptions, and through a gap the sun lanced rays that dazzled off the surface of the ocean and spread silver along the coast. As the light strengthened and filled their vision Toni said,

'Go to it. Go into that beautiful light. That is your place now.'

He understood, rather than heard, the response. 'What about my family?'

Toni felt great love for this lost being, and it shone out from him, coating the entity and soothing it.

'Some of your family are waiting for you, in the light. Some will come later. It's all right. It's your time. Do not fear. Others will follow when it's their time.'

The entity floated before him as if undecided. Toni continued,

'You need healing now. You have suffered terribly in this life. You know the pain of a stillborn child, and you know what it's like to lose a father and a son. You have blamed yourself for letting your son go off to war, but this was not your fault, or even your choice. Now you need healing from this pain. You need insight to understand that it's not your fault.'

Toni felt the emotions fall away from the entity. It became calm, and without a backward glance it began to drift in the direction of the light. In seconds it was over the sea, the clouds came across it and he knew it was gone.

He sat down against the cottage and felt as complete, and at peace, as he ever had in his life.

He sat much longer than he intended, staring out to sea. When he stirred himself and resumed his climb he had none of the urgency of before. He climbed steadily, as if he knew what to expect, aware that events would run their course whether or not he rushed. Eventually he passed the cave, picking his way through the corpses of soldiers and abandoned boxes of ammunition, and as he crested the brow of the hill he encountered the ruined village.

He could see fighting up on Monte Gardo, and there was plenty going on around Borgo, though the rest of the ruins were relatively calm. As he got closer he could see the soldiers were British and they had set up a line just beyond their house on the saddle leading to Zollara. They were crouched behind buildings and broken vehicles, but the line was beyond Casa Mazzanti, so he was able to creep up to the stall unnoticed, hidden by the remains of their house.

Now he says to Mama, 'I think it's all right to come out of the cellar, but we are very close to the front line and could easily be shot. We should move into the main part of the village. I think that's occupied by the British.'

Francesca takes his hand. 'You need to come and look at Lorenzo. I can't do anything for him.'

Toni kneels beside the stricken man. He is only semi-conscious and is burning up with fever. Toni unwraps the bandage and winces at the putrid smell from the wound. The flesh around it is fiercely red, tight and shiny, and there are black patches around the edge of it and pus emerging at several points.

Toni puts his hands upon Lorenzo and finds himself confused. He wants to insert himself into the muscles and the organs but he doesn't know where to start. There is the fever, scalding his left hand like the embers of a fire. There is the pain, initiating in the leg, but expanding so that it swarms all over Lorenzo like bees. Then there is the sickness itself, festering and swelling around the wound, plunging deeper into the bone and muscle. He lets himself be drawn towards it and as he gets close the sickness rounds on him and leaps at him like a virus, assaulting him and making him wilt. It rages at him for interfering with its work, and lances pain into his brain.

Yet he knows what to do. The energy builds in his chest and, carefully controlled, it begins to flow from him into the wound, forcing the sickness back. Now it is his turn to assault it. He drives the pain down and then spreads his energy throughout Lorenzo's body, easing and calming until there is little more than a dull ache – for Toni finds he can tell what Lorenzo feels now. Then he turns his attention to the wound itself, and worming his way into the swollen, red flesh he calms the cells and slows the progress of the gangrene. Where flesh is healthy he makes it more robust and able to defend itself. Where it is damaged he slows the rate of disintegration, his energy playing amongst the cells, finding the healthy ones and helping them to turn and fight. Where flesh is dead he can do no more, but he can tell that the tension is slipping out of Lorenzo's body. When he's done all he can he turns to the fever and his energy becomes cool, blue-white, sliding into Lorenzo's skull and forehead, extinguishing the heat that was burning him up. When he is finished he is tired, and takes a minute to regroup. He turns to Francesca.

'You must find some British soldiers and get a doctor. Also fresh bandages.'

'But he seems so much better. Look how peaceful he is.'

Tony shakes his head, 'It has gone too far. He needs a doctor. Come, we'll find one together.'

Angela says, 'I'll come too.'

The three of them climb cautiously out of the hatch. Here in the stall, sunken behind the house, it feels relatively safe. He can hear soldiers moving in the street but they are still so busy securing the newly won territory that they haven't got round to searching the ruins. Through a gap in the wall he glimpses British uniforms. One of them turns and glances at Toni, assessing him. In not seeing him as a threat the soldier obviously ceases to see him at all. Toni leans back into the hatch and tells Mama it is all right for them to come up, as long as they stay hidden in the stall. Once he finds a safe place he'll come and get them.

Keeping behind houses, away from the road, they creep towards the village, the Collision Brothers at heel. At a certain point they must step onto the road in order to get up to the town gate, and Toni cautiously sticks his head around the corner of a house. There is a hiss nearby. It is Father Morelli, sheltering in a doorway; he has been praying over a corpse.

'Watch out, there are snipers. They don't care who they shoot.'

'My family is in the cellar, but we need to find somewhere safer, and also a doctor for an injured man.'

'If you have a cellar, believe me, that's the safest place for now. As for the doctor, they're bringing the wounded to the remains of the church. Can you bring him to us there?'

'We can try, but how do we get past here?'

'So you have to get over here, to me. You have to be quick. Very quick!'

Father Morelli steps back from the doorway, and Toni tells the girls to wait for him, making them hold the dogs. Then he leaps for the next doorway where Father Morelli catches him and pulls him in.

'First I'll show you the way. Then you fetch the injured.'

Father Morelli leads him through the house to a side door. They slip out and find themselves more or less under the remains of the wall of Gemmano.

'The shelling has uncovered a secret passage.'

Father Morelli leads him into some rubble and Toni can see where an entrance has been cleared.

'It's not much of a tunnel but it means you can come up inside the walls next to the gate, and there is no more shooting in there now. I think it was an escape route in the middle ages, in case the besieged village was taken.'

They make their way up the tunnel, which is steep and in places has one or two rough steps cut into the floor. It doesn't take long before they emerge in the piazza, as Father Morelli promised, with the gate on their right.

Toni stares around at the destruction. Almost nothing remains standing, apart from some walls that will have to be pulled down, their windows and doors opening onto fresh air on the other side. There isn't a roof in place, though a couple of beams point starkly at the sky. The gate is intact, but all it supports is a ruined piece of wall. One or two people are picking their way through the ruins, searching for anything that might be of use. Mostly there are enormous piles of rubble everywhere, and he can see two uniformed corpses huddled in a corner.

Nodding to Father Morelli, he returns to where he left Francesca and Angela. They have gone. Believing they've taken the dogs back to the cellar he hurries back. When he arrives he finds everybody, even Lorenzo, lying in the stall enjoying the fresh air, though there is no sign of either girls or dogs. Lorenzo waves to him and stands.

'What a fine job you've done on me. I feel so much better.'

'But you're not better. Your leg is very bad.'

Lorenzo glances down. 'I grant you it doesn't look pretty but it feels all right. Look, I can walk.'

Toni knows the weight of his next words but cannot take the time to soften the blow. 'I must take you to the doctor in the church. It is gangrene. I think it will have to be amputated. Where are Francesca and Angela?'

Lorenzo goes pale and slumps back against the stairs that lead up to the kitchen. 'Christ almighty.'

Toni ignores him. 'Where are Francesca and Angela?'

Mama says, 'The girls were with you.'

Toni explains and Mama says, 'Ay, something has happened. I know it!'

Lorenzo shouts, 'Francesca!'

Telling one of the Paisani kids to bring his pack from the cellar he pulls the gun from it and jams it in his belt. 'Come, Toni. We must find them. Right now. Who knows what has happened?'

At that moment the Collision Brothers reappear, panting and agitated. Romolo in particular is whining, running off and then coming back a way, ignoring his ruined leg.

'What's the matter with them?' snaps Lorenzo.

'It means they want me to follow them.'

'Well for Christ sake, let's get on with it.'

The two of them make their way through the rubble to where Toni left the girls. Lorenzo is hobbling but refuses to stop.

They get to the doorway and the two dogs part company. Remo turns left, towards the tunnel, but Romolo darts across the street and down a gap between two buildings on the other side of the saddle. Toni is in no doubt who to follow and points for Lorenzo's benefit. Without even pausing to check for snipers, Lorenzo launches himself across the street, Toni close behind. They tumble down the rubble-filled gap between the two houses, suffering cuts and grazes as they go, and then Romolo halts before a house that is almost intact. He paws insistently at the door.

Lorenzo doesn't hesitate. He bursts through the door, Toni at his heels. The room's furnishings are covered in dust and rubble from the caved-in roof. Lorenzo throws his head back and lets out something that is half a roar, and a cry filled with anguish and self-castigation. There is a large sofa at the back of the room and on it a British soldier has pinned Angela down and is forcing himself upon her. She is struggling and wriggling, but he has straddled her so that she can't get up and he is now in the act of taking off his trousers.

It is not this man that Romolo targets. Beside them there is a second soldier and he has Francesca down on the ground. She remains fully clothed and he has one knee on her throat so that she cannot move. Her eyes bulge as she struggles for breath, her hands grasping and scrabbling at his boot. The soldier is not even looking at her, for he is fixed on what his comrade is doing, though he pushes down even harder as she fights.

Romolo hurls himself at the soldier, knocking him off Francesca and onto the floor. Turning, snarling, the dog is about to leap again but the soldier has drawn a bayonet from his belt and is holding it above his head. Toni raises a hand and is crying out when there is a shot, blood explodes from the soldier's head, and he falls dead on the floor.

The other soldier looks up to find Romolo in his face, and the dog bites him savagely on his chin. He rolls off Angela and the sofa, forcing Romolo away, groping for his knife. The dog is on him again but this time the soldier is ready and deals Romolo a backhand that hurls him across the room with a yelp. Toni catches Romolo and holds him, while in the centre of the room the soldier looks up and freezes. Lorenzo is standing over him and has the gun pointed directly at his head.

'Don't,' croaks Toni, 'don't shoot.'

It is as though they are on a stage, and the director has asked the protagonists to hold their positions while he deals with some scenery issues. Lorenzo is absolutely still, leaning on his strong leg, his finger on the trigger of his gun, mere feet from the British soldier. The soldier is lying on his back, blood dripping from a deep wound in his face. He has released his knife and it lies beside him, still within reach. Francesca gets up and helps Angela off the sofa and away from the shot body. Toni holds onto Romolo who, although he doesn't struggle, barks furiously.

Lorenzo says to Francesca, 'Take Angela outside.'

The two girls step over the corpse to get to the door and Toni pushes the reluctant Romolo out with them. Then he turns back and says more clearly,

'Lorenzo, you cannot shoot him.'

There is a silence and sweat has appeared across Lorenzo's brow.

'Why should I not?'

'It is not the answer. It's not the right way.'

'Toni, what are you saying? You know what they were going to do. You saw it. And afterwards they would have murdered them!'

Toni has moved over so he is standing beside Lorenzo who will not take his eyes off the soldier. The latter has got to his knees and watches them carefully.

'That does not justify murder by us. If we murder the murderer we are no better. In any case, they are not murdered.'

'It is not murder. It's war. They would say the same about what they are doing.'

The soldier makes a noise and touches his tunic pocket as if to indicate there is something inside. Lorenzo looks at him suspiciously, puts the gun to the soldier's forehead and nods once. The soldier, moving with infinite care, reaches inside and pulls out a fistful of American dollars, which he holds up to them.

Lorenzo's eyes widen. 'Filth,' he hisses. 'You are filth,' and he stands back ready to fire.

Toni gropes for words. 'Wait! Look at him. Who is he? Have you thought of that? Who are his family? He is a victim of his circumstances too.'

'A victim! How can you say that?'

'He did not ask to be here in this war, fighting Germans in a far off country. He did not ask to be filled with hatred.'

'Toni, for fuck's sake!'

Toni holds up a hand. 'What about the church? What would Father Morelli say?'

Lorenzo doesn't pull the trigger.

'Come on, Lorenzo. Would he say, "Yes, butcher that man?" Or would he say, "Find some forgiveness in your heart"?'

Lorenzo throws his head back and roars again. 'You ask too much. You want too much.'

Toni lays his hand on Lorenzo's arm. 'Listen to me. Do as I say. Look at this man as a five year old. Perhaps his father was a drunk. Perhaps this little boy was forced to watch his father do terrible things to his mother or his sister for all the years of his childhood. And each time he watched a terrible feeling of helplessness and hatred grew in his breast. The little boy only wanted to play with his sisters in the yard outside. Instead he grew into a man filled with hatred.'

'This is just speculation. Bad things happen to everybody. Not everybody becomes like him. Not everybody turns their hatred onto helpless women.'

The soldier has been watching this exchange with an apprehensive expression on his face, and now Toni sees his hand is edging towards the knife. Knowing this will reignite Lorenzo,

Toni leaps forward and kicks the knife across the room.

Lorenzo speaks with contempt. 'You see, he still tries to kill us.'

Toni says quickly, 'You would do the same in his shoes. He probably thinks we're working out how to dispose of his body.'

Lorenzo snorts and raises the gun again. Toni shouts, 'But what will you do? Increase your own suffering with murder? Or will you find your compassion? If we take this man to the authorities, they will deal with him. At least show him justice.'

'I do not feel it. In my head I think maybe you are right, but I do not feel it in my bones. Only his death will satisfy me.'

'It will satisfy you now, but that won't last. Later it will torture and torment you, and as you get older you will think back and know it was wrong. Deeply wrong. You will feel it staining your soul.'

Lorenzo slowly, as slowly as grass growing, lowers the gun a fraction.

'I remember death. I can't forget. Those I've killed. The deaths of people I knew, and those I didn't...'

'You will remember them always. They will accumulate in your memory. The burden will build.'

'Toni, tell me. Tell me now. Are you serious? Are you truly serious that we should allow this man to live? This was your sister on the floor!'

'I have never been more serious about anything in my life.'

Lorenzo lets go a long, slow breath. 'I don't know why I am doing this. I truly do not understand why.'

He steps back, though with the gun still trained on their prisoner, and Toni motions the soldier to rise. He says, to Lorenzo, 'You are doing it for yourself.'

The girls and Romolo are outside. Toni is forced to find a piece of rope with which to hold Romolo for the dog is determined to resume his assault. Then he leads the way back to the road and they follow, Lorenzo bringing up the rear. When they get to the road Toni dashes across and a bullet pings off the cobbled stone at his feet. He calls to Francesca, 'One at a time.'

Before they come over Francesca turns and spits at the soldier.

'Our liberators,' she says contemptuously.

The girls rush over, one after the other, and perhaps the sniper is reloading, or notices they are girls, for he does not fire.

'I want to take the girls and Romolo back to Mama,' Toni calls across the road. 'Then we'll take him to the authorities at the church, and there is a doctor for you.'

'We'll wait for you here,' Lorenzo says, grimly.

Toni hesitates. 'Lorenzo, you…'

'I won't kill him. At least…as long as he doesn't try to escape.'

Toni doesn't even stop to tell to Mama what has happened, leaving the girls to explain it for themselves while he ties Romolo up. He races back to the road and there is Lorenzo, with the soldier face down in the mud in front of him. Lorenzo kicks his prisoner and makes him get up, and they dash across the road provoking another sniper's bullet.

Toni leads the way to the tunnel and they climb it without incident, though Lorenzo struggles on the steep steps. They pick their way through the rubble to the remains of the church. A lot of its facade still stands but there is no roof and when they enter the rest is almost destroyed.

Wounded line the walls between the mounds of rubble. An officer comes over, and Lorenzo explains what has happened. The officer calls two guards to take the soldier away.

'He'll be tried. We'll need you as witnesses.'

Toni spots the doctor who he asks to look at Lorenzo. The examination takes less than a minute before the doctor says, 'This will have to come off. However, if I am quick I can probably take it below the knee, and save the joint. We should prepare him for surgery now.'

Toni waits until two soldiers carry Lorenzo away on a stretcher. Then he says quietly to the doctor, 'You think 'e 'as good chance?'

The doctor is kind. 'In a hospital, with proper equipment, certainly. But in this place…' he glances around, 'infection you see. It's everywhere. He'll need good care.'

'I give him all care,' says Toni.

Toni is about to assist the doctor when, to his astonishment, Francesca turns up.

'I will stay with him. Mama wants you to go back, to find Papa.'

Toni sighs. It is getting late in the day and there is still plenty of fighting going on up at Monte Gardo. It will be difficult to do anything useful now. Nevertheless he wishes Lorenzo well and leaves Francesca clasping his hand in hers as the surgeon starts to prepare.

When he gets back to the stall the adrenalin has run out of him. He sits for a moment in the straw between the dogs who grin and lick him. Mama comes over and gives him some water.

'Here, drink. You must be so tired. You have not even told me your story yet. Where have you been for five days?'

'Mama, I will tell you everything tomorrow, but now I have to do something.'

He goes down into the cellar. He feels around the bread oven until, sure enough, he finds a couple of loose bricks. There inside is a little cavity containing a tin box. He steps into the light from the hatch and opens the tin. There are two old coins, and a ring. There is a lock of hair, wrapped in a wilted violet ribbon, and a tiny pair of earrings with pearls in the centre. There is also a piece of embroidery, of a house with a pond in front of it. There is a little signature stitched into the bottom left hand corner. SB.

Here then, maybe, is a brother. The connection seems immensely important to him suddenly. Tomorrow he will scour the hillside with the dogs. He will not rest until they find Papa.

He puts the embroidery into his pocket and comes up to see Mama standing alone, looking out over the valley, hands on hips. He kisses and hugs her, and promises her again that at break of light he and the Collision Brothers will hunt for Papa, all day if need be. The dogs will show him the way.

He heads back to the church. In one corner the doctor has Lorenzo on a bare wooden table. There is an anaesthetic mask over the patient's face and Francesca cradles his head and mops his brow as the doctor works on the leg. Toni sees him reach out and pick up a hacksaw and turns sharply away.

His attention is caught by a statue of the Madonna, which he can see through a damaged archway. She is standing, her arms at her side, her face at peace, and somebody has placed a British soldier's helmet upon her head. He goes up and stands before her, gazing upon her face.

He pulls the little piece of embroidery from his pocket and examines it. Lorenzo and Francesca must see it, and he will know from Lorenzo's reaction if he is indeed Papa's son. He turns and looks at the wounded around the church. He feels strength in himself, the right kind of strength. He glances up at the sky, framed by the broken edges of the church's roof. He is aware of at least two entities there, though they do not approach. It is as if they await his permission.

He reaches up and gently removes the helmet from the Madonna. He goes over to a large jerry can and fills the helmet with water. He kneels beside the first wounded soldier, raises his head, and gives him a drink.

He has work to do.

The End

About the Author
David Will

David Will was born and raised in Edinburgh but has lived and worked extensively in Australia, China and Italy. He now lives in Devon.

His father fought with the London Scottish in the Gemmano campaign and this novel is based on a detailed diary he kept of the terrible fighting that went on over a period of two weeks. The local Commune has also published a comprehensive account of the battle, and together with the diary this has provided a rich source of material.

On visits to the village, David has spoken to witnesses of the battle. He was struck by the horror of watching powerless as two foriegn powers destroy your village, and the shock of collectively becoming instant refugees in your own land. It is this which inspired the novel.

More Books From
ThunderPoint Publishing Ltd.

The Last Wolf
David Shaw Mackenzie
ISBN: 978-1-910946-39-8 (Kindle)
ISBN: 978-1-910946-38-1 (Paperback)

'So what is the novelist's duty then?'
  'Oh, to tell the truth of course.'
But what is the truth when there are at least two sides to every story?

Brothers Maurice and Christopher have not spoken to each other for over 40 years, despite living on the same small island. And nobody talks about Maurice's first wife, Hester – until an apparently unconnected act of vengeance reverberates across the generations and carefully guarded secrets begin to unravel.

Moving from 1930s Capri to Paris, London and the Isle of Glass off the Scottish coast, *The Last Wolf* is a subtly crafted tale of lies and betrayals.

'*The Last Wolf* is an intimate tale of lies and betrayals lightly and deftly told by a master storyteller.'

Mere
Carol Fenlon
ISBN: 978-1-910946-37-4 (Kindle)
ISBN: 978-1-910946-36-7 (Paperback)

'There's something about this place. It's going to destroy us if we don't get away.'

Reclaimed from the bed of an ancient mere, drained by their forbears 150 years ago, New Cut Farm is home to the Askin family. Life is hard, but the land and its dark history is theirs, and up till now that has always been enough.

But Con Worrall can't make it pay. Pressured by his new wife following his mother's death, Con reluctantly sells up.

For Lynn Waters, New Cut Farm is the life she has always dreamed of, though her husband Dan has misgivings about the isolated farmhouse.

As Con's life disintegrates and Dan's unease increases, the past that is always there takes over and Lynn discovers the terrible hold that the land exerts over people – and the lengths to which they will go to keep it.

'...a well-written and engaging novel about marriage, genealogy and attachment to land' – Anne Goodwin

The Bogeyman Chronicles
Craig Watson

ISBN: 978-1-910946-11-4 (eBook)
ISBN: 978-1-910946-10-7 (Paperback)

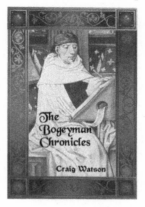

In 14th Century Scotland, amidst the wars of independence, hatred, murder and betrayal are commonplace. People are driven to extraordinary lengths to survive, whilst those with power exercise it with cruel pleasure.

Royal Prince Alexander Stewart, son of King Robert II and plagued by rumours of his illegitimacy, becomes infamous as the Wolf of Badenoch, while young Andrew Christie commits an unforgivable sin and lay Brother Brodie Affleck in the Restenneth Priory pieces together the mystery that links them all together.

From the horror of the times and the changing fortunes of the characters, the legend of the Bogeyman is born and Craig Watson cleverly weaves together the disparate lives of the characters into a compelling historical mystery that will keep you gripped throughout.

Over 80 years the lives of three men are inextricably entwined, and through their hatreds, murders and betrayals the legend of Christie Cleek, the bogeyman, is born.

'The Bogeyman Chronicles haunted our imagination long after we finished it' – iScot Magazine

The False Men
Mhairead MacLeod

ISBN: 978-1-910946-27-5 (eBook)
ISBN: 978-1-910946-25-1 (Paperback)

North Uist, Outer Hebrides, 1848

Jess MacKay has led a privileged life as the daughter of a local landowner, sheltered from the harsher aspects of life. Courted by the eligible Patrick Cooper, the Laird's new commissioner, Jess's future is mapped out, until Lachlan Macdonald arrives on North Uist, amid rumours of forced evictions on islands just to the south.

As the uncompromising brutality of the Clearances reaches the islands, and Jess sees her friends ripped from their homes, she must decide where her heart, and her loyalties, truly lie.

Set against the evocative backdrop of the Hebrides and inspired by a true story, *The False Men* is a compelling tale of love in a turbulent past that resonates with the upheavals of the modern world.

'...an engaging tale of powerlessness, love and disillusionment in the context of the type of injustice that, sadly, continues to this day' – Anne Goodwin

Dead Cat Bounce
Kevin Scott

ISBN: 978-1-910946-17-6 (eBook)
ISBN: 978-1-910946-15-2 (Paperback)

"Well, either way, you'll have to speak to your brother today because…unless I get my money by tomorrow morning there's not going to be a funeral."

When your 11 year old brother has been tragically killed in a car accident, you might think that organising his funeral would take priority. But when Nicky's coffin, complete with Nicky's body, goes missing, deadbeat loser Matt has only 26 hours in which to find the £20,000 he owes a Glasgow gangster or explain to his grieving mother why there's not going to be a funeral.

Enter middle brother, Pete, successful City trader with an expensive wife, expensive children, and an expensive villa in Tuscany. Pete's watches cost £20,000, but he has his own problems, and Matt doesn't want his help anyway.

Seething with old resentments, the betrayals of the past and the double-dealings of the present, the two brothers must find a way to work together to retrieve Nicky's body, discovering along the way that they are not so different after all.

'Underplaying the comic potential to highlight the troubled relationship between the equally flawed brothers. It's one of those books that keeps the reader hooked right to the end' – The Herald

The Oystercatcher Girl
Gabrielle Barnby
ISBN: 978-1-910946-17-6 (eBook)
ISBN: 978-1-910946-15-2 (Paperback)

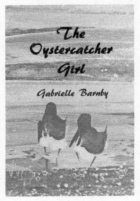

In the medieval splendour of St Magnus Cathedral, three women gather to mourn the untimely passing of Robbie: Robbie's widow, Tessa; Tessa's old childhood friend, Christine, and Christine's unstable and unreliable sister, Lindsay.

But all is not as it seems: what is the relationship between the three women, and Robbie? What secrets do they hide? And who has really betrayed who?

Set amidst the spectacular scenery of the Orkney Islands, Gabrielle Barnby's skilfully plotted first novel is a beautifully understated story of deception and forgiveness, love and redemption.

With poetic and precise language Barnby draws you in to the lives, loves and losses of the characters till you feel a part of the story.

'The Oystercatcher Girl is a wonderfully evocative and deftly woven story' – Sara Bailey

The House with the Lilac Shutters

Gabrielle Barnby

ISBN: 978-1-910946-02-2 (eBook)
ISBN: 978-0-9929768-8-0 (Paperback)

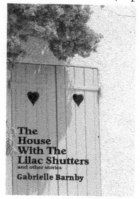

Irma Lagrasse has taught piano to three generations of villagers, whilst slowly twisting the knife of vengeance; Nico knows a secret; and M. Lenoir has discovered a suppressed and dangerous passion.

Revolving around the Café Rose, opposite The House with the Lilac Shutters, this collection of contemporary short stories links a small town in France with a small town in England, traces the unexpected connections between the people of both places and explores the unpredictable influences that the past can have on the present.

Characters weave in and out of each other's stories, secrets are concealed and new connections are made.

With a keenly observant eye, Barnby illustrates the everyday tragedies, sorrows, hopes and joys of ordinary people in this vividly understated and unsentimental collection.

'The more I read, and the more descriptions I encountered, the more I was put in mind of one of my all time favourite texts – Dylan Thomas' Under Milk Wood' – lindasbookbag.com

Changed Times
Ethyl Smith

ISBN: 978-1-910946-09-1 (eBook)
ISBN: 978-1-910946-08-4 (Paperback)

1679 – The Killing Times: Charles II is on the throne, the Episcopacy has been restored, and southern Scotland is in ferment.

The King is demanding superiority over all things spiritual and temporal and rebellious Ministers are being ousted from their parishes for refusing to bend the knee.

When John Steel steps in to help one such Minister in his home village of Lesmahagow he finds himself caught up in events that reverberate not just through the parish, but throughout the whole of southern Scotland.

From the Battle of Drumclog to the Battle of Bothwell Bridge, John's platoon of farmers and villagers find themselves in the heart of the action over that fateful summer where the people fight the King for their religion, their freedom, and their lives.

Set amid the tumult and intrigue of Scotland's Killing Times, John Steele's story powerfully reflects the changes that took place across 17th century Scotland, and stunningly brings this period of history to life.

'Smith writes with a fine ear for Scots speech, and with a sensitive awareness to the different ways in which history intrudes upon the lives of men and women, soldiers and civilians, adults and children' – James Robertson

Dark Times
Ethyl Smith
ISBN: 978-1-910946-26-8 (eBook)
ISBN: 978-1-910946-24-4 (Paperback)

The summer of 1679 is a dark one for the Covenanters, routed by government troops at the Battle of Bothwell Brig. John Steel is on the run, hunted for his part in the battle by the vindictive Earl of Airlie. And life is no easier for the hapless Sandy Gillon, curate of Lesmahagow Kirk, in the Earl's sights for aiding John Steel's escape.

Outlawed and hounded, the surviving rebels have no choice but to take to the hills and moors to evade capture and deportation. And as a hard winter approaches, Marion Steel discovers she's pregnant with her third child.

Dark Times is the second part of Ethyl Smith's sweeping *Times* series that follows the lives of ordinary people in extraordinary times.

'What really sets Smith's novel apart, however, is her superb use of Scots dialogue. From the educated Scots of the gentry and nobility to the broader brogues of everyday folk, the dialogue sparkles and demands to be read out loud.' – Shirley Whiteside (The National)

A Good Death
Helen Davis

ISBN: 978-0-9575689-7-6 (eBook)
ISBN: 978-0-9575689-6-9 (Paperback)

'*A good death is better than a bad conscience,*' said Sophie.

1983 – Georgie, Theo, Sophie and Helena, four disparate young Cambridge undergraduates, set out to scale Ausangate, one of the highest and most sacred peaks in the Andes.

Seduced into employing the handsome and enigmatic Wamani as a guide, the four women are initiated into the mystically dangerous side of Peru, Wamani and themselves as they travel from Cuzco to the mountain, a journey that will shape their lives forever.

2013 – though the women are still close, the secrets and betrayals of Ausangate chafe at the friendship.

A girls' weekend at a lonely Fenland farmhouse descends into conflict with the insensitive inclusion of an overbearing young academic toyboy brought along by Theo. Sparked by his unexpected presence, pent up petty jealousies, recriminations and bitterness finally explode the truth of Ausangate, setting the women on a new and dangerous path.

Sharply observant and darkly comic, Helen Davis's début novel is an elegant tale of murder, seduction, vengeance, and the value of a good friendship.

'The prose is crisp, adept, and emotionally evocative' – Lesbrary.com

QueerBashing
Tim Morrison
ISBN: 978-1-910946-06-0 (eBook)
ISBN: 978-0-9929768-9-7 (Paperback)

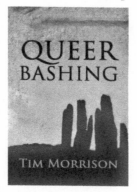

The first queerbasher McGillivray ever met was in the mirror.

From the revivalist churches of Orkney in the 1970s, to the gay bars of London and Northern England in the 90s, via the divinity school at Aberdeen, this is the story of McGillivray, a self-centred, promiscuous hypocrite, failed Church of Scotland minister, and his own worst enemy.

Determined to live life on his own terms, McGillivray's grasp on reality slides into psychosis and a sense of his own invulnerability, resulting in a brutal attack ending life as he knows it.

Raw and uncompromising, this is a viciously funny but ultimately moving account of one man's desire to come to terms with himself and live his life as he sees fit.

'...an arresting novel of pain and self-discovery' – Alastair Mabbott (The Herald)

The Birds That Never Flew
Margot McCuaig
Shortlisted for the
Dundee International Book Prize 2012
Longlisted for the Polari First Book Prize 2014
ISBN: 978-0-9929768-5-9 (eBook)
ISBN: 978-0-9929768-4-2 (Paperback)

'Have you got a light hen? I'm totally gaspin.'

Battered and bruised, Elizabeth has taken her daughter and left her abusive husband Patrick. Again. In the bleak and impersonal Glasgow housing office Elizabeth meets the provocatively intriguing drug addict Sadie, who is desperate to get her own life back on track.

The two women forge a fierce and interdependent relationship as they try to rebuild their shattered lives, but despite their bold, and sometimes illegal attempts it seems impossible to escape from the abuse they have always known, and tragedy strikes.

More than a decade later Elizabeth has started to implement her perfect revenge – until a surreal Glaswegian Virgin Mary steps in with imperfect timing and a less than divine attitude to stick a spoke in the wheel of retribution.

Tragic, darkly funny and irreverent, *The Birds That Never Flew* ushers in a new and vibrant voice in Scottish literature.

'...dark, beautiful and moving, I wholeheartedly recommend' scanoir.co.uk

Over Here
Jane Taylor
ISBN: 978-0-9929768-3-5 (eBook)
ISBN: 978-0-9929768-2-8 (Paperback)

It's coming up to twenty-four hours since the boy stepped down from the big passenger liner – it must be, he reckons foggily – because morning has come around once more with the awful irrevocability of time destined to lead nowhere in this worrying new situation. His temporary minder on board – last spotted heading for the bar some while before the lumbering process of docking got underway – seems to have vanished for good. Where does that leave him now? All on his own in a new country: that's where it leaves him. He is just nine years old.

An eloquently written novel tracing the social transformations of a century where possibilities were opened up by two world wars that saw millions of men move around the world to fight, and mass migration to the new worlds of Canada and Australia by tens of thousands of people looking for a better life.

Through the eyes of three generations of women, the tragic story of the nine year old boy on Liverpool docks is brought to life in saddeningly evocative prose.

'…a sweeping haunting first novel that spans four generations and two continents…' – Cristina Odone/Catholic Herald

Toxic
Jackie McLean
Shortlisted for the Yeovil Book Prize 2011
ISBN: 978-0-9575689-8-3 (eBook)
ISBN: 978-0-9575689-9-0 (Paperback)

The recklessly brilliant DI Donna Davenport, struggling to hide a secret from police colleagues and get over the break-up with her partner, has been suspended from duty for a fiery and inappropriate outburst to the press.

DI Evanton, an old-fashioned, hard-living misogynistic copper has been newly demoted for thumping a suspect, and transferred to Dundee with a final warning ringing in his ears and a reputation that precedes him.

And in the peaceful, rolling Tayside farmland a deadly store of MIC, the toxin that devastated Bhopal, is being illegally stored by a criminal gang smuggling the valuable substance necessary for making cheap pesticides.

An anonymous tip-off starts a desperate search for the MIC that is complicated by the uneasy partnership between Davenport and Evanton and their growing mistrust of each others actions.

Compelling and authentic, Toxic is a tense and fast paced crime thriller.

'...a humdinger of a plot that is as realistic as it is frightening' – crimefictionlover.com

Shadows
Jackie McLean
ISBN: 978-0-9575689-8-3 (eBook)
ISBN: 978-0-9575689-9-0 (Paperback)

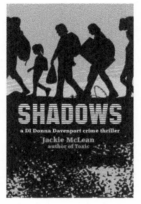

When DI Donna Davenport is called out to investigate a body washed up on Arbroath beach, it looks like a routine murder inquiry. But then the enquiry takes on a more sinister form.

There are similarities with a previous murder, and now a woman connected to them both has also gone missing.

For Donna, this is becoming personal, and with the added pressure of feeling watched at every turn, she is convinced that Jonas Evanton has returned to seek his revenge on her for his downfall.

Fearing they may be looking for a serial killer, Donna and her new team are taken in a horrifying and unexpected direction. Because it's not a serial killer – it's worse.

Moving from Dundee to the south coast of Turkey and the Syrian border, this is a fast paced novel about those who live their lives in the shadows, and those who exploit them.

'…a frank and unapologetic depiction of the ways human trafficking affects societies worldwide' – The Lesbian Review

The Wrong Box
Andrew C Ferguson

ISBN: 978-1-910946-14-5 (Paperback)
ISBN: 978-1-910946-16-9 (eBook)

All I know is, I'm in exile in Scotland, and there's a dead Scouser businessman in my bath. With his toe up the tap.

Meet Simon English, corporate lawyer, heavy drinker and Scotophobe, banished from London after being caught misbehaving with one of the young associates on the corporate desk. As if that wasn't bad enough, English finds himself acting for a spiralling money laundering racket that could put not just his career, but his life, on the line.

Enter Karen Clamp, an 18 stone, well-read wann be couturier from the Auchendrossan estate, with an encyclopedic knowledge of Council misdeeds and 19th century Scottish fiction. With no one to trust but each other, this mismatched pair must work together to investigate a series of apparently unrelated frauds and discover how everything connects to the mysterious Wrong Box.

Manically funny, *The Wrong Box* is a chaotic story of lust, money, power and greed, and the importance of being able to sew a really good hem.

'...the makings of a new Caledonian Comic Noir genre: Rebus with jokes, Val McDiarmid with buddha belly laughs, or Trainspotting for the professional classes'

Talk of the Toun

Helen MacKinven

ISBN: 978-1-910946-00-8 (eBook)
ISBN: 978-0-9929768-7-3 (Paperback)

She was greetin' again. But there's no need for Lorraine to be feart, since the first day of primary school, Angela has always been there to mop up her tears and snotters.

An uplifting black comedy of love, family life and friendship, Talk of the Toun is a bittersweet coming-of-age tale set in the summer of 1985, in working class, central belt Scotland.

Lifelong friends Angela and Lorraine are two very different girls, with a growing divide in their aspirations and ambitions putting their friendship under increasing strain.

Artistically gifted Angela has her sights set on art school, but lassies like Angela, from a small town council scheme, are expected to settle for a nice wee secretarial job at the local factory. Her only ally is her gallus gran, Senga, the pet psychic, who firmly believes that her granddaughter can be whatever she wants.

Though Lorraine's ambitions are focused closer to home Angela has plans for her too, and a caravan holiday to Filey with Angela's family tests the dynamics of their relationship and has lifelong consequences for them both.

Effortlessly capturing the religious and social intricacies of 1980s Scotland, Talk of the Toun is the perfect mix of pathos and humour as the two girls wrestle with the complications of growing up and exploring who they really are.

'Fresh, fierce and funny…a sharp and poignant study of growing up in 1980s Scotland. You'll laugh, you'll cry…you'll cringe' – KAREN CAMPBELL